Rhubarb without Sugar – Pamela Cartlidge

Books by Pamela Cartlidge

Bluebells and Tin Hats – the Prequel to Rhubarb without Sugar

Set in Wrexham a small mining town in North Wales, this romantic historical novel traces the life of fourteen year old Louisa caught up in the clash of old and new traditions during the nineteen thirties. Unable to change her mother's entrenched belief that working in service was her best career choice Louisa finds herself living and working away from home in a job she detests. Whilst struggling to change her destiny the impact of a mining explosion in Gresford and the arrival of a young man from Liverpool changes Louisa's life forever. Running alongside the developing stages of romance, the years leading up to and through world war two pushes Louisa down a turbulent path of tragedy and love.

Restless Yew Tree Cottage – a ghost story

Amanda was unaware that she had inherited her grandmother's extra sensory powers. Yet throughout her childhood and early teens she always sensed a weirdness about herself. It was a strangeness that she couldn't define. She was very artistic and when she became a gifted art student, she put her strange feelings down to her creative talent. Meanwhile her mother was exploring the internet to try to find her own birth parents. Soon after her mother made contact with her long lost brother, Amanda's latent powers came to the surface. Whilst Amanda comes to terms with the unexplained phenomena that surrounds her, other events revive the wrath of a ghost

Rhubarb Without Sugar

Chapter One

Louisa was on her way to Dodman's the shoe shop
in Wrexham. Her two little girls accompanying her
were as excited as their mother. However the pure
excitement of buying new shoes was not the only
emotional issue that occupied Louisa's thoughts.
She was looking forward to the next day when her
beloved brother Arthur was returning home from the
war.

The minister of Labour and National Service –
Ernest Bevin had been put in charge of demobilising
the troops and now it was Arthur's turn to return
home. The whole family were overjoyed that they
would be reunited again soon and they had pooled
their rations to make a welcome meal for him.

Louisa had been saving her coupons for months so
that she could buy Christine and Susan new shoes.
In any case Christine needed new shoes for school in
September. Louisa reckoned that the occasion of her
brother's return seemed an appropriate time to buy
them. Both Christine and Susan would be able to
wear their new shoes to Arthur's welcome home
meal. Louisa was fortunate that she didn't have to
use coupons for Susan's shoes as the Government

had seen fit not to ration clothes for children under four. Of course she still had to pay for them.

The little girls pressed their faces in the High Street shop window and stared at the shoes on display. There wasn't a lot to choose from, yet this didn't diminish the children's excitement. Both girls liked the idea of having something new.

"I like those brown ones on the end mummy." Six year old Christine said. She pointed to the corner of the window display and Louisa was pleased that she was able to afford them. Susan at the age of two was bewildered when they walked into the shop. She looked up mischievously at the proprietor with her wide beguiling eyes and Mr. Dodman at once fell helplessly under her spell. Many people did. She was a wild child though very lovable.

Her sister Christine, though sharing Susan's inquisitiveness was more reserved around men she didn't know. It had taken her a long time to build up a relationship with her father who had returned from the war several months earlier. She had been nine months old when Fred had joined the Navy to fight for his country. He had missed a lot of her early years growing up. Each snatched short visit due to sick leave or survivor's leave had not given him the opportunity to bond with Christine. Fred had been heartbroken when she had shied away from him each time he returned home but understood that he had to be patient with his daughter.

Mr. Dodman was good-natured with the two children even when they started to run around the shop poking their prying little fingers at the boxes on the shelves. Both Christine and Susan were easily pleased and didn't need any encouragement to walk around the shop to try out their footwear.

Satisfied with her purchases, Louisa led her children to King Street to get the Chester bus home to Pandy. The bus was almost full. The two little girls squeezed together on one available seat whilst Louisa sat on the seat's edge. It was just a two mile journey to Pandy from Wrexham so Louisa didn't mind the slight discomfort. She smiled at her children who had engaged in chatter with their fellow woman passenger. Louisa realised it was Mrs. Penson who had helped deliver both her children. She often wondered how many babies she had delivered over the years. As far as she was aware, Mrs. Penson was not a qualified midwife. However she was so experienced that many mothers trusted her to attend to them when giving birth. She was also cheaper than the midwife. Louisa caught her eye and they exchanged smiles.

They left the bus on Chester Road at the Smithy stop and walked past the dairy towards Bluebell Lane to their home. Theirs was the last house at the end of a terrace of eight. The children ran in to see their grandmother and excitedly told her about their new shoes. Mary Ellen watched them open the boxes as she stood washing her hands after skinning two rabbits. She caught Louisa's glance as her daughter's eyes fell upon the raw meat.

"I'm going to make a rabbit pie for tomorrow. We've plenty of potatoes and carrots in the garden and Mrs. Taylor has saved her sugar ration so we can have blackcurrant tart too."

Louisa grimaced at the thought of blackcurrants. The fruit brought back to her too many bad memories of her youth.

"There's rhubarb too if you prefer though we may have to go easy on the sugar."

Mary Ellen smiled at her daughter. She could never understand her daughter's aversion to eating blackcurrants. She recalled that Louisa had always liked them as a child.

"Thanks mother." Louisa smiled. "Dot is bringing some sugar so maybe there will be enough."

Mary Ellen sighed. "The war is over and still we have to be rationed. I hope it will end soon. I'm just grateful that at least we can grow our own vegetables here and we don't do too badly for meat. I dread to think how Fred's family in Liverpool are faring. They are not as lucky as we are." She sat down at the kitchen table to rest for a while and to examine the shoes that her grandchildren were proudly showing her.

"Jim and Annie were very pleased with the chicken Fred took for them last week. I'm hoping we can spare a couple more for his other brothers, not that we have heard when they are coming home yet. Fred is hopeful it will be soon." Louisa said. She put her apron on and started to make herself and her mother some weak tea. They had got used to weak tea over the years though still drank it very sparingly. Her mother watched her quietly, and Louisa noticed a sad expression fleet across Mary Ellen's face. She kept her eyes fixed on Louisa as she poured water in the kettle. Louisa stole a quick glance at her mother to observe her faraway countenance. She turned away quickly and put the kettle on the open fire at the side of the range. Though it was a warm summer day, the fire was lit as it provided heat for baking as well as water for tea and bathing. Mary Ellen didn't usually light the fire until mid-day to save on coal.

Louisa knew that as soon as she had mentioned Fred's brothers, that her mother would start thinking about Harry. She often thought about him too. People kept saying "no news is good news". But it didn't help when they hadn't heard anything about her brother since he had been taken prisoner by the Japanese in nineteen forty two. Dot would be very pleased to see the safe return of her brother-in-law Arthur tomorrow but Louisa knew that she would be desperate for news of her husband Harry. They all were.

The next day was Saturday and the atmosphere in the house was charged with emotion in anticipation of seeing Arthur again. Mary Ellen worried that he might not come at all. Louisa worried that the trains wouldn't be on time, or that Arthur wouldn't be able to get on a train. She had read that the trains were always packed when a new surge of demobbed service men and women arrived in Britain.

To help to take her mind off Arthur, Louisa busied herself with her sewing. She wanted to finish the skirt she was making for one of her friends. Since the war ended it seemed everyone wanted to cheer themselves up with new clothes. Not that the clothing coupons could buy much. Yet somehow or other Louisa and some of her friends managed to buy the fabrics they needed. Then Louisa would re-create the styles they had seen advertised in the fashion magazines.

Fred did his best to try to calm his wife, though he himself shared her anxiety. He was looking forward to seeing his brother-in-law again after so many years. He hoped that the war hadn't changed him too much. He was well aware how it had mentally affected so many people that he knew. He was also hoping to see his own brothers again too. A month earlier he had received a letter from his oldest brother Jim to say he was now home. He had been demobbed a few weeks earlier. Owing to his age Jim hadn't been posted overseas after his training in Ballymena. He had spent a huge part of the war in the army based near the aerodrome in Lincoln.

Fred had been pleased to hear the news and had managed to get the train to Seacombe so that he could see him. Jim was now living in New Brighton with his wife Annie and their two children Louisa and Alfred. But Fred was still anxious about his other three brothers. Neither he nor Jim had news to pass on about Tom, Bob and John. However Jim was able to assure Fred that both their sisters, Mary and Cissy were safe. So too were the wives and young families of their brothers. Somehow or other they had all survived the Liverpool blitz.

By the middle of the afternoon Louisa had finished the polka dot pencil skirt and held it up for Mary Ellen to see. She examined the garment absently but Louisa could see that her mother was not concentrating. She was desperate to go to Acton to see if Arthur had arrived. She was unable to settle in her chair and kept glancing at the door. William and Fred said it was only fair to wait for Arthur to arrive with Gladys and their children. They had arranged this days ago when Gladys had given them the news of Arthur's demobilisation.

Louisa hung the skirt up on a hanger and put her sewing notions away. At four o clock Dot arrived with her two children Malcolm and Gordon. She too was tense with excitement. Both boys went into the garden to play with Christine and Susan. The children had only been in the garden five minutes when the adults heard Gordon shout "Brian, Maureen, we are over here."

Upon hearing the names of her son's children, Mary Ellen could not contain herself any longer. She flung open the door and ran into the yard to see Arthur striding towards her. Tears ran down her face as Arthur swept her off her feet. "Hello mother, I'm home." He put her down as she struggled to wipe the tears from her face and smile simultaneously. She stayed by his side whilst it was Louisa's turn to be hugged and kissed. Louisa smiled into her brother's tanned face. His eyes were still the same steely blue she remembered and his black wavy hair inherited from his father was still there. As her eyes roved his face she could see that under the smiles he was tired and his face was a little thinner.

Arthur put her down to greet his father. William strode forward towards his son and hugged him hard. He finally let him go to let Fred greet his brother-in-law. They shook hands warmly, then Arthur caught sight of Dot who had hung back from the others. He took her in his arms and gave her a hug. Over her head he mouthed "Harry" and his eyes searched both the faces of his mother and sister who both shrugged and sadly shook their heads.

Meanwhile Gladys leaned on the garden fence smoking a cigarette. She grinned as she watched the happy reunion of her husband and his family, their faces wreathed with smiles. Her mother Mrs. Taylor stood beside her.

Before going into the house Arthur stepped into the garden to see the children.

Christine didn't recognise him and held back with Maureen and Brian. Even her little cousins were wary of the man who was their father. Malcolm stared at Arthur long and hard but kept his distance. He instinctively moved towards his cousins. It was Gordon and Susan who were willing to greet their uncle. Susan was her usual affable self with strangers and Gordon now aged eleven had a better understanding of what was happening. He regarded Arthur with a faintly cautious expression on his face. Observing him Louisa realised sadly that the boy was probably thinking, who was this man? A man who resembled Gordon's father but wasn't he. His thought processes finally helped him to identify the man before him. Gordon politely offered Arthur his hand to shake. Somewhat bemused Arthur held out his own hand and shook the boy's hand affectionately.

"Hello." Gordon said. "I thought you were my dad."

Arthur knelt down in front of the boy. "I'm your dad's brother. Don't you remember me?" He smiled gently at the boy.

Gordon nodded his head. "I do now Uncle Arthur. Have you seen my dad?"

Arthur got up before he answered. "I haven't seen him for a while, but I hope we will soon."

11

Scarcely had Arthur finished talking to Gordon when he was jumped upon by his youngest sister Dorothy. She had just got off the Chester bus having finished work and had run all the way home hoping that her brother would have arrived in Pandy. When she saw him in the garden she was so overcome with emotion she hurled herself at Arthur and nearly knocked him over. He just managed to save himself from falling into canes of peas which were lining the side of the garden. William's brows shot up as he saw this spectacle and went to examine his peas. Meanwhile Arthur disentangled his youngest sister from her kisses and hugs.

"Arthur, I'm so glad you are home." Dorothy said as she linked her arm in his and they went into the house for supper.

Arthur grinned, his blue eyes shining brightly. "Not as much as I am I bet."

Over their meal Gordon explained to his mother that he had at first mistaken Arthur for his father. Louisa noticed that he kept giving Arthur side long glances and her heart went out to him. She knew how much he missed his father. The rest of the family agreed that there was a strong likeness between both Arthur and Harry.

Dot glanced cautiously at her two sons before explaining to Arthur that they were still unsure of Harry's whereabouts. She didn't usually talk about Harry in front of the two boys because they constantly asked her when he was coming home and she was unable to tell them. The worry was making her ill.

Fred shared her concern about his three brothers. He informed Arthur that he had received letters from his two sisters Cissy and Mary and was relieved that at least they were both safe. He explained that three of his brothers were still abroad and he had no idea when he would see them again. To help lighten the mood Fred changed the subject from demobilisation. He asked Arthur what his plans were now he was home.

"I've been offered my old job back at Clark's garage, though fewer hours and less money." Arthur replied. "I'm lucky to get that really. It will have to do for now." He glanced at Gladys and she smiled.

"What about you Fred? Have you got work?" Arthur asked as he put another piece of rabbit pie in his mouth.

Fred nodded. "I've been lucky too. When I was discharged last September I was given work down Gresford pit – that was a condition of my discharge, - but since the war ended in Europe I also got my old job back. I'm working again with Roberts and Son the builders. I've been there a month already. We are very busy." Fred put down his knife and fork then helped Susan to eat her own meal.

Louisa took the dinner plates away and Dorothy squeezed past her into the tiny kitchen to bring out the fruit tarts.

"That was a lovely meal mother, thank you. I've missed your cooking. It is nice to get some home cooked meals again." Arthur said.

Mary Ellen glowed at the compliment and smiled at her son. "It's good to have you home."

Gladys laughed. "Well I know my cooking isn't up to much. I just don't seem to have the knack. However my sewing has improved. Louie has given me some tips."

Mrs. Taylor said nothing. She was very competitive when it came to cooking. However, she managed a thin smile.

Arthur beamed at his wife then turned to Fred again. "What about transport. Have you still got your old motorbike?"

Fred grinned. "Yes and the side car. Though petrol is still rationed. I manage to get enough to get me to work and sometimes there is a bit left to take Louie and the kids to Farndon for a walk on the river side."

"Hmm." Arthur paused with his spoon in the air before putting in a mouthful of blackcurrant tart. "I wonder if my old jalopy will start again after so many years idle. At least it is in the yard, I hope, unless Mr. Clark has scrapped it." He laughed.

"Well it is in the right place for you to strip it down and put it back in order again." Fred commented. He finished eating his tart and looked across the table at all the smiling faces cramped around the kitchen table. The one thing on his own mind was how long he and Louie would have to wait before they could move back into their own home.

Arthur must have read his mind. "So what is happening about your house? Is Joan still living there with her children?" Arthur searched Fred's face then Louisa's.

Louisa nodded. "Yes she is still renting it from us until she can go back to Liverpool. But it looks like it is going to be ages before the government can start re-building Liverpool so we will just have to wait. The housing shortage there is terrible. We don't want to put pressure on her." She sighed and Arthur shrugged sympathetically.

"As long as everyone is safe, that's all that matters." Mary Ellen said cheerfully as she cleared away the dishes. Dot helped her.

"We manage really." Dorothy said. "I don't mind sleeping with my nieces. We have a lot to be thankful for."

After the meal they went outside again as it was still a very warm evening. Fred lit a cigarette and Dorothy and Arthur both took one from his proffered packet. Arthur looked surprised to see his younger sister smoking. She shook her head at him defiantly. "I've been smoking ever since I worked at the munitions factory in Wolverhampton. Most of the girls did actually."

"What about you Louie?" Arthur asked.

Louisa shook her head. "I tried it a long time ago but I didn't like it. Besides I've got better things to spend my money on."

Arthur shrugged. "I dare say." He shifted his gaze across the garden where William had rows of vegetables growing in every small patch of soil he could find.

"Father has worked hard here. At least you can rely on fruit and vegetables if nothing else."

Louisa agreed. "Yes that's true and we have chickens too. At the end of the garden he has made a chicken coop with a small run fenced off to protect them from the foxes." She pointed to a ramshackle affair in the corner of the garden where two chickens could be seen pecking at the ground.

Arthur grinned. His eyes twinkling. "Very enterprising of father."

Dot came out just then with her boys and said goodbye as they were walking back home to

Rhosrobin. "Good to see you Arthur. Welcome home." She kissed him goodbye and they waved as she walked towards the Pandy fields.

Gladys joined them just then with their two children and her mother. She and Arthur got ready to leave too.

"We'll walk with you as far as Acton Smithy." Fred said. He raised his brows for confirmation from his wife. Louisa agreed and rounded up their two daughters.

Mary Ellen hugged Arthur again before they left and he promised to come and see her again soon. There were tears of joy in her eyes as she watched them walk down the lane at the side of the house. She just prayed she would see Harry again soon.

Chapter Two

A few weeks later on the sixth August Fred called Louisa to listen to the wireless as it was announced that the United States of America had dropped a bomb on Hiroshima killing thousands of people. Louisa stared at her husband in horror. There were mixed emotions running through her. The death of so many people shocked her.

"Does this mean the war in the Pacific has ended at last?"

Fred shrugged. "It could be the beginning of the end."

Louisa's thoughts turned to Harry still somewhere in Asia. The usual questions she could get no answers to whirled around in her head. Would he be alright? Would this bomb make things better or worse for him? She didn't know where Hiroshima was, would it be near his prison? Three years with no news and she had no idea for certain where he was.

Three days later another bomb was dropped. This time in Nagasaki. Apparently this bomb was even bigger than the first one.

"An awful loss of life will be taken in this senseless war." This was the only comment William would say about it.

The subsequent surrender of the Japanese gave the family new hope. No-one dared to mention Harry in case he wasn't alive. They dreaded a telegram coming to say he was dead.

Weeks passed without a word from Harry. There was no news about Fred's three brothers either. Then at the beginning of September they heard about the formal surrender of the Japanese. This had occurred on the second of September. On the same day, Fred received letters from Robert and Thomas. Tom had signed up for another two years in the army and would not be coming home for a while. He said he was fine and would visit Fred when he was on leave. He knew that the government were struggling to get the troops home and felt that at least he was one less to worry about. His decision to stay in the army was nothing to do with demobilisation he assured Fred. He reminded Fred that he was already serving in the army before the war started and had adapted to that way of life.

Bob on the other hand wrote to say that he was waiting for a troop ship to bring him home.

Fred put down the letters on the kitchen table after reading the short messages with pleasure. "That's good. I was beginning to worry about them. We just need to hear about John now. It's a shame that Tom isn't coming home yet though."

Louisa put a comforting arm on his shoulder. "Do you think Bob will be shipped to Liverpool or will he have to make his own way from Southampton like so many soldiers have had to do? Our Arthur being one of them."

"I hope they can get to Liverpool for their sake. But if he has to go to Southampton, at least I know he is on his way home."

"Do you think Bob and John will both be on the same ship?" Louisa asked.

Fred frowned. "It's hardly likely. Bob was a gunner in the artillery and John was in the guards. They are both in different regiments. But you never know. There are so many ships coming to and fro."

Two days later Fred was informed that John was also waiting for a troop ship. He felt it was likely that the ship would be destined for Southampton. He had no idea when.

"So he will have to make his way back to Liverpool?" Louisa asked. "Where will he stay? That place where he had digs was bombed and you know there is difficulty in getting housing."

Fred frowned. "I will write to Cissy and Mary to tell them. Perhaps they can help." Fred looked exasperated.

Louisa nodded. "It will be lovely to see them all again. Perhaps you should write to Maggie to see if she has heard anything else from Bob."

Fred wrote to his sister in law that very evening as well as to his two sisters. He posted the letters on his way to work the next day. Two weeks later Louisa received a letter from Cissy. She was looking forward to seeing her brothers again but had no more information to give. She hoped that both John and Bob would arrive in Southampton within days of each other.

When she knew more about their arrival Cissy was planning on going to stay with Maggie the night before with her two boys Neville and Michael. They planned to go to the train station to meet Bob and hopefully John too. Mary was also going to go to the station.

Fred frowned. "They have no idea what time the troop ship will arrive in Southampton. Neither do they have any idea how long it would take Bob and John to get home to Liverpool. They might not get a train the same day. Maggie and the rest of them could be waiting all day and probably the next." He sighed. "We don't know anything concrete except that they are safe. That will have to do."

Once they had a firm date for the ship's arrival, they agreed to allow a few days and then travel up to Liverpool.

"There won't be room for us all at Bob's" Fred said. "Perhaps we could stay with Jim and Annie – if you want to?" He looked at his wife anxiously."

"Of course I do. I'm sure they will welcome us and it means you can see all your brothers and sisters." She clapped her hands with glee. "Oh this is exciting. I just wish we could hear from Harry though."

Fred held up Cissy's letter in the air and hugged her. "Maybe this is the beginning of good news."

"I hope you are right." Louisa sighed.

However all Fred's plans to visit his brothers were dashed when Maggie got in touch to say that Bob and probably John would not be coming home directly after their ships docked in Southampton. Bob would be taken to a military disembarkation camp in Oxford. From there he would be transferred to another camp in Hereford called Bradbury Lines. They assumed this would be the same for John.

"We will just have to wait until we hear more." Fred sighed. "I'll be happier when I know they are on British soil."

"All these delays are frustrating." Louisa said. "Why will they have to go to Oxford and Hereford?" Fred breathed heavily. "I suppose they will need to get their papers signed and their wages sorted out. I daresay there will be thousands waiting to be sorted. And of course they will get their demob suits." Fred smirked at that comment. "Good luck with that!

The next day in the middle of September, Dot came rushing through the door with a letter in her hand. Her face was covered in smiles. She was out of breath because she had run all the way from Rhosrobin and could hardly speak. The children were in school and all she could say was Harry. Unable to breathe properly, she handed the letter to Mary Ellen. Louisa looked over her shoulder to read the tiny message that said. "I am coming home soon. Waiting for a hospital ship. All my love Harry X.

Mary Ellen collapsed in Louisa's arms with relief. Louisa was overcome with joy too and scarcely had the strength to guide her mother to a chair before she herself slumped into a chair by the kitchen table. She took hold of Dot's hands over the table and promptly wept. Mary Ellen too was silently weeping tears of joy.

Eventually Dot spoke. She wiped the tears from her face and said "I think we need a cup of tea, don't you?" She began to laugh hysterically and Louisa joined her too.

21

"Yes, let's have some tea. Make it a strong one and hell to the rations. I will go without tea for two days to compensate. This news is the best we have had for such a long time."

Mary Ellen took off her glasses and wiped them with the end of her apron. "Yes, it is very good news indeed." She sniffed. "Your father will be so pleased when he comes home from work tonight."

"Why wait mother?" Louisa said. "Why don't we walk up to Stansty farm and tell him?"

Mary Ellen began to smile as she let Louisa's words sink in. "Yes. He deserves to know. Let's have our tea first and then after we have told your father you must go and tell Arthur."

Wanting to share her happiness Dot said she would go with them and then she would get a bus from Stansty with Louisa to tell Arthur.

As they drank their tea they began to wonder what state of health Harry was in if he had to wait for a hospital ship.

"Maybe it was the only ship available." Louisa mused. "We lost so many ships during the war. It might not be a British ship. It might be Australian or American."

Mary Ellen laughed. "I don't care what ship it is as long as it brings Harry home." Her gaze fell on her youngest granddaughter who had just wandered into the kitchen clutching a rag doll. Her dark hair had been plaited with a ribbon and the child was now sucking the end of the ribbon. "Your uncle Harry is coming home Susan."

The little girl smiled and then climbed on to her mother's knee. "Harry." She repeated. Her mother beamed at her daughter. "Yes. Harry."

Together, the three women walked the two miles over the fields to Stansty farm. The two younger women stood with Susan a little way back in the field as they saw William with his beloved shire horses. They could see his anxious face when his wife approached him. His expression fell into a grin as he hugged Mary Ellen with obvious relief. He beckoned to Louisa and Dot to join them. He hugged Dot who began to cry again. "This is good news isn't it? At last."

Presently they said goodbye to William who wore a smile on his face for the rest of the day. They walked to the Mold road to get the bus into Wrexham. Mary Ellen had decided to go with the younger women to tell Arthur the good news. His reaction was similar to his father's and when they finally let go of him they returned to the bus stop in King Street. Dot said she would go straight home to Rhosrobin and so they said goodbye whilst Mary Ellen and Louisa waited with Susan for the Chester bus.

As they waited, Mary Ellen asked Louisa if she ought to go and tell Fred. She shook her head. "I don't know which building site he is on today. I could be walking all over Wrexham and still not find him. He will be home at six o clock I will tell him then." She exhaled heavily. Her emotions had taken a lot of her strength. Mary Ellen too said she felt drained.

"What about Gladys?" Louisa suggested.

Mary Ellen shook her head. "Let Arthur tell her. Besides, it is getting late and we need to get back to pick up Christine from school."

The day seemed to fly by. Louisa saw Dot again at the school where she waited for Gordon and Malcolm. The smile had not left her face and somehow Dot looked younger. The three years of waiting had left its mark on Dot's face, but today the strain was no longer in evidence and she was radiant. She waited until Christine had joined the little group before telling the children the good news. Gordon was ecstatic. However Malcolm and Christine received the news without much display of emotion. Both Dot and Louisa were saddened to witness their lack lustre reaction but acknowledged that the children had not seen Harry for almost four years when both Christine and Malcolm were only two years of age.

The younger children's reaction was sharp contrast to that of Dorothy and Fred who were both delighted with the news.

"So how long will the ship take to come from Singapore to Britain Fred?" Dorothy asked excitedly.

"Depends on the size of the ship and the weather. A couple of weeks I expect." Fred replied. "Always supposing they have sent in mine sweepers first." He breathed heavily thinking about the narrow escapes he himself had experienced only a year earlier whilst serving in the Royal Navy. His ship had hit a mine when in Normandy. Fortunately the ship had not been too badly damaged and no-one was hurt. His memories made him think of his youngest brother. Eddie had been killed whilst carrying out mine sweeping at the end of nineteen forty two.

As the days went by there was no more further news about Harry. Then on the twelfth of September Dot received a more detailed letter from Harry. It seemed that there were a shortage of ships and that he would have to wait a bit longer. Those who were in most need of medical attention were being taken first to medical centres in other parts of the country and the rest had to wait their turn. The ex-prisoners were being transported in alphabetical order according to their surnames, so he hoped he wouldn't have to wait too long since 'Edwards' was towards the beginning of the alphabet. It was three weeks later when Dot received a letter to say that Harry had left Singapore on the twenty seventh of September on a Polish ship called Sobieski. Prior to that he had been taken to Rangoon to be 'fattened up' as he and his fellow prisoners of war had not been fed properly.

"What does that mean?" Louisa asked indignantly. "Why haven't they been fed properly?"

Dot could only shake her head in wonder when she told Louisa and Mary Ellen.

The weeks seemed to drag by as they waited for more news. It was the newspapers that told them that the ship Sobieski was due to dock in Liverpool on twenty third of October. There was still no news about Bob and John's demobilisation and they assumed that they were still waiting for a troop ship.

Meanwhile Louisa was excitedly making plans to go to Liverpool docks.

"We must go." Louisa said to her mother. Mary Ellen agreed whole heartedly that they should accompany Dot. William said he would go too. Fred who had originally planned to take two days off work without pay to see his own brothers decided he would go to Liverpool too. He felt it was too important a day to miss. Dorothy also decided to accompany them. She too took a day off from work without pay.

They got an early train on the twenty third of October. Dot had packed as much food as she could spare to greet her husband. Her sister Ivy was looking after her two sons. Gordon had wanted to go with them but Dot wasn't sure what state of health Harry would be in and whether it would be too overwhelming for Harry to have so many of his family to greet him. He hadn't seen his sons for such a long time. Meanwhile, at the last minute Arthur decided to go with them. He wanted to use up his petrol ration to take everyone in the car. Fred advised him to leave the car at home.

"Liverpool is in a mess." Fred said. "You won't be able to park anywhere near the pier and if the crowds are anything like when I came home to Southampton you won't be able to use the roads safely. Not that the roads are much better. There is still rubble lying around everywhere."

So Arthur took Fred's advice and he accompanied the little party travelling by train.

The small group assembled themselves early at the docks and happily waited hours for the ship to arrive. They were grateful for the sandwiches and flasks of stewed tea. As the time went on more and more people gathered on the quayside. Eventually the ship arrived greeted by shrieks and hand waving as they watched the disembarkation of the survivors.

"Can you see him?" Louisa asked excitedly. Her companions shook their heads all of them straining their eyes to catch a glimpse of Harry. All they could see were hundreds of gaunt looking men and women being greeted by loved ones and walking away arms entwined.

More and more walking skeletons seemed to pass them by and Louisa began to worry that if these men were ex-prisoners of war, then what would Harry look like. She cast an anxious look at Arthur's face and she could see her concern mirrored in his eyes. She gulped trying to prepare herself for the worst. As she turned towards her parents and Dot she felt and saw their uneasiness whilst more and more under nourished men and women walked past them. Still they strained their eyes hoping to catch sight of the man they had not seen for nearly four years.

In the end it was Harry who found them. A lean man with a pinched face walked straight up to Dot and threw his arms around her. At his approach Dot had stared at his face in disbelief. Only when in his tight embrace did she catch sight of the familiar blue eyes and dark wavy hair similar to his brother and father. Then she recognised him and yielded to his grip.

"Harry, Harry!" is all Dot could say and they stood together encircled in each other's arms for several minutes whilst the rest of his family were transfixed on the emotional display they were witnessing. Eventually Harry released Dot and one by one he hugged the rest of his family. First his mother who he hugged tightly, then his father then his sisters. Finally his brother and his brother-in-law.

"Good to see you Harry." Arthur said gruffly breaking the spell. Fred agreed.

"Yes, yes it is." The others repeated smiling through their tears. Mary Ellen could not hold back her tears and William comforted her with his arm around her shoulders. Harry's eyes glittered and took his mother from his father's grip and held her closely to him again. She clung on to him openly weeping noisily. Louisa handed her a clean handkerchief and eventually Mary Ellen managed to smile again.

Arthur took charge of the little reunion. "Come on what we all need is a cup of tea. Fred can you show us the way to a café?" They followed Fred and Louisa away from the quay side towards the centre of the city where Fred managed to find a little café.

Once settled they poured the tea and Arthur bought some buns. At sight of the buns Harry's eyes lit up. "I haven't seen one of them for a long time." They all laughed and were delighted to see him tuck into the confection.

"Here have mine." William said. "You look as if you need fattening up."

Harry forced a laugh and willingly took his father's bun. "If you had seen me two months ago…," he hesitated,"I was a lot thinner than this."

They stared at him appalled at what he had said.

"Didn't they feed you?" Mary Ellen cried.

Harry shook his head. "Not much."

Louisa looked into her brother's emaciated face and held back more tears that were threatening to burst down her cheeks.

Dot beamed a tearful smile. "We'll feed you up again as soon as we get you home. She squeezed his hand lovingly. "We've missed you so much."

When they arrived in Wrexham much later, Dot and Harry got a taxi home. Arthur said he would walk home to Acton because he felt the walk would do him good. Louisa guessed he was upset about

28

seeing the withered body of his brother and wanted to compose himself before seeing Gladys. The rest of the party caught a bus to Acton Smithy and strolled up the lane back to Pandy.

Mary Ellen was happy to have her son home again but sad at seeing how frail he was. William was angry at the way his son had been neglected. The others shared their views but decided not to say anything else.

They each realised that it was going to be a long time before Harry got back to the way he used to be. They decided to leave him in peace for a day or two to spend time with Dot and his children.

"I'm just glad he's home. That's enough for me for now." Mary Ellen said.

Louisa agreed that it was wonderful that Harry was home. She added that he would need a lot of nourishment to get him back to the way he was. Everyone vowed they would do their best to help restore Harry to his previous self.

There was no-one more devoted than Dot and Mary Ellen to provide nourishment for Harry. Over the next two months they worked hard to provide him with the nutrition he needed. With the help of Dot's family and Harry's family he began to look healthier and by Christmas his face had begun to fill out again bringing with it some semblance of the vigour that once marked his features. As his energy levels increased his relationship with his two sons improved. Harry had experienced the same disappointment that both Fred and Arthur had felt, when their children had looked upon them as strangers. Gordon had been easier to bond with even though the young boy scarcely recognised his father.

Malcolm on the other hand reacted to Harry in the same way as Christine had reacted to Fred's home coming.

At the beginning of December Harry began to lose the haunting shadow that masked his features. His bone structure was less prominent and from time to time Louisa caught glimpses of the man he used to be. She hoped with time he would return completely to his old self.

So it was an emotional time for all when one dry but cold day in mid-December Harry summoned up enough energy to play football with his two sons. The very next day they accompanied Fred, Arthur and Brian to a football match to watch Wrexham play Shrewsbury in the FA cup where they witnessed a draw.

Earlier that same month the long awaited arrival of Bob and John finally arrived. It seems that miraculously they had both made contact with each other at the demobilisation centre in Hereford and would be travelling together on the same train to Liverpool. Fred was pleased to hear that the brothers had managed to reunite with each other. However he was somewhat disappointed to discover that John would be leaving the train at Crewe. Apparently his sweetheart Joan lived in Crewe and her parents had offered him accommodation. They had a box room where he could sleep. Joan's father said he would help John get a job at the same factory where he worked. He also planned to marry Joan as soon as possible.

"I can't blame him. In a way I'm relieved." Fred said. "He's got somewhere to stay and the prospect of a job."

Louisa hugged him. She knew he was fond of his younger brother. "Well at least we can give Bob a good welcome. I think we should go to Liverpool to meet the train."

Fred looked pleased then a worried expression shadowed his face. "The trouble is we don't know what time he will be leaving Hereford. We might miss him. The train will be heaving with returning troops."

"Well, if we miss him we can go to the house. Just for a few minutes at least." Louisa suggested. "If Maggie isn't at the station we know he has been and gone home."

Fred arranged with his boss to take a day off work and he and Louisa got the early train to Liverpool. Fred warned Louisa that there would be thousands of people on the platforms and thousands of people getting off the trains. It would be difficult to find each other. He laughed. "We might not see him. We might not recognise him."

A voice behind him laughed. "We will. Don't you worry! There are too many of us to let him slip past. If we are all together, he won't fail to see us."

Fred and Louisa turned round in astonishment.

"Cissy!" Fred said. His face beamed and hugged his sister. His smile widened when over her shoulder he saw Mary and then Maggie and then Jim.

Cissy lit a cigarette whilst Fred and Louisa greeted and hugged the others in turn. The cigarettes were passed around and all but Louisa took one.

"Do you know what time he will get here?" Fred asked his sister-in-law.

Maggie shook her head. "He said it depended on how easy it was to get on the train. The poor sod might have to stand all the way." She glanced at a train that had just pulled in where newly demobbed troops were virtually tumbling out of the doors. They followed her gaze all of them straining to see if they could see Bob.

Louisa felt suffocated there was hardly room to move. The platform became more and more packed as one by one the uniformed occupants of the train passed them by. Most of them falling into the arms of their loved ones. But no Bob. Eventually the platform was less crowded as the first tranche of the demobbed left.

Two more hours later Bob finally arrived. Maggie pounced on him. Fred took his kitbag from him and carried it for him off the platform. Amidst tears and laughter they all walked away from the station so that they could talk. There were so many people hugging and kissing with children running around them they created a moving human wave as they headed towards the rubbled city.

Most of the cafes they found had little room for them to sit down but by sharing chairs and sitting on the edge of tables and then squashing themselves together they managed to gather themselves into a large corner of a café. There they managed to chat over endless cups of weak tea and coffee.

The scene was similar to the arrival of Harry. The customers in the café hailed the men in uniform as heroes and made way for them all. Bob bemused by the fuss finally sank on a chair next to his wife.

With an arm around Maggie he leaned across the table to chat to Fred and Jim. Mary and Cissy leaned over the back of Fred and Jim's chairs. Louisa sat on Fred's knee and gazed around the café at all the smiling faces. Taking up space besides the excited human bodies were the temporarily abandoned kitbags, some of them were stored under the tables.

As she contemplated the family through the sea of uniformed men and women and the haze of cigarette smoke that engulfed them all Louisa felt content. More than once whilst waiting on the platform had she reflected how grateful she was that her husband had returned home from the war alive.

As the hours passed the café became even more shrouded with clouds of nicotine and happy faces. It soon became time for Fred and Louisa to say goodbye. They promised to keep in touch.

When they eventually returned to Pandy, Louisa described to her mother the emotional scenes she had witnessed.

"It was as if Liverpool was wetter than the docks, not with the sea but the tears of love and gladness."

The description moved Mary Ellen to tears. William shook Fred's hand and said how pleased he was for him.

Chapter Three

1946

Harry continued to improve in health and by the end of February he felt fit enough to resume working for his old employer as a painter and decorator. It seemed everything was slowly getting back to normal or at least something nearer to what it was like before the war broke out.

"If only this Labour Government would increase the rations." Mary Ellen complained bitterly one March afternoon.

Louisa had heard her mother grumble about rationing for so long that she ignored her comment. Instead she tried to say something positive about the Government. She knew her mother had voted Liberal as she always had but she and Fred had voted Labour in the General election the previous summer.

"Well Clement Atlee has said he will improve welfare for ordinary people and start a house building programme. Hopefully we will see the evidence of that soon."

Mary Ellen said nothing. She was concentrating on turning the collar and cuffs of one of William's shirts. Louisa was doing something similar for Fred. She tried again to engage her mother in conversation.

"At least Fred, Arthur and Harry have got their old jobs back. So many people are still out of work you know."

Mary Ellen sighed. "Yes, I know. I shouldn't grumble. We are luckier than most. It just seems that even though the war is over we still can't live the way we were in 1939. Maybe when they start building houses, Joan will be able to move back to Liverpool and you can have your old house back." She looked up suddenly to gaze at her daughter. "I'm sorry I didn't mean to say that I am fed up of you and Fred and the children staying here. I just mean I want everything to be back the way it was."

It was Louisa's turn to sigh. "It would be nice to move back. Joan is very grateful you know. She is also very kind to let us use her bathroom too. After all she is paying us rent." She put a pin in her mouth whilst she arranged the cuff.

"But that only just covers your mortgage doesn't it?" Louisa took the pin out of her mouth and turned the cuff around another inch. "Yes it does, but at least we are not in debt and we have a stake in some property. Joan's four children are looking a lot better too. She's managed to get a part time job as a music teacher in Grove Park School, and she is enjoying it very much. Apparently that is what she did before she got married."

Mary Ellen looked up from her darning. "If that is the case, she may not want to return to Liverpool."

Louisa met her mother's eyes and shrugged. "Possibly not. In any case the way things are going it will be a long time before she gets the option to move back. The housing shortage there is as bad as London and there doesn't seem to be much effort being made for shifting the rubble and re-building."

Louisa put away her mending and got up to get her coat. "I'm going to fetch Christine from school. Susan is still asleep."

Mary Ellen nodded. This was the usual format of the week day afternoons. Sometimes Louisa took Susan with her to the school if she was awake.

Outside Gwersyllt primary school Louisa met up with Dot who was there to collect Gordon and Malcolm. Together they walked down the lane towards Rhosrobin which was en route to Pandy.

Whilst the children were out of earshot Dot confided in Louisa that both of her boys had accidently witnessed Harry having a wash in their tiny washroom downstairs. He had stripped off his shirt to the waist and the boys had seen the lash marks on his back. They were very distressed about it.

Louisa was distressed too when she was reminded of the beatings that Harry had taken whilst being a prisoner of war.

"What did Harry say?" Louisa asked.

"He tried to shrug it off and said it looked worse than it was."

"Well we both know that isn't true!" exclaimed Louisa. Her eyes filled with tears.

"Harry doesn't want to upset them anymore. He feels they have gone through enough." She hesitated. "The thing is Gordon has taken it very badly and has become withdrawn. He's older, as you know and he's heard stories from his classmates about the Japanese prisoner of war camps."

Louisa pulled in her lips in dismay. She was instinctively protective of her brother. "Harry has been through a lot too. I know he doesn't complain, he's so grateful to be back home."

Dot smiled. "Yes he is grateful beyond words. Sometimes though he looks as if his mind is far away and I know he is thinking about the war. He is very bitter that they had to surrender."

"They were obeying orders, he had no choice!" Louisa protested.

Dot nodded her head. "I know, I keep telling him that. I suppose time will heal. As for Gordon I hope in time he will get better too. He follows Harry around everywhere when he can, as if he is expecting him to go away again."

Louisa didn't know what to say to make things better. All she could manage was to repeat Dot's words "time will heal." She sincerely hoped it would.

During early summer Dorothy declared that she was going to spend the night in Wolverhampton in her old digs. She explained that her old colleagues from the munitions factory where she had worked had organised a reunion.

"There's going to be a band playing as well as a lot of the girls I used to work with in munitions. Some have got married now and are bringing their husbands." Dorothy confided in Louisa who was watching her sister get ready.

"This dress will have to do. It's one that you made for me with the material that was left over from the blackout curtains." She grinned mischievously at her sister "with a bit of help from me." She held up a flared cotton dress with three quarter length sleeves. Louisa had inserted panels of black and white polka dots into the skirt part of the dress and had added a polka dot collar. Two rows of large white buttons six inches apart ran down the front of the top of the dress to finish it off.

Louisa rolled her eyes good humouredly and replied with a hint of sarcasm. "What you mean is you helped to sew the buttons on!" She lifted up the dress from the bed to feel the material.

"I like this style of dress and it suits you. It seems everyone is wearing polka dots these days." She helped her sister into it and zipped her up at the back. Dorothy smoothed down the dress and looked at herself in the mirror. Satisfied with her appearance she began to put some red lipstick on. There was scarcely any left in the container and she dabbed her finger on the top to smooth it on to her lips. She scowled. "We are going to run out of this very soon."

Louisa picked up the near empty lipstick container and carefully put it back in the makeup box she shared with her sister. She changed her mind and took it out again staring ruefully at the lipstick. "Do you want to take it with you? There is hardly anything left now. You may as well finish it off."

"Are you sure you don't mind?" Dorothy took it from her eagerly and put it in her clutch bag. Louisa shook her head. "No, I'm not going anywhere special. Fred and I are probably going to see a film later but I don't need to wear lipstick for that. Anyway you know he doesn't really like it."

Dorothy laughed. "No he doesn't does he? He always has to say why are you wearing that stuff? He is a bit old fashioned like that, even though his two sisters wear it all the time."

Louisa shrugged. "At least he doesn't try to stop me using it."

Dorothy grinned at her sister. "He wouldn't dare to try." They both laughed.

After Dorothy had left to get the train to Wolverhampton, Arthur and Gladys arrived in Pandy to see if Louisa and Fred would like to go and see a film with them.

As usual they debated which cinema to go to and ended up deciding on the Odeon to see *Gilda*. "Who is playing Gilda?" Louisa asked as she draped her cardigan over her shoulders. It was a mild summery evening but she knew it would be cold when they returned home later.

"Rita Hayworth!" Arthur replied. "It should be a good film."

Fred agreed. "It has had some good reviews."

They followed Arthur and Gladys out to Arthur's car. He had managed to get his old Austin Seven to function again and they all happily slid into the vehicle to get to the cinema.

Two hours later they emerged from the cinema just as the light was fading outside.

"Well that was good. I enjoyed that." Louisa stated when they left the cinema. Gladys agreed. "It's a shame Harry and Dot couldn't come, it would be just like old times."

Arthur shrugged and then sighed. "I think old Harry would have enjoyed it too – and Dot. They don't get out much these days."

39

"Can't Dot's mother look after the two boys?" Gladys asked as she lit up a cigarette. She inhaled deeply and blew out the smoke above their heads as they walked to the car.

"It's not that so much." Louisa explained. "Harry likes to spend as much time as he can with the boys and Dot is happy that they are all together."

Neither Arthur nor Fred made any other remark. Both of them had seen atrocities during their service in the war and they were glad to be home. They knew that Harry had endured a lot of suffering when he was a prisoner of war and was having difficulty still to come to terms with the fact that he was now free.

"What shall we see next week?" Fred said trying to be cheerful. Louisa squeezed his hand affectionately. He always tried to be positive.

As expected the group began to argue which film would be best to watch and which was the best cinema. When Arthur finally drove them back to Pandy, Fred and Louisa quietly crept upstairs to bed. Louisa checked on the two girls sleeping alone in the double bed. They seemed lost in the big bed without Dorothy who was no doubt dancing the night away Louisa mused. She kissed both girls on their foreheads and then went to join Fred. She felt lucky to be loved and have two lovely children. She snuggled up in bed with Fred's arms around her and for some reason began to think about her sister.

When Dorothy arrived home late on Sunday evening she couldn't wait to tell Louisa about her reunion party the night before. She waited until the little girls were asleep and beckoned Louisa into her bedroom where they whispered conspiratorially.

"I've met the most wonderful man Louisa! She confided. Her eyes were sparkling and Louisa was immediately enthralled by her sister's enthusiasm. "What's he like?"

Dorothy sidled around the bed hanging up her clothes in the wardrobe as she spoke. "He's very very tall, he has thick dark hair and is really good looking."

"I see, so he's tall dark and handsome." Louisa smirked. They both laughed.

"Yes I know it is a bit clichéd but he really is Louisa."

"So who is he and what's his name? Are you going to see him again?"

"His name is William Linton and he's a friend of Joyce's husband George. They don't call him William though they call him Bill. He hasn't long come back from Palestine. Before that he was in Greece."

"Joyce is one of the women you worked with isn't she? I seem to recall you mentioning her name."

"Yes she lives in Ellesmere Port now with her husband. They have rooms in her parent's house. They were engaged before the war and he was one of the fortunate ones who came back." She sighed ruefully as she thought of the people who did not return from the war. Louisa was thinking the same thoughts. However neither girls wanted to dwell on such sad events. They had both spent too many years shedding too many tears over those they had known and lost whilst serving their country. Almost as if they had read each other's minds both of them made an effort to push away these unhappy events and tried to be cheerful.

"So are you going to see him again soon?" Louisa asked.

Dorothy nodded ecstatically. "Yes next Saturday. We are going to meet in Chester. He lives in Mold but works in Chester. He's got a temporary job as a shop assistant in the draper's shop not far from where I work in Greene's Stores. It makes it easier for both of us to travel home from Chester." She whirled around quickly from the wardrobe. "I'm not going to tell mum and dad yet. You won't say anything will you?"

Louisa got off the edge of the bed and tiptoed to the bedroom door. "Of course not. I'm glad you are happy. Pleasant dreams." Smiling broadly, she tiptoed back to her own bedroom and got in next to Fred. He was nearly asleep so she decided to keep her news until the next day.

As the following day was Monday and Fred had to get up early to go to work, Louisa had little chance to tell Fred the news about Dorothy. She waited until he had eaten his supper. Then they went outside in the garden to get some fresh air. She wanted to make sure they were out of earshot of her parents. Fred was delighted that Dorothy had met someone who she thought she might love.

"After the heartache she went through after losing Frank, that's good news isn't it?" He commented as he took his cigarettes out of his pocket and lit one. He inhaled appreciatively.

"Yes it is, but she doesn't want mother and father to know just yet. She's being cautious after Frank."

Fred shrugged. "Understandable I suppose."

Much later they went upstairs to bed. Louisa took the clips out of her dark hair and brushed it in front of the mirror. Satisfied with this action she got into bed.

"By the way I got a letter from Olive today. She and Sidney would like to come to Wrexham to see us. Sidney is going to visit some family members in the area – Ruabon – I think and they thought we could meet up somewhere and spend the day together."

"Olive is the girl you used to work with in Broughton Hall?"

Louisa nodded. Fred raised his eyebrows mischievously whilst he gazed at his wife's face before continuing. "And she is the woman who almost broke up Arthur and Gladys?"

Louisa laughed. "Well not really, but her appearance did put a spoke in the wheel. Still it all worked out well in the end."

"I take it you won't be asking Arthur and Gladys to meet up with them." Fred smiled jovially. He bent down to unlace his shoes then after removing them looked up again with a question in his expression.

"Have you any idea where we should meet?"

Louisa looked into her husband's eyes and smiled. "Actually yes. I mean no I am not inviting Arthur and Glad, and yes I have thought where we could meet. I was thinking we could get the bus to Froncysylte and walk over the aqueduct. It is a wonderful piece of engineering and you have always said you would like to see it."

"Good idea. Perhaps we should ask Harry and Dot to come too. Their boys would love to see the canal. I'm sure our girls would too. We will have to watch Susan doesn't try to jump in the water."

Louisa grimaced as she thought about Susan's wild antics. She acknowledged that it would be just like her to walk along the high aqueduct wall then fall off into the valley.

"I will write to Olive tomorrow and try to arrange something for next Saturday afternoon. You will be home from work in time to get changed."

Upon reading Olive's return letter, Louisa was pleased that Olive and Sidney liked Louisa's idea of walking over the aqueduct. It would be easy to get there from Ruabon. So on the following Sunday the little party met near the canal at the agreed time of three o clock.

At the meeting point Fred stood gazing at the plaque which read that the Aqueduct sat on nineteen cast iron sections and was one hundred and twenty six feet high. The aqueduct had taken nearly ten years to build. Construction had started in seventeen ninety five and was finished around eighteen hundred and eight.

"It took ten years to build the Mersey tunnel." Fred mused to no-one in particular. He carried on reading the plaque which informed him that the civil engineers Thomas Telford and William Jessop were responsible for the aqueduct's construction. Ever since its completion it had been used to transport coal, iron, slate and limestone across Dee Valley.

Harry came to stand next to him, Gordon and Malcolm in his wake. "This is a wonderful achievement. I've only been here once before, and that was a very long time ago." Harry rested a hand on each shoulder of his sons. "This is a piece of history that tells us all about the canal age in this country. We are very privileged to have it more or less on our doorstep."

He smiled at his sons who gazed at their father in awe. They were soon distracted though by the capers of Christine and Susan who were running and skipping up and down the canal path. The two boys joined them. Gordon gave a backward glance at his father reassuring himself that Harry was following, then ran off to play with his brother and his cousins.

Ahead of the children walked Louisa, Dot, Olive and Sidney. Olive was three months pregnant and was giving an account of the house she and Sidney were renting in Fairwater a small village just a few miles outside Cardiff.

"We were very lucky to get re-housed so quickly." Olive said. "In fact I was lucky I wasn't in the house in Pearl Street when the bomb dropped. I was working in Bridgend at the time in the munitions factory."

"Yes, I remember hearing about that bomb raid in Cardiff." Louisa said. "I know that some people in Pearl Street were not so fortunate."

Sidney shook his head. "No, it was tragic that many people lost their lives. The Luftwaffe were aiming for the port so parts of Cardiff caught the tail end of the raid." He put his arm protectively around Olive. "I'm just glad that we have each other. We are the lucky ones."

They strolled along the towpath towards a nearby wood and watched the children run around playing in the trees. Fred took out a map he had brought with him and studied it. Standing up to look around he remarked that if they were to walk up the little hill that he could see a few hundred yards ahead, they would be able to see a section of Offa's Dyke and Dinas Bran castle in the distance.

Louisa linked her arm in Fred and smiled at him adoringly. "Come on then. Let's go." She and Fred took the lead and the rest followed enthusiastically whilst the children weaved themselves around the adults as they walked. Meanwhile the sun continued to shine and everyone lifted their faces to the sky enjoying the warmth and the simple pleasure of being outdoors.

Eventually they found a tea shop which sold ice lollies and the children happily sat down near the river Dee eating their carrot flavoured ices.

The view across the river was beautiful with the fading evening sun etching shadows across the water. Whilst the adults enjoyed their tea, Louisa thought how idyllic everything was and how just two years ago they were all apart from each other and unsure what the future would bring. She looked across at her handsome husband with pride and then at her brother who seemed to have brightened up considerably that day. He was looking much healthier than he had been eight months earlier. He caught her gazing at him and beamed a wide smile. "Happy Louie?"

She nodded. "Now my family are home and well, yes I am." She turned towards Fred and he put his arm around her shoulders then kissed her head. "It's been a good day. I'm hoping this is the beginning of many to come."

Harry agreed. "We deserve it."

Olive and Sidney declared they needed to catch a bus back to Ruabon where they were staying with Sidney's aunt and uncle. Before getting on the bus Olive promised to write to Louisa to tell her when her baby had arrived. The two friends hugged each other. The rest of the party decided to stay another hour. They were enjoying the day out with the children.

Before heading for home in his old car, Harry said he and Dot would wait with Fred and Louisa at the bus stop until the Chester bus arrived from Llangollen. The bus would stop at Acton Smithy making it easier for the little party to walk from there to get back to Pandy. They sat down on the bench and Louisa pulled a very sleepy Susan on to her knee.

"Olive looks well." Dot remarked as she squeezed up besides Harry on the wooden bench. "Pregnancy suits her. It was nice to see her again. A shame Arthur and Glad couldn't come too."

At this comment Harry suddenly burst out laughing and Louisa looked at him in surprise. It was good to hear him laugh but she was astonished at the force of his guffaw. It was almost as if something had been gurgling inside him for some time and was now spurting out.

Dot stared at her husband somewhat dumbfounded at his outburst. "What's so funny?"

"Don't you remember how jealous Gladys was, when Arthur brought Olive to Pandy that Christmas time?" Harry replied. He almost choked as he tried to restrain his laughter which eventually faded into a wide grin. It was as if that innocent comment from Dot had unleashed a knot in Harry's stomach and he laughed so loudly and heartily, that it became infectious.

Fred grinned broadly too and Louisa began to laugh too as she recalled the fury on her sister-in-law's face when she saw Olive sitting on the chair in Pandy.

"It wasn't so funny at the time." Louisa said wiping the tears from her eyes. She struggled to control herself and stared blearily at Christine's bemused face who had pushed herself towards her mother at the sound of everyone laughing. The little girl leaned over her sleeping sister slumped on her mother's knee. Just then they saw the bus arriving. Fred hurriedly lifted Susan up into his arms whilst Christine hung on to her mother's arm and together they got on the bus. They turned to wave goodbye through the window and Louisa could see that both Dot and Harry still wore wide beams of laughter on their faces.

Settled on the bus Louisa recalled the days when she and Olive had worked together in Wallasey. She had been very homesick and miserable. Olive was the only person who had been kind to her. When Arthur had arrived to visit her, he had made a decision to take her home again much to the disgust of the housekeeper. Olive had had to take over the scrubbing of the floor in Louisa's place. Meanwhile Arthur had marched Louisa through the main entrance door catching sight of Olive kneeling on the floor. Despite her distress Louisa had detected a hint of chemistry between Arthur and Olive. A year later when circumstances had brought Olive to Wrexham they had become re-acquainted. By that time Arthur was in a serious relationship with Gladys who was unhappy with the appearance of Olive in Pandy. Both Arthur and Olive had always insisted that their friendship was purely platonic. Things came to a head when Gladys discovered that

Arthur had taken Olive to see a film. A huge row had ensued which days later ended with them becoming engaged to be married. Louisa smiled as she remembered those halcyon years before she herself was married. She looked up at Fred who caught her smiling.

"I bet you are thinking about Arthur and Olive." He said.

Louisa nodded and squeezed his hand. Her thoughts drifted on to Dorothy. She hoped that her secret romance with Bill Linton would make her happy.

It was very soon after Dorothy's birthday in November when Dorothy decided to tell Mary Ellen and William about her romance with Bill. He had bought her a gold locket and she was anxious to show it off. They were astonished and thrilled to hear that she had found a new love in her life.

"So when are we going to meet him?" Mary Ellen asked.

Dorothy replied that she hoped he could come for tea one Sunday before Christmas.

Mary Ellen happily agreed to that suggestion. Meanwhile she began prepare for Christmas. She was also determined to make a special tea for the mysterious Bill Linton.

Louisa felt a little bit sorry for the man to have to deal with so many of Dorothy's relations all at once. She smiled to herself when she recalled the day she had met all of Fred's brothers and sisters for the first time in Liverpool.

Bill seemed to take things in his stride when he arrived with Dorothy. She had gone to the Chester road to wait by the Smithy bus stop to meet him.

They came in through the kitchen door arm in arm both faces wreathed in smiles.

It was evident to Louisa that her sister was in love. She hoped everything would work out well for her. At least Bill looked healthy unlike Frank who when Dorothy had first introduced them a few years ago, had always looked frail. Dorothy had been hopelessly in love with him and devastated when he died of pneumonia.

Bill seemed at his ease sitting round the table with the rest of the family. He said he had a sister and brother of his own who were both married with children and so he was used to big family gatherings. He also had another brother living at home in Mold and an aunt and uncle who lived in London.

"Mold isn't too far from here." Mary Ellen commented. "Do you visit the family in London much?"

Bill shrugged. "The whole family used to visit regularly when I was younger. We lost touch during the war but I went to see them recently. They are both in good health. They escaped the bombs."

Fred engaged him in conversation about films as was his wont and was delighted that Bill was also enthusiastic about the cinema.

"I'm hoping to take Dorothy to see "*Great Expectations*" when it comes out in Chester." Bill confided.

"Yes we are looking forward to seeing that too." Fred remarked as his eyes searched Louisa's for confirmation. She met his glance and nodded her agreement and passed around some mince pies.

Both Mary Ellen and William seemed satisfied that Dorothy and Bill appeared to be happy. After Dorothy had left the house to walk Bill back to the bus stop Mary Ellen commented to Louisa as they cleared away the dishes that she was pleased to see Dorothy happy again.

"She's found her sparkle again and Harry is getting his back too thank God."

Louisa agreed. "Let's hope the New Year will be a new and happy beginning for her and for all of us."

Chapter Four

1947

At the beginning of the New Year the government announced that they were going to nationalise the coal mines. This announcement precipitated discussion in Pandy and villages all across Wrexham. The announcement brought back to the surface the memories of the disaster that had occurred in nearby Gresford colliery. Those old enough to remember easily recalled vividly that tragic early morning in September in nineteen thirty four where 265 men had died.

"Do you think this plan of Sir Stafford Cripps will make mining safer than it was?" William asked Fred. "He's been talking about nationalising the mines ever since he defended the miners during the Gresford disaster inquiry."

Fred didn't hesitate. "If it means the health and safety of miners is taken from the hands of greedy private mine owners, then yes I think it will."

"Does this mean that Gresford will have to change its name?" Louisa asked.

Fred shook his head. "No it will be still Gresford but it will come under the umbrella of the National Coal Board."

Fred's expression was sad as he recalled the day he read about the explosion in the Liverpool Echo. Louisa too recalled vividly that terrible day. She had been working in Broughton Hall at the time as a housemaid. She had been woken in the early hours of the morning to be told that there had been an explosion. Days later when she had visited her family in Pandy there had been an awful sense of loss and grief everywhere she went.

She shivered, partly from her memories and partly because despite her father having built up a fire that Sunday morning it was still cold in the draughty kitchen. She was not the only one who shivered. They were all huddled around the fire trying to keep warm. She stared at the coal bucket remembering how the widows of the coal miners struggled to get through that first winter without money and without coal. There had been a collection which had raised a lot of money but that didn't go very far. Besides, the money in no way replaced the lives of loved ones. The explosion had affected the lives of almost everyone she knew.

Her father had talked of a man he once knew who had been killed. His name was David Lloyd Jones. He was upset when he saw his name listed in the newspaper. In the same newspaper Louisa had read that a Mrs. Clutton had lost three sons. Some women had lost husbands and sons.

Mary Ellen got up out of her chair and poked the fire then put some more coal on. "I've never known a cold winter as much as this one." She said.

Later that month, it was still cold. But the weather didn't stop Fred, Arthur and Harry going to watch Wrexham Dragons play Halifax at the Racecourse. The three came back jubilant that Wrexham had won with a score of 2-0.

As they sat in the kitchen drinking tea and eating the scones that Louisa had baked their conversation moved from football to cars. Arthur was trying to persuade Fred to buy a car and to get rid of his beloved motorcycle and side car.

Louisa sat down at the table to listen to the conversation. In her hands was an old shirt of Fred's. She was unstitching the collar which was almost threadbare. She was going to turn the collar so that the good side would be visible around Fred's neck. Apart from the remnants of his naval uniform when he was discharged from the navy he had been given a demob suit and a couple of shirts. He still had the clothes that he had owned before the war but they were now becoming very thin. At least the shirts had double cuffs not like the utility shirts that the government had decreed manufacturers should make.

On these post war shirts, the cuffs had to be single. The men disliked these but not as much as their dislike of the trousers being shorter and with no turn ups. Fred's demob suit had been much too big for him and the trousers were too long. Louisa had managed to shorten them to the correct length. She had done the same for Harry and Arthur. It seemed that none of them had been given the right size clothes, but at least they weren't too small.

Arthur was always trying to sell Fred a car and he usually resisted. She knew that he was trying to save some money towards buying a bigger house. Even though Joan was still living in their old home, they knew one day that she would move back to Liverpool. But as the house they rented to Joan was a small two bedroomed house, both she and Fred had agreed that now their little girls were growing up they would need more space. They also agreed that maybe they would eventually have more children, and if that were the case they would certainly need a house that was a bit bigger. She sighed and the sound distracted her husband and brothers so they all set their eyes on Louisa.

Fred glanced at Louisa intently and before she knew what she was saying she asked her brother how much would the car cost.

Arthur looked at her in surprise. His badgering Fred about cars had become a habit more than anything and so he was taken aback when Louisa asked the question. So was her husband.

"I could get you a good deal." Arthur replied warily. He shot a hesitant glance at his brother-in-law.

Louisa faced her husband squarely. "Maybe we should consider buying a car instead of saving for another house. We know we will eventually get back the other one. Even if we have another baby we still have a few years to save up."

Fred looked excitedly at his wife. "Are you sure about this? I mean it would be nice for the whole family to go out together instead of worrying about buses."

Louisa nodded her head and her two brothers and husband focused on her again.

This time Harry spoke. "I think it would be a good idea. As long as you are living here you need to have a bit of fun." He looked over his shoulder to make sure his parents were not in earshot. Satisfied that they could continue the conversation without being heard he said "we know that if you can get baby sitters, Louie is willing to ride pillion. But the girls are too big now in the side car with her, and she won't let them travel in it without her." He glanced at Louisa for confirmation. She nodded her head. She was always uneasy letting the girls travel in the sidecar without her.

"So that means you have to get buses to go everywhere." Harry finished.

"Is there no news about Joan going back to Liverpool?" Arthur interrupted.

Both Louisa and Fred shook their heads.

"Re-construction in Liverpool is very slow. There is a huge waiting list." Fred said.

"We can't expect her to move when she has four children under the age of ten. Even she is cramped in our little two bedroomed house. But the house is in good condition. I check it regularly." Fred paused and said soberly. "Her old man was in the navy. He was badly injured in Normandy. They couldn't save him."

All the men sighed. "Bad luck." Arthur said. His brother agreed.

"So what do you think Louisa? Are you serious?" Fred asked.

Louisa read the excitement in her husband's eyes and before she could think anymore said "yes let's do it."

Arthur thumped the table in obvious delight. Harry also grinned. He got up and put on his coat. "I have to go. Just wait until I tell Dot."

He opened the door letting in a blast of cold air. He shivered and pulled his old army coat tightly around him. He wound his hand knitted scarf around his face to protect him from the biting wind. The scarf had been hand knitted by his mother several years earlier and he was appreciating the warmth of it this very cold winter. He was also very grateful for his old trench coat. As he pulled up the collar he recalled suddenly a memory of the cold winter and spring he and his comrades had endured in Belgium during the early part of the war. He shook his head as if trying to shake the nightmares from his mind. He wanted to stop the thought processes which would inevitably force him to recall his years as a prisoner of war in Changi. Whilst he stood on the doorstep his parents came round the side entrance. They too were swathed in scarves and hats as well as thick coats to keep out the cold. That winter seemed to them to be the worst they had ever endured. Harry held the door open for them and then re-entered the kitchen so he could snatch a few words with his parents. They had been shopping and they carried in the meagre amounts of food they had queued up for hours to buy. A tin of spam escaped from Mary Ellen's basket and Harry bent down to pick it up. "There you are mother." He dropped it in to her bag and then kissed her forehead. Harry edged towards the door again shaking hands with his father as he did so.

"Do you have to go now?" He asked wistfully.

"Dot and the boys are expecting me." Harry replied. "We are coming tomorrow for dinner." He looked over his father's shoulder to get confirmation from his mother who smiled and nodded her head. Returning his gaze to his father's face, he saw William's countenance brighten. Every time William saw his two sons together he always felt grateful that they both had returned from the war. Yet he couldn't relax for long without seeing them. He worried they may be taken away from him again.

He sat down wearily at the table. It was tiring and time consuming having to queue up for basic items. It was also exasperating that it still had to be done even nearly two years after the war was over.

Arthur laid a hand on his father's shoulder. "Fred and Louisa are going to buy a car Father."

William jerked up his head in surprise. "So when did you decide that?"

"Just now." Fred laughed.

"Did you hear that mother?" William said to Mary Ellen as she took off her coat and seized the teapot from the table. Louisa got up and moved her sewing to make space for her to sit down.

"I will put the kettle on again mother. You sit there." Louisa said.

William repeated the news to Mary Ellen.

"Well that's good. Maybe you will be able to take us shopping in it." Mary Ellen said. She slumped gratefully into the chair Louisa had offered her.

Fred grinned. "Of course."

Mary Ellen rummaged in her bag and then handed Louisa a brown paper bag full of ribbons and small off cuts of felt.

"Since they are not on ration and Oliver on the market stall was selling these off for next to nothing, I thought you could do something with them Louie."

Louisa pounced on the bits of haberdashery with glee. She was very inventive with pieces of cloth and trimmings and was able to transform some of her old clothes into fashionable garments. The pieces of felt were also useful for covering threadbare sections.

"Thank you mother. I'm sure these will come in handy."

She fondled the haberdashery with delight whilst she listened to her husband and brother discussing Austin cars.

"We've got one car that would suit you Fred. It's old stock but still in good condition. The price when new was around a hundred and seventy five pounds…"

"What? I can't afford that!" Fred exclaimed. Louisa looked up from making tea in horror. She wasn't expecting to pay that much either.

"Calm down." Arthur said excitedly. "As I said, it is old stock. I could get it for you for probably much less than half that price. Plus a bit of discount."

Arthur winked and Fred looked relieved. Louisa glanced at him with an amused smile spreading on her face.

Much later after she was sure Christine and Susan were asleep in Dorothy's bed, Louisa told Fred about an idea she had been thinking of to make money. They were both in their own bedroom getting ready for bed.

"Buying fabric to make clothes costs less coupons than buying readymade clothes. A few people have asked me to make clothes for them because they can't sew. Iris and Doris have said they would rather pay me some extra money to make something fashionable. Obviously I would adhere to the government guidelines so I won't waste material. They are fed up of utility clothes and making do with their siren suits."

"Is it going to be worth your time?" Fred asked as he got into bed. He knew his wife was skilled with a needle and thread but to start a little business would be hard work.

"I would like to try it and see. Iris is well off so she can afford to pay me well, and as you know you may have a lot of money but you still need clothing coupons. Iris also has some well off friends, so it might be lucrative."

"What about Doris?" Fred said doubtfully.

"Doris would pay me well I'm sure, though she would probably be a one off customer, whereas Iris and her friends would give me more orders."

Fred could see that Louisa was serious about sewing to order, so not wanting to discourage her he asked her just one more question.

"What about space? Would your mother mind having fabric everywhere and customers coming to the house for fittings?"

"I think she would welcome it. Knowing mother she would want to help me!"

Fred turned the light out and put his arm around his wife. "If you are sure, then why not give it a go? It's worth a try."

In the darkened room Louisa smiled. She was following her dreams.

Chapter Five

As anticipated Mary Ellen was as enthusiastic about Louisa's sewing venture as her daughter. She even moved furniture in her back parlour to give Louisa more space. The huge dining table used for Sunday dinners was to be for cutting fabric. Usually the table was covered in a linen table cloth. On top of that were various dishes and mixing bowls that both Mary Ellen and Louisa used for cooking. All these were carefully stowed away under the table. When a client arrived they would be out of sight, concealed by a huge patchwork quilt. This would be removed whenever Louisa or Mary Ellen needed to use a utensil for cooking. The table top provided space not just for cutting out patterns, but for the sewing machine.

As soon as Fred and Mary Ellen had given her the encouragement she needed, Louisa lost no time telling Iris and Doris that she would make the clothes for their friends if they bought the fabric themselves with their own clothing coupons.

Within a few weeks Louisa had become swamped with orders and appeared to be perpetually in the back parlour sewing. She tried to manage her time so that she was able to take and collect Christine from school. In any case she needed the break from her work. It was good to take Susan out with her on both these two mile round trips. When Louisa was really busy she was grateful that her mother looked after Susan. The little girl was very energetic and was always wandering off away from the footpath when they walked home. She seemed to take delight in walking in the opposite direction from where Louisa was taking her. Then she would hide behind trees or bushes. Louisa felt guilty that she didn't allow her daughter enough time to play when they walked over the fields to the school. She frequently argued with herself that the income she earned, small though it was, would be for Susan and Christine's benefit as well as for her and Fred's. It wasn't as if she was neglecting her children. At least she had the support of her family. Her mother encouraged her with her enterprise. Pleased though both women were with the arrangement, they were always glad when Susan had an afternoon nap. This was usually around twelve thirty after she had something to eat. When she was asleep the two women had a couple of blissful hours of peace and quiet.

Meanwhile Louisa was happy and excited that at last she was doing what she really wanted to do with her life. It had been her dream from an early age to design and make clothes for a living. She wasn't making a vast amount of money just yet, but it was the beginning of something new. She was a hard worker and she worked tirelessly.

Towards the end of March just before Susan's fourth birthday Arthur delivered the Austin Ten Saloon to Fred. He promised he would try to sell the motorbike and side car for him. Susan's birthday was on a Tuesday, so Fred said that the four of them would go out somewhere at the week end. Arthur had arranged for Fred to register the car at Clark's Garage in Wrexham so that he could get his rationed petrol. They decided to drive to Ellesmere to see Louisa's Aunt Nancy and her husband Alf.

Though Mary Ellen would have loved to see her young sister again she declined to accompany them when Fred offered to take her. She said it would be a nice family outing for just the four of them. Louisa and Fred appreciated her generous decision. It wasn't often they were able to get out together with just the two of them and their children.

As Fred drove up the lane past Ellesmere mere and to the spacious cottage where Nancy and Alf lived, his mind went back to the last time he had driven a car up the track. It had been during his survivor's leave in 1942 when American soldiers had been billeted nearby. They had thrown them some food which they had gratefully received. He wished they were there now as rations had become even tighter than they were then. It was obvious that Nancy too was missing the Americans. She missed their company as well as the extra foodstuffs they gave her. She was always happy to share what she had with Louisa and Fred. Miraculously she still had a stock of bottles of fizzy drinks and served the two delighted girls with them.

"Alf and I don't like it very much and Pat only drinks it when she is really thirsty. I've also still got a good supply of tea." Nancy said. "But when that goes I will just have to limit myself to one good pot a day." She laughed. "I just drink a lot of water. I miss the Americans. Most of them have gone back now, there are just a few still recovering here from their war wounds though poor things. Their families have been to visit them and one or two have called here. They brought me some good supplies of tea and coffee too."

Louisa and Fred were sympathetic.

"Those injured in the war have another battle to fight now." Fred said. "So many disabled people have returned. Life is not the same for them."

Nancy shook her head sadly. "I hope the government recognise the sacrifices they made."

Fred said nothing. He was sceptical about any compensation for ex-servicemen who were now disabled.

"Maybe the Marshall Plan will help, if it goes through." Nancy suggested. She poured the tea and handed a cup and saucer to both her guests.

Nancy disappeared upstairs in her cottage for a little while then re-appeared with two silk dresses. She showed them to Louisa and she gasped when she saw them.

"They are beautiful."

"Can you do something with them? They are too big for me. Besides I don't wear these kind of clothes. But you are so good with sewing."

Louisa looked at her aunt incredulously. "But where did you get them?"

"Two well off American wives brought them over for me when they visited their husbands. I have to say they seemed to reek wealth." Nancy smirked as she draped the clothes over a chair.

"They were very grateful to me for looking after their husbands when they were sick. Other relatives brought me lots of little food stuffs including the tea and these biscuits."

Nancy opened a large bag of chocolate chip cookies. "I only received these a week ago. We have been limiting ourselves to one a day. They are very nice. Please help yourselves."

The little family needed not to be told twice to eat the sweet biscuits. Unaccustomed to sweet treats the children nibbled them warily, then smiled as the sweetness tingled their taste buds. With a knowing twinkle in her eye, Nancy put them away again out of Susan's and Christine's reach.

Louisa examined the dresses that her great aunt had given her. "These look haute couture."

"Probably. Just look at all the fabric and embellishments. Nothing utility about these."

Louisa picked up one of the dresses. It had a very full skirt with a long wide matching scarf attached to the shoulder. Her aunt had wound it several times around the hanger. Nancy fumbled at the top of each dress for the labels. "This black and white one is an Italian designer, I think the other one is French." She casually tossed it back on to the arm of the chair. It slipped across the red dress which cascaded unceremoniously on to the floor.

Louisa gently pulled the red pleated cocktail dress towards her. The pleats were very generous and as she pulled the dress towards her the fullness of the skirt billowed out across her face. She grinned as she pushed it off to check the label.

"Yes it is French." She traced the intricately pleated bodice carefully her fingers gliding over the beaded trimming. "They must have cost a fortune. How on earth could they afford them and want to give them away?" She gasped as she realised that on the chair underneath the dresses where Nancy had flung them there was also a full length silk cape to match the red dress.

Nancy shrugged. "I suspect our American friends were good at bartering with food when they were in France." She said no more and Louisa didn't pursue the matter. Fred said nothing. He remembered too well how the American soldiers had been generous with their food. He guessed that if the American GI's found themselves in liberated Paris, they would have used their food as currency to buy dresses for their wives. How legal that would have been he wasn't able to judge. The war had forced hungry people into desperate situations.

Fred conceded that the families of the sick soldiers may be extremely rich and well placed to discard their unwanted clothes. Undoubtedly they were grateful to Nancy for looking after their sick relatives.

Louisa was overjoyed to get two beautiful dresses. The amount of fabric used to make them seemed obscenely abundant. Louisa reckoned that if she was careful how she unpicked the garments she could remake them in to three or possibly four dresses. They wouldn't be as luxurious as these in front of her but they would still be glamourous dresses. She was sure she would manage to make something for her little girls too.

When they arrived home in Pandy later that day, both Mary Ellen and Dorothy admired the dresses enviously.

"These look like they have come out of a fashion magazine. I have seen similar stuff in the newspapers that people leave behind in the waiting room at the train station. I suppose the designers in the haute couture business never stopped working even during the war. But where did they get the silk? I thought it all went on parachutes."

Dorothy finished speaking as she seized the red silk dress and held it towards her. She whirled herself around the kitchen allowing the dress to float around her. Then she did the same with the black and white dress. Her mother smiled as she watched her.

Dorothy's display of enthusiasm with the twirling dresses sparked Louisa's imagination. Her mind was at work cutting and sewing clothes. Louisa gauged there was enough fabric to make something for the three women and two little girls. She just had to be very careful when unpicking the seams and removing the beaded trim.

"From what I can gather the silk trade in Italy after 1943 was doing quite well! Louisa commented coming out of her reverie. "I know that the Americans started using nylon. In fact the American dress designers probably had some impact on these dresses." She added smugly. She couldn't wait to get started on her own inventions. However her designs had to wait as she still had orders to fulfill.

The following few weeks Louisa became more and more busy with her sewing. As spring turned into summer, more weddings seemed to be taking place and she was asked to make bridal dresses, bridesmaid dresses as well as outfits for those guests attending the weddings. So she had little time for creating clothes for herself, though she and her mother managed to unpick the silk dresses. Dot helped too. She often called on her way home from work. She had started working in Woolinghams the department store again part time.

Meanwhile Louisa was saving all the money she earned from her sewing and whilst she was pleased that she could contribute to her husband's salary, she knew that she was working all hours of the day and evenings to do it. So much so that by the end of August she was exhausted and still had not made her own dresses.

One Saturday evening Fred persuaded her to go to the cinema with him to see a film. Reluctantly she agreed, then was pleased to see that he had arranged for Arthur, Gladys, Harry and Dot to accompany them. They had all crowded in to the small kitchen in Pandy to discuss which film they would see.

Harry sat down and produced a copy of the *Wrexham Leade*r and pursued the Entertainment page. "What do you fancy Louie? Drama, comedy, romance?"

Louisa looked at Fred for inspiration. "I suppose you would prefer a thriller or crime?"

"I don't mind. You choose. I just want to get you out of the house."

"What about a horror?" Arthur suggested. "That would shake you up a bit." He grinned at his sister, and she gave him a cold look rolling her eyes at the same time.

"That's put the kiss of death on that then." Fred replied returning Arthur's grin.

"Ha ha. Very funny Fred." Harry laughed. "That's supposed to be a good film too."

"What is?" Dot asked looking from Harry to Fred.

"The film "*The Kiss of Death* with Humphrey Bogart," said Arthur.

"Actually it is Richard Widmark." Harry corrected him reading from the newspaper. Dot looked over Harry's shoulder at the newspaper. "How about *The ghost of Mrs. Muir*?" She suggested to Louisa.

"That sounds like a horror movie to me." Louisa hesitated.

"No it's a comedy romance." Dot replied. "Rex Harrison is in it.

"Alright then let's see that. If everybody agrees." She looked at her husband and brothers for confirmation. She sensed they were not over the moon about the proposal but no-one challenged her.

"Right come on then let's go." Arthur said. Decision made they all whirled out of the kitchen in a wave of activity leaving Mary Ellen bemused as she sat by the range with her knitting. William had still not returned home from work so she had another half an hour of peace to herself. Christine and Susan had been taken to Dot and Harry's that afternoon and would be staying there with Dot's mother who would look after them. The little girls were excited to be staying overnight at their cousin's house. The four got on well together.

In the cinema the group of six settled down to watch the film. Whilst the adverts were screened, Dot suddenly asked Louisa why Dorothy hadn't joined them.

"She's meeting Bill in Chester."

"Doesn't he ever come to Wrexham to take her out? Dot asked.

Louisa nodded. "Sometimes, but Saturday nights are easier for both of them. Dorothy stays behind in Chester after work and Bill travels from Ellesmere Port to meet her. He has started work as a truck driver and the company he works for is based there. He actually lives in Mold. It is easy for Dorothy to get a train or a bus back from Chester to Wrexham. Sometimes she catches the last bus to Wrexham and gets off at the Smithy. Bill has a scooter to take him back to Mold. Sometimes he brings her back to Pandy. He has to be careful because of petrol rationing."

"We hardly see her these days. I suppose she must be happy." Dot said.

"They are in love." Louisa whispered just as the film was about to start.

Dot managed to whisper back "I suppose we will hear wedding bells soon."

In the dim light of the cinema Louisa nodded her agreement and shared a conspiratorial grin with her sister-in-law.

Louisa's and Dot's speculations were soon confirmed.

A few months later on Dorothy's birthday in November, Dorothy burst in to the house at Pandy with Bill and excitedly announced that they were getting married. There were exclamations of joy and surprise and Dorothy paraded her diamond engagement ring around the family so that they could see it. Her eyes were sparkling and Louisa was pleased to see how happy she was. Dorothy had

71

been heartbroken when her fiancé Frank had died of pneumonia in1944.

They set a date for 5th June for the wedding the following year.

When Christine heard about this she exclaimed that it was her ninth birthday on that day and in the same breath asked if she could be a bridesmaid. Dorothy said whilst winking at Louisa that being a bridesmaid was going to be Christine's birthday present. However when Christine pointed out that Susan was to be a bridesmaid too and it wasn't her birthday, she was appeased when Dorothy said that Christine would be the chief bridesmaid.

Louisa was going to be making all the dresses for the wedding as well as the bridal dress.

Meanwhile now late November, she had a bit more time. All her orders had been fulfilled and though some of her wealthy clients wanted new garments for Christmas a lack of coupons limited how much material they could buy. So taking advantage of the lull in orders Louisa excitedly used the time to make the new garments she had long been planning. She had waited a long time to use the material she had salvaged from the dresses aunt Nancy had donated to her.

The two haute couture dresses had been unpicked and all the adornments put aside for re-using. Louisa realised she had enough fabric to make a dress for herself, Dorothy and their mother as well as one each for Christine and Susan. Using the three colours of red, black and white silk she had contrasted the fabric to make three individual designs. Her own dress and the children's were red, whilst those for her mother and Dorothy were black and white. The scraps left were also put to good use. Dot was presented with a camisole that was white on the front and black at the back. The neckline was decorated with tiny red bows made from ribbon. She was delighted when she saw it a week before Christmas.

"Louisa it is beautiful. "I didn't expect to get anything you know."

"I'm glad you like it. You helped to unpick the silk so I thought you would like this as a thank you. And don't worry. I have something for Gladys. I just hope she sees the practical side of it." Dot frowned not understanding Louisa's wry comment until she showed her what she had made. She held up another camisole made with six panels of silk. The front and back middle sections were black and the side panels were red and white lace.

"Louisa that is a work of art!" Dot exclaimed. "I'm sure Gladys will love it!"

"I must admit I had fun making it, though there were a lot of French seams to sew. Working with lace is very tricky."

"You have utilised the lace well. If I dare use that horrible word utility! I remember removing the lace from the bodices of both those dresses. They were very extravagantly decorated. You don't see much lace about in this country even though it is off the ration. Only the rich can afford it." She sighed as her finger gently traced the lace on the camisole.

Louisa agreed. "The lace was a bonus, plus the fact that the two women who wore the original dresses must have been quite large around the chest!"

Gladys was indeed overjoyed to get the silk and lace garment from Louisa and was close to tears when she saw it. Louisa was pleased she had made the effort to make it. The week before Christmas heralded the last of Louisa's orders and thankfully she put away her sewing machine and notions to make room for the Christmas preparations. She was pleased to give herself a rest and promised the family she would not take any more orders until the New Year.

So when Fred said that there was a Christmas pantomime on at the Majestic theatre and had suggested they take Christine and Susan to see it she agreed whole heartedly. The production was '*Robinson Crusoe.*' Louisa had read the book and was as eager as the two children to see the pantomime. The four of them laughed at the antics of the clowns in the show which had nothing at all to do with the story but it was good fun anyway. It took Louisa's mind off her sewing for a couple of hours. Fred was pleased to see her relaxed and enjoying herself.

Louisa had kept the dresses for her mother and sister hidden away until Christmas Eve. She had made many alterations of their old clothes several times over the years and knew their measurements well enough. When Mary Ellen saw her dress she was overwhelmed with pleasure and held it against her whilst William looked on with a supportive smile on his face.

"I didn't think you would have enough material to do this." Mary Ellen said ecstatically.

"There was more fabric than I first thought in the bodice. It had been ruched up very thickly, so when I unpicked the lace and beads that were covering it, I discovered much more material underneath.

Although I had to adjust a lot of the pieces, I discovered in total that I had more than nine yards of fabric to play with as well as the lace and bead trimmings. There was also the wrap and the scarf that gave me more fabric too. So the government can't complain that I haven't re-cycled anything. I have used more than the recommended two yards per person per dress but it is recycled fabric!"

"Well the government can't complain you have broken the austerity rules. The clothes were second hand." William commented with a grin.

"Good quality second hand!" Louisa agreed.

Dorothy's reaction to her dress was the same as her mothers. She was impatient to try it on and whisked it upstairs immediately. She came down a few minutes earlier to show it off. "I will wear this tomorrow on Christmas day. Thank you Louie." She kissed her sister affectionately.

Louisa laughed. "We can all wear our dresses tomorrow! The government ministers are not invited!"

Chapter Six

1948

Preparations for the wedding soon started and Louisa busied herself with dressmaking and planning the wedding details with her sister and mother.

When Mary Ellen learned that Dorothy and Bill would be moving to Mold to live after the wedding, she became upset.

"I always thought my children would be living close by after they were married." Mary Ellen said as she took a pin out of her mouth. She had a length of green satin in her hands which would be the small bridesmaid dress for Susan.

Louisa glanced at her mother in surprise at this comment. She couldn't help thinking about when Mary Ellen had happily packed her off to Wallasey at the age of fourteen to work in service. Despite her protests she had been forced to go. Years later Dorothy had worked away from home quite a lot during the last two years of the war. They rarely saw her except on snatched leave from working in Wolverhampton in the munitions factory. She tried to cheer her mother up.

"It's only two bus rides away. The whole journey probably won't be more than an hour and a half." She risked a glance at her mother. "They are lucky to have somewhere to live. It will be a squeeze though. Bill's parents, his grandparents all in the same house. I know they have a three bedroomed house. But it is very small and Bill still has one grown up brother living at home too."

"Apparently they are going to live downstairs in the back parlour. They could have done that here." Mary Ellen sniffed

Louisa made no other comment. She too was concerned about her sister's future happiness but there was little she could do to change things. Her mother seemed to have forgotten that she had designated the back parlour for Louisa's sewing. If Dorothy and Bill had moved in there would have been no space to sew. Fortunately Dorothy had already realised that living in Pandy with Bill would be disruptive. She had assured Louie that she had no intention of upsetting her little sewing business.

Louisa shook out the bridesmaid dress she had been making for Christine and laid it aside. She glanced at the clock and hurriedly got up. "I will have to go and fetch Christine from school. Susan is still asleep, I think I will leave her. Do you mind?"

Mary Ellen shook her head. "Don't worry I will look after her. You will be quicker without her."

Louisa raced across the Pandy fields to the school in Gwersyllt. At the gates she saw Dot with Gordon and Malcom. There was no sign of Christine yet. Eventually she came out arm in arm with her friend Joyce.

"How's the sewing coming along Louie?" Dot asked as she watched her sister-in-law untangle herself from Christine's satchel and her coat which she had not bothered to put on despite the cold weather. Louisa bent to push Christine's reluctant arms into the coat. She gave up resisting when she realised her mother was determined she should wear it.

"Rushed off my feet, but I am enjoying the challenge." Louisa looked up at Dot and smiled brightly.

"Well if you need help don't' hesitate to ask. Don't wear yourself out. You do look a bit tired."

Louisa laughed. "I am a bit tired but I am enjoying what I am doing. It's nice to have a little bit of independence. I'm doing what I always wanted to do."

"I understand about your feeling of independence. I enjoy working part-time at Woolinghams. I feel as if I am contributing to the household expenses, though I don't know what I would do without my mother if she didn't look after Gordon and Malcolm."

"Same here." Louisa acknowledged. "I'm grateful that my mother looks after Susan when I am sewing."

Despite her work and the balancing act for childcare arrangements, Louisa loved what she was doing, and still managed to help with the usual domestic chores of washing, cleaning and dusting. However by the end of March she had to admit she was feeling more exhausted than usual and when her mother suggested a break with a cup of tea before collecting Christine one afternoon, she agreed. Later that evening just after Fred had arrived home, Louisa fainted.

"I think you are over doing it. You must be exhausted." Fred said. Louisa was adamant she was fine. However she agreed to take no more orders for clothes for a few weeks. She told her existing clients that there would be a couple of days delay in their orders being finished. She had built up a good relationship with her small clientele and they were understanding. However a few days later Louisa fainted again. With rising suspicions about her condition she went to see a doctor who confirmed that she was pregnant again.

Fred was ecstatic. "Maybe this time it will be a boy." He said.

"That would be nice." Louisa replied. She was lying on their bed sipping a very weak tea and Fred sat on a chair facing her. His expression changed and Louisa's own features looked troubled as she contemplated his serious countenance.

"I think we ought to start thinking about moving out of here to a place of our own now that we are having another child."

Louisa gazed at him. "But where? I thought we agreed we would wait for Joan to move out of our old home."

Fred nodded. "Yes but she is determined to return to Liverpool, and the way things are going with reconstruction it could take another few years. I think we should put our names down for one of those prefabricated houses the Wrexham council are building in Gwersyllt. Just as a temporary measure. Then we can move out when Joan goes to Liverpool."

"A steel house? Wouldn't you rather have a brick house?"

Fred grimaced. "Of course I would. It goes against the grain to live in a prefabricated house when I am a qualified builder and come from a family of builders. But in the short term it would be beneficial for our growing family."

Louisa saw the earnestness in his face and knew he was right. He had worked hard to save money for a deposit on a house before they had got married, and they had both been very proud of it. Yet now here they were years later living in cramped conditions with her parents and her own sister. Even when Dorothy moved out to get married she knew it would make sense to get somewhere of their own now there was a new baby on the way. If it hadn't been for the war they wouldn't be in this predicament.

"Damm Hitler." She sighed.

Fred shrugged. "Yes damn Hitler for a lot of things. We are luckier than many, I know, but we have to move forward to help ourselves." He got up to hold her hand. "You know it makes sense don't you?

Louisa nodded. Fred kissed her on the forehead. He bent to take her empty cup and saucer away then went downstairs.

At the end of the week Fred finished work early and went to the council to put his name on the waiting list for a house in Gwersyllt. Although it was a prefabricated building, he was excited that he was moving forward again. He saw it as a new beginning. After enduring a six year war which had destroyed all the major cities and towns killing millions of innocent people; then living nearly four more years with his in-laws this was the opportunity they needed to rebuild their lives. So he was a bit more cheerful than usual on Saturday afternoon when Arthur came round to Pandy to visit his parents before going with Fred to the football match. They planned to meet Harry at the racecourse. Arthur often called on a Saturday afternoon to see his parents. On this occasion William was out. He had cycled to Highfield to see his brothers who shared a large house together. William was from a large family. Three of his four sisters had married and lived locally. Just one of his three brothers had married. The rest of the siblings lived together. The whole family had followed William from their hometown of Oswestry to Stansty to work on the farm.

William being well respected by the farm manager Mr. Fern had been happy to employ William's four brothers. They had found work before world war two started and had remained there throughout the war. William had helped them find a place to live.

Their sister Gertrude and her husband also moved to Wrexham where they had bought a house in the small village of Bradley just two and a half miles away from the town. Fanny had stayed in Oswestry, however when both sisters lost their husbands in the army during the war, Fanny moved in with her sister. After pooling their resources they decided to share the house in Bradley. Their home was a pleasant stone house with a garden that backed on to a stream. It had a bonus of having two apple trees.

Each autumn they gave William a bag of apples to help make Mary Ellen's blackberry jam. In return she gave them a jar or two of the precious preserve. Sugar was still on ration and so each year they came to an arrangement about sugar contributions.

"You are happy today aren't you Fred?" Arthur commented as he stirred the weak tea that his mother had put before him on the table. She sat opposite him and listened to their conversation as she began to knit a pair of bootees.

"Do you think Wrexham have a chance to win today then?" Arthur grinned.

Fred glanced at Louisa who was sitting on an easy chair at the side of the range. A nod of assent passed between them before Fred replied.

"Well we have two pieces of news for you. First of all we're going to have another baby."

Arthur laughed. "Congratulations. So are we."

"What? Exclaimed Mary Ellen and Louisa together.

"We have just found out." Arthur confirmed. "Gladys didn't want me to say anything but well you will find out soon enough. It is due in November."

"So is ours!" Louisa said.

Mary Ellen began to knit faster as if she had to get the bootees finished for one baby before she could start on the next. Her face curved into a happy and excited smile.

"So what was the other piece of news?" Arthur asked once the excitement had died down again about the new babies. Fred told him about their plan to apply for a council house in Gwersyllt.

"Hmm that's not a bad idea Fred, what with your expanding family." He allowed himself to grin before continuing. "It looks like it could be a few more years before the country is back on its feet again and there is less of a housing shortage. I think you are very wise to do this as a short measure."

Harry agreed with them and said as much to Louisa when he called at Pandy on his way home to Rhosrobin after the match. All three men were jubilant as Wrexham had beaten Hartlepool United with a score of two nil.

"Fred's been telling me about your plans Louie. I think you are very wise to try to get one of those houses in Gwersyllt. I've heard that they will have three bedrooms and a bathroom upstairs as well as a downstairs toilet. The gardens are going to be generous too."

Louisa smiled and then to her surprise Harry lifted her up and said "congratulations on the new baby. Dot will be pleased when I tell her."

Louisa's smile broadened as he put her down again. "Thank you."

At that moment William returned from Highfield and always glad to see his two sons sat down to join in the conversation.

"This Marshall Aid the government are getting from America should help boost the housing shortage." Harry continued after he and Arthur had greeted their father.

"It all depends on Ernest Bevin and Aneurin Bevan getting their proposals through parliament." William commented.

"If Aneurin Bevan nationalises the Health Service as he promised he would, then that would be a great achievement." Fred said. "I voted for the Labour party in the 1945 elections because they said they would put the welfare of working class people first and look after returning servicemen and women. Health, housing and jobs must be a priority surely. I'm sure that is what they said in their manifesto." He glanced at Louisa who was listening intently to the conversation. She acknowledged Fred's remarks with a vigorous nod of her head before replying.

"Yes you are right Fred. I remember because I was going to vote Liberal and you convinced me that it would be better to vote Labour."

William who had voted Liberal all his life grunted but refused to get drawn into party politics with his family. He smoked his pipe with good humour and listened to his son.

"The lack of housing in the cities was bad enough before the war and now it is a hell of a lot worse after all the bombing." Arthur commented darkly. "They also have to clear away all the rubble too and demolish any houses that look unsafe. If you ask me, I think it is going to take years. Aneurin Bevan is Housing minister as well as health minister. He will have to come up with some kind of nationalisation of houses if we are going to re-build this country again. There are refugees and evacuees displaced all over Britain poor sods. Thank god we live here and not in Liverpool." He looked at his brother-in-law with affection. "Are your family looking for accommodation in Liverpool Fred?"

Fred shook his head. "Fortunately they have all returned to their original homes except for Cissy and Mary. The buildings they are living in are not in a good state of repair though. They may have escaped the bombs, but god knows what affect the blasts have had on the foundations of those houses left standing."

Fred looked uneasy. Louisa knew he was worrying about his two sisters.

"The government have got a huge task on their hands to try to accommodate those people who lost their homes. Plus they have to help those returning from the war with nowhere to go. All this on top of the slums that were in existence in the first place. I don't envy them." Arthur said with a sigh.

"One good thing about building these prefabricated houses is that they are easy to erect." Fred said. "They can be ready within a few days with enough labour to do it. Then of course there is the decorating and fitting up with gas, water and electricity."

"So what are they made of and where is the material coming from?" Harry asked. His father too started to ask the same question.

They all looked at Fred expectantly. He came from a long line of builders so they supposed he would know. Actually Fred did know, but not because of his background but more to do with the fact that he had taken an interest in the work being carried out in Gwersyllt. He had physically visited the building site to talk to the workers. He had seen the panels of pre-cast reinforced concrete which were reinforced with steel. These panels he had been told were bolted together with a steel frame.

When Fred had explained all this he was bombarded with more questions. Harry asked him where the steel was coming from.

Arthur asked about the provenance of the concrete materials.

Louisa wanted to know where each component was being made.

Fred laughed. "Hang on a minute, don't all talk at once. I am not an expert but from what I can gather the material is being imported from abroad, and the government, or rather Aneurin Bevan on behalf of the government is negotiating with the local councils." Fred got up and put his hands around the teapot to see if it was still warm. "All this talking has made me thirsty. Shall I make some more tea?"

Mary Ellen got up to make it but he said he would do it. He picked up the kettle from the fire in the range and went into the small ante room. This room was so small it barely had room for one person. There was a large enamel sink where Louisa bathed her children and where all the family washed. At the side was a newly installed electric oven which was rarely used. Mary Ellen preferred to use the range and whilst Louisa was happy to try modern appliances she was frequently over-ruled by Mary Ellen who favoured the heat provided by the coal fire and the range for cooking.

Fred filled the kettle with water and returned to put the kettle on the fire. He was surprised to see his two brothers-in-law pulling on their coats and scarves ready to leave. "Sorry Fred I have to go." Arthur said.

"I have to go too." Harry echoed his brother. He bent down to kiss his mother goodbye. Arthur dutifully did the same. "See you next week." They both said. They both braced themselves as they opened the door to step out into the cold evening.

Inside Louisa wanted to know more about the houses she may have the good fortune to live in.

"The idea came from an engineer in Leeds." Fred said. "In fact they have already built hundreds of steel houses in Leeds already. Leeds took a hammering in the war just like all the major cities in Britain."

"Who was the engineer?" William asked.

"His name is Edwin Airey. Apparently he works in a company called William Airey and Son Limited."

"So Edwin is the son?" William asked.

"I don't know I'm afraid to say." Fred said. "All I know is that the development of these houses is providing accommodation for a lot of families who need homes."

All the talk about housing made Louisa hopeful that she and Fred would be lucky enough to get one of the houses being constructed in Gwersyllt. She knew that Fred was optimistic, but for the moment they just had to wait.

Chapter Seven

The bitterly cold months from the end of the preceding year which had continued into the beginning of the following year soon became a phenomena of the past. The lighter months of April and May in 1948 brightened people up with hope that the future would be better. However Louisa's pregnancy caused her many a morning bout of vomiting. She became anxious that her sewing would suffer as she had to delay some of her orders for her customers. Thankfully she hadn't taken on too many after Christmas because she wanted to concentrate on Dorothy's wedding.

Fortunately the few customers who had placed orders with her for clothes were sympathetic. This however didn't placate Louisa who liked to get things done on time. She was always anxious when she asked for more time even though she knew there was little they or she could do about it.

Eventually by the middle of April she had cleared all her orders and was almost finished with the four bridesmaid dresses for the wedding. Dorothy had managed to save up enough coupons and money to buy her own wedding dress. This was one item less for Louisa to worry about. Dorothy was going to borrow Louisa's shoes and a veil from Gladys. The wedding was to be on the fifth of June in Rhosddu Church.

On the morning of the wedding various members of the family began to arrive in Pandy. Mary Ellen's sisters Nancy, Patricia, Betty and Susan along with their husbands had travelled up together from Oswestry. Mary Ellen's brother Alf and his wife Pat arrived sometime later.

Whilst everyone was served cups of tea and anticipated the excitement of the day, Christine took it upon herself to remind everyone that it was her birthday that day and that she was nine years old. Some of her great aunts indulged her giving her a penny for a treat. These aunts probably would never have bothered about her birthday any other time but got caught up with the excitement of the day. Mary Ellen told Christine off when she found out what she was doing so the little girl ran off outside in the garden to sulk. Here however she struck gold because her grandfather was out in the garden with his brothers-in-law and when they saw her petulant face readily put their hands in their pockets to find some loose change. The great uncles proved to be less generous than their wives and managed only to find half pennies to give Christine, though this put a smile on her face again. They patted her head kindly and she ran off to show her sister her booty.

On the back of Christine's campaign for a birthday treat, five year old Susan decided to try her luck too. She told everyone that she was a bridesmaid and that she should be given some presents. She was fobbed off with a few half pennies and some peas from the garden.

Soon it was time for the bride and bridesmaids to get ready to leave for the church. All the guests went ahead then Dorothy and her father got into the car that Arthur had procured. The three young bridesmaids had been whisked away by Louisa and Fred in their own car. The church was just two miles away so it wasn't far to travel. Louisa helped her two daughters and her niece Maureen to straighten their dresses outside the church whilst they waited for the bride. When Dorothy arrived Louisa put her arms around her sister.

"Good luck. You look beautiful."

Dorothy smiled nervously then took William's steady arm to walk down the aisle.

After the ceremony Dorothy and Bill stepped out of the church in to bright sunshine. The married couple and various family members posed in groups to take photographs outside the church. Fred had bought a new camera and was experimenting with photographs. He had elected himself to be the photographer. Photography was something he continued to do for many years later and would encourage his children to learn about developing negatives. Rolls of film hanging from pegs in the bathroom would become the norm.

The wedding reception such as it was based on the meagre rations that were available was held in the church hall. Mary Ellen, Dorothy, Louisa and Dot had all helped with the food. Some of the neighbours had also popped into the small kitchen in Pandy to help make small sandwiches. Bread was now on ration so they had to make sure everyone got at least a taste of bread. As Fred said "two bites and it is all gone."

Mary Ellen was tearful when she finally said goodbye to her daughter and new husband. Dorothy hugged her parents and sister and brothers then with a huge smile drove off with Bill for their Honeymoon in Blackpool.

"The last one married." Mary Ellen turned to William as she spoke. Her husband nodded his head and put his arm around his wife. "She will be alright. Don't worry."

At the end of the day Arthur and Harry along with their wives and children settled into the kitchen in Pandy. It was still light outside and the children were encouraged to go outside into the garden for half an hour. Louisa put little aprons over the bridesmaids' dresses to that they would be protected from being soiled. The last thing she wanted was blackcurrant stains on the dresses. She knew the children had a habit of wandering along the vegetable patch and helping themselves to peas and currants. They had even tried sticks of rhubarb which though sour they had gallantly chewed. Their faces were usually screwed up in distaste at the bitter tang.

"Well that went well!" Arthur said as he accepted a bottle of beer from his father. "All down to you mother."

Mary Ellen still tearful accepted his compliments.

"It's good that both of them have somewhere to live and that they are both working." Harry observed.

"It's a start. They will soon be able to save up for a place of their own. It's what Dot and I did. Sorry

Fred I didn't mean to upset you. I know your circumstances are different now."

Fred wasn't ruffled. He knew his brother-in-law meant no malice in his comment. He was pleased that Dorothy and Bill had somewhere to live. It would have been difficult if they had not managed to find somewhere to live and they were forced to live in Pandy. Mary Ellen had planned on converting the back parlour into another bedroom if necessary. Fred couldn't see how that would work, what with Louisa's sewing and the fact that she was expecting another baby. The only good outcome would have been that his two little girls could share a bed with each other instead of sharing with their aunt Dorothy.

"I'm expecting to hear from the local council soon about one of those houses in Gwersyllt. They have already finished the first phase in Wheatsheaf Lane. The builders are now working on another phase near the school. Hopefully we will be lucky enough to get one." He swigged his beer thirstily.

"It will be handy for school for the little ones if you do." Arthur agreed.

A few days later Fred received a letter from the council to say that his application had been accepted and that as soon as the houses were ready they would be allocated a three bedroomed house. They anticipated that the houses would be ready in September.

Louisa and Fred hugged each other with joy when they heard the news.

"That means we will have time to get the house ready before the baby is born in November." Louisa said joyfully. She patted her stomach. Though she was four months pregnant the baby was barely visible. She was feeling much healthier now the first few months had gone by. The early morning sickness had stopped and she had set about her sewing with re-newed energy.

"We will have to spend our savings on some new furniture." She said. "Mother has said we can have the double bed that we are sleeping on but she would like to keep the other one in case she has visitors. So we will need to get some beds for the children. Luckily we still have a cot for the baby. Father put it in the attic when Susan started sleeping with Dorothy and Christine. I will have to wash it down."

"We should have enough money to buy something to sit on and we need things for the kitchen too." Fred said. A worried expression fell on his face. "Even if we had a lot of money there is still a shortage of basic things in the shops. What is available is the utility stuff that the government have commissioned."

"We'll manage somehow." Louisa replied. "We can borrow Mother's chairs from the parlour and I have a few kitchen items that I kept before Joan moved into our house. I left her with just the basics. We did very well for wedding presents and I have stored them away in the attic too. We just need a stove." She kissed him. "Everything will be fine you see."

Fred hugged her. "It will be like starting married life again."

So the following Saturday when Louisa's brothers came to Pandy they were able to tell them their good news. The football season was now over, however

Arthur and Harry continued to visit their parents in Pandy every Saturday afternoon. This particular day Gladys accompanied Arthur with their two children Brian and Maureen. The two children went out in to the garden with Christine and Susan whilst the adults enjoyed their conversation.

"I'm pleased that you will have your own place again." Gladys said. She propped herself up half on Arthur's knee there being no extra chairs in the room. He put his arm around her expanding waist to support her. She refused to let him get up so that she could have the chair. She was quite content.

"I'm not an invalid you know. I'm quite healthy just as Louisa though she is looking a bit peaky."

"I'm fine. I have had a few busy days catching up with my sewing orders. I am up to date now."

"That's good. I wanted to ask you to make me another two maternity dresses. I have been saving my coupons for later. I didn't keep my old maternity dresses. I gave them to my cousin who in turn gave them to her sister, so I decided I would have two more made. I will of course pay you the going rate." She searched Louisa's face. "I want to be as fashionable as I can despite the austerity we are having placed upon us by this government."

"Of course I will. I am going to make another one for myself. I kept one of my old ones but I altered the other one into a skirt and blouse. It seemed a good idea at the time. Who would have thought that all the rationing would continue even now the war is over."

"Well at least you can thank the Labour Government for the new Health Service." Fred said. "Both you and Gladys will be able to have health care free of charge when you have your babies."

"Yes." Harry said. "I have been reading about that in the papers. Aneurin Bevan the minister for health is responsible for that. It is going to be the National Health Service and it is due to start next week. I think."

"It starts on the fifth July." Arthur said. "I've been reading about it too. Both you women will benefit from it. I'm hoping they are going to include dentistry because I think I have a tooth that needs attention. I've been getting a lot of toothache lately."

"Oil of cloves." Mary Ellen said. She got out of her chair to look in the pantry for the said item. She emerged a few minutes later with a small bottle and a piece of lint. "Here take this home with you. It might help."

Arthur unscrewed the bottle and gingerly lowered his face to smell it.

"It won't kill you." Mary Ellen said.

"Hmm it smells like Christmas." He fastened the bottle again and put it in his pocket. Gladys carefully put the lint in her handbag.

"You are thinking of the bread sauce that I use for the roast dinners." Mary Ellen said with satisfaction. She was pleased her son had taken the herbal remedy and also pleased that he recalled her cooking skills at Christmas.

Harry said nothing about his own teeth. They were in a bad state after spending nearly three years as a Prisoner of War. He had tried his best to look after them under extremely harrowing conditions. For a moment unpleasant memories tried to push themselves into his mind and he screwed up his eyes as if trying to push these mental thoughts out.

William watched him gently. He sensed his son was having a few bad memories. Arthur too glanced at his brother. He knew that expression. He wasn't without his own demons left over from his war experiences. He knew Fred got them too. None of them wanted to talk about it.

William took off his glasses ostensibly to wipe them with his handkerchief and tried to change the subject. "I read that they may include free eye checks and spectacles. I hope so because I could do with a new pair."

"I think that was something the government couldn't agree on, and I'm not sure whether that is included." Fred said. "We will have to wait and see. Ha ha!"

William rolled his eyes. "Very funny!"

Chapter Eight

At the end of August Louisa accompanied her mother and Gladys to go blackberry picking in the bluebell wood. It is something they did every year so that Mary Ellen and Louisa could make jam. Gladys always helped to pick the fruit but as she frequently admitted she wasn't very good at cooking and preserving. She enjoyed the walk in the woods though when the children accompanied them during the school holidays.

"Have you managed to save up enough sugar?" she asked as she helped herself to a blackberry.

Louisa sighed. "I think we can manage. We will reduce the sugar amount like we usually do and we will just have to depend on the sweetness of the fruit and the sweetness of the apples that Gert and Fanny give us. I will be glad when the rationing is over though. The government said they are waiting for the sugar plantations in the Philippines and elsewhere in the world to grow back after they were destroyed during the war."

"I wonder how long that will take." Gladys replied. "I suppose they have to clear the burnt out fields and replant the sugar canes or whatever they have to do."

"I just wish they would hurry up about it." Mary Ellen grumbled.

"Arthur said that during the war sugar was used to make tyres for the aeroplanes that were used for bombing."

Louisa looked at Gladys with a perplexed expression on her face. "Tyres! How did they do that?"

"I've no idea." Gladys laughed. "That's what some of the Americans told him. They also said that it was used for making medical supplies too. Most of the sugar from Cuba went to America's armed services for their own food rations."

Gladys stood up and stretched, then shook her small basket of berries to level them off. She popped one in her mouth.

"Well if that's the case I don't begrudge my sugar ration." Louisa said. She examined a blackberry for tiny grubs before handing it to Susan to eat. Christine was already trained in the skill of blackberrying and carefully examined every berry. Most of them went into her mouth rather than in the basket.

"I don't either." Gladys straightened up again and put an arm on her back to rest. She looked down at her swollen stomach then made a sidelong look at Louisa's stomach.

"When are you due Louie?" She asked as if she didn't know that Louisa's baby was due the middle of November.

"November. Two weeks before you I believe." Louisa knew what was coming. Gladys kept

98

comparing her swollen stomach to her own. Mary Ellen looked up when she heard Gladys ask the question and studied her daughter's expression. She too was concerned that Louisa seemed to be quite slight in comparison with Gladys. She said nothing and waited for Louisa to speak.

"Not everyone is the same you know." Louisa said. "I feel fine. There's nothing to worry about, so stop going on about it."

"Sorry. As long as you are alright." Gladys looked away, glanced at Mary Ellen and said nothing more.

The atmosphere was tense between them for the rest of the afternoon, and soon after they had gathered all the fruit Gladys left with Brian and Maureen. Normally she returned to the house in Pandy for a drink but on this occasion she took the children with her to the Chester Road to get the bus to Wrexham. From there she would get another bus to Acton.

Inside the house at Pandy Mary Ellen began to pick over the fruit to prepare for the jam. Louisa began weighing the sugar, but saying she was feeling a little dizzy she sat on a chair to peel the apples.

Mary Ellen looked at her daughter anxiously. She didn't usually sit down to peel apples and she did look paler than usual.

"Are you sure you are well?"

"Quite sure Mother. Just tired that's all."

A few weeks later at the beginning of September Louisa's body seemed to swell and at last she was showing signs of being over six and a half months pregnant.

"You see." She said happily to Fred and Mary Ellen. "Nothing to worry about. The baby is growing now."

Their relief was short lived. When Louisa had reached just seven months in her pregnancy, her ankles began to swell at an alarming rate and she felt nauseous and dizzy. She felt so ill that Fred took her to the Trevalyn maternity hospital in Rossett where she was immediately admitted.

Upon examining her the Doctor said that he feared she had picked up an infection and that she should rest. He also said that her blood pressure was rather high. Arrangements were made for her to stay overnight in hospital. Not wanting to leave her Fred stayed with her. During the night Louisa's condition worsened and the doctor advised him that Louisa had Toxaemia.

"So is there a cure for it?" Fred asked. He was very worried.

"I'm afraid we will have to induce the baby."

Fred paled. "Will she be alright? Will it harm the baby?" He fired a lot of questions at the doctor.

"As soon as we deliver the baby, your wife has a good chance of recovery. The baby will be premature and we will do all we can to save it."

Fred had no option but to allow the doctor to do what they needed to do.

The next few hours for Fred were some of the worst he had endured in his life. Whilst he waited, both Harry and Arthur arrived at the hospital. They took it in turns to go outside to have a smoke. Eventually the doctor returned to tell Fred that Louisa was fine but very weak. He congratulated him on having a baby son but warned him that he would have to be in an incubator for several weeks so that they could monitor him.

Fred and Arthur received this news, just as Harry rejoined them in the waiting room. His anxious countenance relaxed a little as he saw Fred then Arthur shake hands with the doctor. His brother turned towards him. "She's alright. She's given birth to a boy."

"Can I see her?" Fred asked. The doctor nodded. "Yes just for a few minutes but she is very tired."

Fred turned towards his two brothers-in-law. "Thanks for your support. I'll see you soon."

Fred could see that Arthur and Harry were relieved that their sister was fine. "Will you call at Pandy and tell them the news?"

Both men readily agreed and said they would go together.

Louisa was indeed very tired but managed a smile when she saw her husband. "We have a son." She whispered.

Fred kissed her on her forehead. "What shall we call him?"

"I think we should call him Michael."

"Good name. It was Eddie's middle name."

"I know." Louisa replied then closed her eyes and went to sleep.

After a few anxious days and nights the baby made progress. Louisa herself began to recover her strength too though she was advised to remain in hospital for at least another week.

"The maddening thing is that I can't hold him or feed him." Louisa confided in Dorothy when she visited her on the following Sunday afternoon. "He is so tiny he can't suck on a normal size teat and so the nurses are feeding him from the feeder that is used in a fountain pen!

Dorothy blinked in surprise. "How strange." She bent over to her sister and whispered "What are they feeding him on?"

Louisa hesitated before answering. Dorothy sensed her sister's uncomfortable composure and turned to ask Bill if he minded leaving her with her sister for a few minutes.

Bill obligingly got up from his chair and said he would wait in the waiting room. Both sisters smiled when he had departed from the ward.

"I think he was relieved to go." Dorothy said mischievously.

"I suppose being surrounded with women and their babies is not every man's cup of tea." Louisa replied. She couldn't help thinking how different Fred's reaction was to seeing so many women in the ward. Some were in various stages of pregnancy, others were actually holding their babies. One or two had curtains around their bed so that they could have privacy breast feeding. She thought that Fred's easy reaction to being in the maternity ward was because he was now a father of three children. He probably felt he could share the excitement with the other mothers and their babies. He took a lot of interest in the new born babies. Louisa turned to her sister to explain about the feeding.

"Because Michael is in an incubator they have to make sure no germs are carried in. The nurses have to wear masks when they feed him. The milk they are using is mine. I have to express it every day and they freeze it in big freezers, so they have a supply for every four hours.

"Is that painful?" Dorothy asked anxiously. She worried if the same thing might happen to her. She wanted children in the future and wanted to know as much as possible about child birth. She hadn't taken much notice when Christine and Susan were born. Her mother had taken charge, but things were different now. She had a suspicion that she herself might be expecting though it had not been confirmed. It was too early to tell yet. She longed to confide in her sister but felt that the current moment was not the right time. She had read that stress could upset her menstrual cycle, and she had had a stressful few months. First there was her wedding, changing homes twice, and worrying about her sister.

"It does make me sore, but at least he is getting my milk, and they have assured me that once he puts on a few pounds I will be able to continue feeding him with my own breast milk."

"How long will that be?" Dorothy asked.

Louisa sighed. "A few weeks yet. I will be coming home next week but without my baby."

Dorothy put her arm around her sister's shoulder. "Cheer up at least you and he are alive and you are both doing well even if it is slowly."

Louisa wiped a tear from her face and smiled. "I know. I'm just a bit emotional. He is so tiny. I have to look at him through a glass partition and I can't help thinking how fragile he is."

"It is a miracle he is alive. The hospital staff have been wonderful from what I hear from Fred." Dorothy held on to her sister's hand. "What would you have done without the new National Health Service Louie?"

"We would have spent all our savings on his health and mine and then would have to start saving all over again. We haven't saved a huge amount and we will need to buy some furniture when we move house."

"Oh yes. Any news on that yet?" Dorothy asked. Louisa shook her head. "Not yet."

Dorothy took a deep breath and looked at her sister with such an anxious expression that Louisa became alarmed.

"What's wrong? Has something happened?"

"The thing is Bill and I have come back to Pandy to live. There's been a burst pipe in the house in Mold and part of the ceiling has collapsed over the back parlour. Bill's grandparents have had to move in with neighbours until it is fixed. You don't mind do you? We are in the back parlour in Pandy."

"Oh my god you poor thing. Of course I don't mind. What a dreadful thing to happen." She grinned. I expect mother is glad to have you back."

Dorothy hugged her sister and Louisa could tell she had been worrying about telling her. The look of relief on her face was evident.

"Do you need to buy another bed?" Louisa asked anxiously. She knew that they had bought a new bed when they moved to Mold.

"Fortunately no. The rubble just missed the bed. Bill's grandparents were lucky too, part of the floor is missing in their bedroom but fortunately not where the bed was. Everything was dusty though. Harry and Arthur helped us to move things. We didn't want to worry you. Fred has been to see the damage. He said it could take a few months to get it repaired. There is a demand for building materials so that could slow down progress."

104

A day later Fred came into the ward with another bunch of flowers for Louisa. He wore an ecstatic smile on his face. He bent down to kiss his wife and then showed her a letter he had received from the Wrexham council. Louisa read it quickly and her eyes shone when she finished reading it. She looked up at her husband.

"We have got a house!"

Fred nodded. "Yes we can move in at the end of October. A new baby and a new house." His eyes glowed with excitement and Louisa could see how relieved he was to be at last moving into their own home. Even though it was not made of bricks and mortar, it was somewhere he could call his own home. He hoped it wouldn't be forever.

But the news was not met with the same enthusiasm from their two daughters. Both Christine and Susan looked upset when Fred told them that they would soon be living in a new house.

"I don't want to go!" Christine said resolutely upon hearing the news. Susan who was not sure about what would happen copied her sister and said she wasn't going either.

Fred tried to persuade them it was a good idea. "Just think you won't have to go outside to go to the lavatory. And you will be able to have a proper bath instead of washing in the kitchen sink."

If the truth were told, Fred was looking forward to having a bathroom and indoor lavatory again. The children would not warm to the idea and Fred thought it was because they missed their mother who had been in hospital a week now. They didn't understand that she had been very ill and even though they had been told they now had a baby brother, they still hadn't seen him. He thought things would be better when Louie was home again.

On a sunny Saturday afternoon in early October, Fred took the little girls to the maternity hospital in Rossett to collect their mother. He decided to take them for a little ride to Chester where Fred parked his car besides the river Dee. They enjoyed a stroll along the riverside looking at the boats and the two little girls ran up and down excitedly along the river edge. Not far away from the river bank there was a teashop so they sat themselves down near a window with a view of the river. As a treat they had a plate of buns as well as a pot of tea and lemonade for the children. Louisa was looking a lot better and Fred held her hand across the table to comfort her.

"We will have to start thinking about furniture for the new house." Fred began. "We have some money saved but we won't be able to furnish every room the way we would like. I have asked the builders to install a gas cooker for us and fortunately the kitchens have cupboards already installed so you won't need to worry where we are going to store everything."

"That's good. I was wondering about cupboards. Mother said we can have our bed, but we will have to buy new ones for the children and sheets and blankets. She said we could have our wardrobe too."

"That's a good start." Fred turned towards the children who were pre-occupied with eating buns. It was a rare treat for them and they were determined to eat every crumb. "Did you hear that girls? New beds for you in the new house."

Christine stopped eating for a few seconds and looked at her mother. "Are we really going to live somewhere else?"

Louisa nodded encouragingly. "Yes in Gwersyllt."

"What about Nan and Grandad? Are they coming too?" Susan asked. She licked her lips slowly, they were sticky from eating the bun. Her face wore an anxious expression. "And Auntie Dorothy and Uncle Bill?"

Louisa shook her head. "No they will stay in Pandy but they will come to see us, and you can visit them as often as you like."

That final statement of Louisa's appeared to appease the girls and they said nothing else about the proposed move. Meanwhile their parents had a lot to think about. Michael was still in hospital though improving, and the new house required several items.

Louisa was also worrying about honouring her sewing commitments. Her friends and clients had been very understanding, but she wanted to make sure that she finished everything before moving to the new home.

"Don't make yourself ill again." Mary Ellen warned her. She had been very worried about her daughter. All the family had rallied around and had been relieved to hear that Louisa and baby were recovering well.

Dot offered to help Louisa with her sewing commitments. As a temporary measure she had taken Louisa's sewing machine to her own home and had put it in her back parlour. Dorothy had been upset about causing havoc but both Dot and Louisa had comforted her. "Your need for somewhere to stay is more important than my sewing." Louisa hugged her sister. "Besides in a few weeks I will be moving out and you and Bill can move upstairs! Both of them wiped tears from their eyes. Their emotions for several reasons were running high.

"In a way I have a reprieve with Michael being in hospital." Louisa said to Dot one evening. "Although I would love to have him here with us, it means I can use the time to concentrate on my sewing orders. Besides now Dorothy is living in Pandy she doesn't mind looking after the girls in the evenings after she finishes work."

Dot concentrated on threading a needle to hem a skirt before replying. "Yes I suppose every cloud has a silver lining."

"I was able to feed Michael with the feeder today." Louisa confided. She wore a huge grin on her face. "I had to wear a mask but it was lovely to hold him in my arms." Louisa was beginning to feel happier. She had a lot going on in her life. She looked forward to having the baby home as well as moving in to a new house.

Chapter Nine

At the end of October the removal day finally
arrived. Amidst catching up with her sewing
commitments and the commotion of packing items
for the new home Louisa still found time to visit
Michael in the hospital. She always tried to go mid-
day so that she could give him a feed and to express
more milk for the freezers.

On the day of the move, she was delighted to be told
that in a week or two she could take him home.
However she would still have to feed him with a
fountain pen feeder for a few more weeks until he
had grown a little more. When she saw Fred and told
him the news he was delighted. His face was sweaty
with the exertion of moving furniture in what would
be their dining room. He still managed a smile when
he heard the news about his son.

Louisa's two brothers were helping with the move.
She found them upstairs setting up the double bed in
the room she would share with Fred. Harry's grin of
pleasure upon hearing the news was immediately
reflected in Arthur's.

"Do you know what day this is today?" Fred asked
his brothers-in-law. He had followed Louisa
upstairs and paused to lean against the doorway. He

continued to talk before either Harry or Arthur could say anything. In any case they both looked a bit puzzled.

"Today is our wedding anniversary. In nineteen thirty eight we got married and moved into our new home. Now here we are ten years later moving into another new home, starting all over again. This time with three children."

He wiped a smear of sweat from his face on his shirt sleeve. A strand of his dark hair fell into his eye and he flicked it away with the back of his hand.

"Congratulations!" both Harry and Arthur said though they said it without much enthusiasm as they could see a grim expression creep over Fred's face.

"It wasn't supposed to be like this though. All those years in the war and then having to start again. Not that I am complaining about your parents they have been wonderful. It just makes me bitter about all the hard work and the dreams we had to be dashed by that terrible war. And we are all still living on rations."

Arthur nodded. "And we are the lucky ones. Those who came home." He turned towards his brother as he spoke. "Despite everything though Fred, we have a roof over our heads and we have Harry back."

Harry put a hand on Fred's shoulder. "I know you lost a brother at sea, and in a way you lost your home, but you and Louie did a wonderful thing helping homeless people. You should be proud of yourselves. At least when Joan and her family are re-housed in Liverpool you will have your property back."

This was a rare moment that the three men talked about the consequences of the war and neither of them wanted to dwell on it.

Fred shrugged and managed a glimmer of a smile. "I know you're right. I am trying to remain positive. I'm not just grumbling for myself. I feel sorry for all those others too."

Louisa realised that Fred was tired. He had been looking forward to the move and he had been worrying about her and Michael. So now all the stresses of the past few months were beginning to wear him out.

"What you all need is a cup of tea." She said cheerfully. This brought a smile to their faces and they began to finish the task they were doing.

By the end of the day everything was ready.

"And now I am going to run a bath!" Fred exclaimed. He had perked up a bit by then. He had been looking forward to a bath all day.

Louisa left him to it and went downstairs to say goodbye to Arthur and Harry. In the dining room she found her two little girls wearing glum faces and being consoled by their uncles.

"You won't have far to walk to school now." Arthur was saying to Christine.

"And you can come and visit me and Dot and Gordon and Malcolm any time you like." Harry said.

Christine brightened up at these remarks. She could see the advantages of the house move. She also liked having her own single bed. No longer did she have to share a bed with anyone. During her earlier years she had shared a bed with her aunt Dorothy, then when Susan was born the three of them shared.

She had got used to sharing with just Susan after Dorothy had got married. Throughout her nine years she had adjusted to all the small changes in her young life. The biggest change was adjusting to having her father home from the war. As a result Christine was a little more adaptable to change than her sister. She was finally satisfied when she realised that her school was just a five minute walk from the house; her cousins were just a ten minute walk away and that she would see her grandparents twice a week.

Susan took more convincing and was unable to settle in her new bed. Louisa lay beside her until the little girl fell asleep. She promised she would show her the way to Pandy the next day and that they would all walk there. This seemed to soothe the child's anxiety and Louisa hoped that she would soon adjust to her new home.

So the next day Louisa left Fred at home to finish the odd jobs in the house and she took the two little girls on the one mile walk to Pandy. She pointed out their school, then showed them how easy it was to get to Harry and Dot's house, then through Rhosrobin, over the Pandy fields to their former home. As soon as they saw the house both girls ran in excitedly to see their grandparents.

It took a few minutes for William and Mary Ellen to disentangle themselves from their grand-daughters. Eventually they settled down and chattered non stop about their new home. Dorothy and Bill encouraged them to talk about this new change in their lives. Louisa hoped that this visit would help them to settle in.

An hour later Fred called in the car to take Louisa to hospital. They left the children in Pandy and Fred collected them later.

They repeated the same routine the following Sunday. However on that particular Sunday Fred returned two hours later at the hospital, to find Louisa waiting for him with the baby in her arms.

"We can take him home." She greeted him. She handed the baby over to Fred who for the first time was able to nurse his tiny son. He felt a lump in his throat and could not speak for a little while. Meanwhile Michael's little sisters were clamouring to see their brother. Fred sat down on a chair in the waiting room with the baby in his arms. That way his daughters could see their brother more easily. He was able to recover his composure whilst the children bonded with the baby. Over their heads he caught Louisa's happy smile and Fred considered himself a lucky man.

In contrast to Michael's premature birth, Gladys went into labour exactly on the date she had been given on the eighteenth of November. She delivered another son who they called Arthur.

"I always thought the first born son would be called after his father." Louisa mused half to herself and half to Dorothy who had called to see her after visiting Gladys in Trevalyn maternity hospital.

"I don't think it is a tradition. I know lots of younger sons named after their fathers." Dorothy said as she sipped her tea. "Anyway Louie I have some important news to tell you myself."

Louisa looked up at her sister expectantly whilst she pinned in a zip on a skirt.

"I'm having a baby too." Dorothy burst out. Her face shone with pride and excitement.

Louisa put aside her sewing and jumped up to hug her sister. "That's wonderful news. When is it due?" She cast her eyes over her sister's stomach looking for a faint bump. There wasn't anything to see.

"August. It will be a summer baby. I haven't told mother yet. I am going home now to tell her."

Dorothy took her cup and saucer to the kitchen to wash up and then seized her coat from behind the chair where she had dumped it. Louisa watched her buttoning up her coat.

"You won't have to worry about maternity clothes. You can have mine. I daresay Gladys will let you have hers too. I made her two brand new ones this time."

Dorothy turned to face her sister. Her face was beaming.

"Thanks. I was hoping you would say that." She leaned against the sink. "Talking of sewing. What are you going to do about your sewing? Or should I say your sewing business for want of a better word? I see you are occupied with a skirt at the moment. Is it for you?"

"No. The skirt is Nora's. I am putting in a new zip for her. As regards the 'business' as you call it, for now I am not taking on any more work except for family. I need to keep myself free for Michael. Maybe later on when he is healthier I will start again."

"That's good. I don't want you to tire yourself out. You will need all your energy now you have another child to look after."

114

Louisa shrugged. "I'm not giving up completely. I still want to sew again eventually."

"I know you do, and you will." Dorothy kissed her sister goodbye. "Thank you in advance for the maternity dresses. I will be glad of them. I must go. It's been a busy day visiting everyone. Thank goodness Wednesday is my day off. Back to normal next week when mother will come to visit you and I will stay at home! Sorry I can't stay to see the children today. I will see them on Saturday."

On the following Saturday afternoon Fred arrived home from work to discover his wife in a panic.

"I can't find Susan. She's vanished. Christine doesn't know where she is either. They were both upstairs reading books an hour ago and now she is nowhere to be seen. She isn't in the garden. I've looked in all her usual hiding places."

Nevertheless Fred looked in the garden again and they both opened their one and only wardrobe in the faint hope she may have burrowed inside. This was indeed a faint hope as the narrow wardrobe contained every piece of clothing the whole family owned. Winter coats and summer dresses jostled together for space, so the chances of finding a little girl hidden in the folds of fabric was very remote indeed. In desperation they both questioned Christine again. She was still calmly reading her book lying on her bed a pillow propped her back up against the wall.

"Are you sure you don't know where Susan is? Are you both playing a game with us?" Fred asked his oldest daughter gently.

Christine shook her head. "No. She was trying to read one of my books and then she said she was fed up."

"What else did she say?"

"Nothing much, except that she wished she could go to Pandy."

"Pandy!" Both Fred and Louisa shrieked the word together.

"The little minx. I bet that's where she has gone." Louisa said.

Fred ran out of the house again to his car. "I will go and look for her."

Driving the car slowly along the road through Rhosrobin, Fred looked both sides of the route in case he saw his daughter lying injured. His imagination played tricks with him as he thought of all the horrible things that could occur to a five year old girl. Passing Harry and Dot's house, he took just a few minutes to see if Susan had called to see them. The door was locked so he assumed the family had gone shopping as they sometimes did on Saturday afternoons if there was no football match at the race course.

Fred continued driving slowly towards the Pandy fields. He hesitated and thought about leaving the car at the side of the road to see if she was on the fields. There was no cattle about so he knew he could cut across the path to Pandy easily. He argued with himself it would be quicker to drive to Pandy to see if she was there and if not leave the car and walk to the fields from the other direction. He accelerated down the Llay road and turned right towards Pandy. When he parked his car outside William and Mary Ellen's house he breathed a sigh of relief when he saw Susan emerging from round the corner of the house with Dorothy and Bill.

"Fred!" Dorothy shouted. "We were just bringing Susan home."

"Daddy!" Susan called excitedly and ran into her father's arms. Fred was so pleased to get his daughter back safely he forgot to be cross with her. He lifted her up and gently said. "You gave your mum and me a fright wandering off like that."

Susan grinned. Fred couldn't resist her impish smile. He put her down again and strolled across the side entrance of the terraced house to greet his sister-in-law and her husband. He also put his head around the door to say hello to his in-laws. Mary Ellen greeted him anxiously. "I'm so glad you came Fred. We were worrying that Susan had walked here by herself. We told her off for not telling Louie where she was going."

Susan jumped out of her father's arms and ran to her grandmother. She kissed her and waved her arm as she ran back to her father. "Ta ra. See you soon."

Outside Fred asked Dorothy and Bill if they were going to visit himself and Louie.

Dorothy shook her head. "Not today. We've had a busy day and got more to do. We would of course have brought Susan back, but now you are here we can do what we intended to do. First of all, we are going to see Arthur and Glad's new baby. Then we are going to Mold to see Bill's mum and dad. We will come and see you next week. Have a good birthday. Its next Friday isn't it?"

Fred grinned. "Yes.

As the weeks passed, Michael was able to feed properly and was putting on weight. Louisa watched over him anxiously. She was forever looking for signs of breathing problems. Sometimes she forgot to breathe herself and found herself inhaling huge gulps of air as she gazed at her son over the side of his cot. She continued to refuse sewing orders so that she could look after her new baby.

Though she missed her sewing routine, she appreciated having the time with her son during the day when both her two daughters were in school. She did not know for sure if she was able to start her sewing business again, such as it was. When the time was right she would try again. She smiled wryly to herself when she recalled Dorothy's description of her sewing activities. It was scarcely a business. It wasn't as if she advertised for work. In any case the agreement on their council house stated that tenants were not allowed to run private businesses from their homes. For the time being Louisa was content with that. After all living in this house was just a temporary arrangement. She wondered if her parents had a similar agreement with their own home in Pandy. The house they lived in was the property of the Colliery owners. They had been built for the workers who they employed either in the mine or on the farm. Most of her parents' male neighbours were coal miners in the Gresford pit.

She doubted there had been a clause that stated the houses were not to be used commercially. Louisa shrugged. That particular issue no longer concerned her.

Soon Louisa and Mary Ellen began to plan their Christmas festivities and once again agreed to pool their rations and resources. Mary Ellen was pleased that Dorothy and Bill were going to spend Christmas with them in Pandy. The rest of the family would join them at various intervals over Christmas and Boxing Day. The family was rapidly expanding and it was no longer feasible for everyone to gather in the small house in Pandy.

Chapter Ten

1949

Rumours that clothes rationing was about to end were rife in the early part of the year. Whilst Louisa and her family speculated on whether they would be able to buy new shoes and coats, the winter months turned into spring with no announcement from the government. Then suddenly at the end of March the president of Trade, Harold Wilson announced on the wireless that clothes were to come off ration at the end of that month. He appealed to people not to buy more than they needed and that clothes shops would be instructed to make sure people didn't buy large amounts. He stressed that he was keen that the country should continue to export goods as much as possible to boost the economy.

"He wants us to recycle our clothes ration books." Louisa commented to Fred. "What will they do with them I wonder?"

"Make them back into paper products again I suppose." Fred remarked.

Meanwhile people around her were discussing more serious topics than clothes.

The previous September Louisa had been too occupied worrying about Michael to take much notice of what was going on in the world. She vaguely remembered Fred telling her that the British government were negotiating some kind of defence agreement with other Western European countries and with the United States of America.

So when it was announced on the wireless that a treaty had been signed early in April in Washington DC she commented to Fred that it seemed to be a good idea. He agreed with her. "Let's hope it prevents another war."

"There are quite a lot of countries signed up to it. Twelve of them as far as I can tell. I read in the newspaper that if an armed attack happened against either one of those countries that all of the rest would defend that country. So we would have to join forces to defend even America or Canada." Louisa said. "It will be known as NATO."

"Yes I read it too. It stands for North Atlantic Treaty Organisation." Fred said. "An impressive title isn't it?"

When Arthur arrived on their doorstep a few days later he too commented upon the Treaty. "It is good that we have some kind of defence mechanism Fred. Don't you think?"

He watched Fred put his coat on as he spoke to him. Brian stood next to him. They were going to the football match to watch Wrexham play New Brighton. Harry was also going with his two sons Gordon and Malcolm and they had arranged to meet in front of the Turf Tavern. This location was just a hundred yards away from the racecourse entrance.

121

"I think so. At least it sounds fine in theory. How much is it going to cost the tax payer?

"It all comes down to money." Arthur agreed. Fred kissed Louisa goodbye and followed his brother-in-law and his son to Arthur's car.

A few minutes later Dot arrived to keep Louisa company.

"Any news from Dorothy?" Dot asked once they had settled down to a cup of tea.

"She is having a difficult time at present. Her morning sickness has come back. That's why she hasn't called to see us lately. When I say morning sickness, she seems to be vomiting any time of the day or night poor thing. She's still got two months to go yet. Well now I think about it, actually she's got another six weeks."

"Has she come up with any names?"

Louisa smiled. "She hasn't mentioned any to me. More tea?"

Dot nodded as Louisa poured. Christine and Susan rushed into the room to see their aunt. Susan thrust a rag doll on to Dot's knee. She had been given it for her sixth birthday two months previously along with a set of doll's clothes that Louisa had made for her. Christine sat beside them and watched as Susan demonstrated how to take off the petticoats from the doll and then re-arrange her attire.

"What's the doll's name?" Dot asked kindly.

"She's Princess Mary." Susan replied.

Christine laughed at her sister. "She can't be a princess. She hasn't got a crown."

"It doesn't matter. I will make her one." Susan said resolutely. She snatched the doll up and ran out of the room then returned later with the doll. She had twisted a thin piece of ribbon and tied it around the doll's head. She showed it to her sister. "She's got a crown now."

"Where did you get that ribbon from?" Louisa asked. She knew very well that Susan had been in her sewing box. Both little girls loved playing with all the haberdashery and sewing notions that Louisa kept in a wicker basket under the stairs.

Susan smiled and ran off again. Christine picked up Susan's Noddy book and began to read it. The book was written for younger children but she liked looking at the colourful pictures.

"Have you thought more about taking orders for sewing again? Dot asked.

Louisa shook her head. "At the moment, with the difficulty of shopping for fabric and looking after the children, I haven't really got the time. Now clothes are off the ration I don't think I will be getting many orders anyhow."

"Well the clothes aren't cheap and there isn't a huge choice at the moment. It will be difficult to ease ourselves off making do and mending after eight years of rationing." Dot remarked. "Having something homemade especially by you Louie, means it is different to what is available in the shops. Something special."

Louisa shrugged. She was pleased with the compliment. Much though she missed her sewing, she still harboured fears over Michael's health. She did not want to neglect him.

"Maybe when Michael starts school, I will start again."

Dot laughed. "That's years before he starts school. The little thing isn't even walking yet! Don't put your dreams on hold Louie."

"It was easier when I was living in Pandy because mother looked after Susan. When I got too busy to go to the school she would walk to the school to meet Christine. She would take Susan with her too if she wasn't asleep. Then she would keep.them both occupied for an hour or two so that I could get on. Fred and I thought that perhaps when we get our old house back we might be able to build an extension and I could have a little room to set up my sewing machine."

"Have you heard from Joan?"

Louisa shook her head.

"I don't know why she didn't put her name down for one of these houses. You know, rather than hang on waiting for something to come up in Liverpool. She will probably have to wait for ages before something comes suitable. It isn't as if she is homeless even though she is living in your house."

Louisa sighed. "I know that. Fred tried to tell her that the only way she is going to get something is if she is actually living in Liverpool in terrible conditions. At the moment she isn't a priority even though she and her family are from that city and are living in cramped conditions in Wrexham. Having four children in a modern two bedroomed house in Wrexham is not Liverpool council's great concern."

"Your house." Dot pointed out.

"I know, but at least they pay us rent which pays the mortgage on the house. We just have to pay rent on this one. Some people in the cities are living in slums and in houses which ought to be demolished.

We will just have to wait. At least we have plenty of space in this house and a large garden where we can grow our own vegetables."

"We seem to spend our lives waiting." Dot said. "We waited for our men to come back, now we are waiting for the rationing to end. And some returning people from the services are still looking for jobs."

"Well at least we can get more fuel now and go out in the car." Louisa said. She sensed that Dot was exasperated with the continuing rationing and wanted things to get back to normal just as it was before the war started. Many of her neighbours and her friends had been complaining about the government over the continued rationing. They were all getting fed up of it. There was a lot of bitterness about the war years and impatience for the rationing to finish.

Michael began to whimper and Louisa went to the cot to see if he was alright. She came back smiling. Louisa always regarded her son as her miracle baby and she was still grateful that both he and she recovered from his birth. As a result she tended to be a little over protective of him still.

"He's crying in his sleep. He's teething."

A few hours later the house began to fill up again when Fred, Harry and his two sons returned with jubilant expressions on their faces from the football match.

"I take it Wrexham won." Dot said smiling as Malcolm and Gordon sat one each side of her on the sofa. Both boys nodded their heads. Louisa went to make more tea whilst Christine and Susan who had been playing in the garden, marched into the house to play with their cousins.

"How is Arthur?" Dot asked Harry. "I haven't seen him for a while. I haven't seen Gladys either."

Fred grinned. "He is getting used to having three youngsters in the house. Just as we are." His gaze dropped on to his daughters at the precise moment they disappeared into the other room with their cousins tagging behind them. Harry grinned too and sat down beside Dot in the space left vacant by one of his sons.

"He's also working hard to save money to buy a bigger house. He is also talking about getting a better job, though I don't know where. He only takes time off work when there is a home football match."

"That sounds like Arthur." Louisa chipped in when she returned with a fresh pot of tea. "He is always looking at ways to improve things. Good luck to him too."

A few months later Bill came knocking on their door in the middle of night frantic with worry. He told Louisa that Dorothy had gone in to labour and that she was asking for Louisa.

"Is it too late to get her to Rossett?" Fred asked Bill as they waited for Louisa to get her things.

"I believe so." Bill said. At least that is what the midwife said. I've just been for her and taken her to Pandy. Mrs. Mathews her name is. She's young and very authoritative. She told me to get out of the way."

Fred put an encouraging hand on his shoulder. "Don't worry. They did that to me too when Christine was born. He recalled the day when Louisa went into labour with their first child. Mary Ellen wouldn't let him near the bedroom and he could hear Louisa's cries coming from the bedroom.

126

Upstairs Louisa hastily got dressed and dragged on her coat as she got on to the back of Bill's scooter to ride back to Pandy.

They found Mary Ellen and William downstairs. William was making a fire and Mary Ellen was boiling some more water. She looked up when she saw her daughter and Bill rush through the door.

"It's nearly all over." She looked at Louisa in dismay. "That nurse won't let me do anything. She keeps telling me to stay away. She said we need to keep things hygienic and has me boiling water all the time. I know what to do. She doesn't have to give me instructions."

Mary Ellen looked affronted as she addressed Louisa. Her daughter gave her a sympathetic look.

"You go up and try to see her. Dorothy has been asking for you."

Louisa went up the stairs two at a time determined to see her sister. She fastened on a clean apron her mother handed to her as she went up the stairs. Being forewarned by her mother she didn't knock on the bedroom door. She barged in to the room and immediately got to Dorothy's bedside. She held her sister's hand just as the midwife said "one more push will do it." She glared at Louisa indignantly, but Louisa took no notice. Dorothy's hand gripped hers tightly as she obeyed the midwife's instructions and they both heard a reassuring slithering noise as the baby emerged into the world. Dorothy sighed and laid back exhausted.

"It's a girl the midwife announced.

"Go and tell Bill." Dorothy whispered to Louisa.

"I will." Louisa kissed her sister on her forehead and left her side. She hurried down the stairs again and found Bill in a very agitated state in the kitchen. She beamed at him. "It's a girl. Go on up. Don't bother knocking."

She said the last few words whilst Bill had already disappeared running up the stairs.

Mary Ellen and Louisa exchanged a triumphant look and hugged each other.

"Come on let's have a pot of tea." Mary Ellen said.

After the midwife had gone, Mary Ellen and Louisa went upstairs with more tea for Bill and Dorothy. They stayed just a few minutes to gaze at the baby then went downstairs again so that William could visit his daughter and new granddaughter.

They were going to call her Ann.

Dawn was breaking and Louisa said she would walk home. "I don't want to trouble Bill. I will call and let Harry and Dot know the good news on my way home."

It was a Saturday morning and Fred still had to go to work. He was ready to go when Louisa returned, though he still had half an hour before he was to leave.

"I got the children ready to bring to Pandy just in case there were problems with the birth." He looked at his tired wife. "You look all in."

Louisa shrugged. "I am, but I don't think I could sleep even if I had time. Maybe I will have a nap this afternoon when you come home from work."

Later that morning Louisa told the children that they had a new cousin and that they were going to Pandy to see her. They had been playing in the garden and had run in to the kitchen to find out more information.

"Is it a girl or a boy?" Christine asked.

"A baby girl. Her name is Ann."

Once Michael was settled in his pram they set off to Pandy. Mary Ellen took hold of Michael who had now woken up and she cradled him as she spoke to her daughter.

"All these grandchildren I am having, they keep multiplying." She smiled. "My knitting needles can't keep up with it all."

Later that same day Fred received a letter from his sister Mary. She too had given birth to a little girl and she had called her Stephanie.

"That's an unusual name." Fred commented. "I had better send her some money for the baby, and tell her we will try to get to Liverpool to see her soon."

"Good idea. She hasn't seen Michael yet. Perhaps we could visit Cissy as well. I don't think we can visit all your brothers too. The children will get tired."

Louisa gave Fred a side long glance. She knew he would like to see more of his brothers in Liverpool. Petrol rations, work and their growing family making extra demands on their time prevented many excursions to Liverpool. She suggested to him that he should get the train from Gwersyllt on his own one day so that he could keep in touch with them all. He agreed he would do that one Saturday soon.

Dorothy looked exhausted but radiant when Louisa walked into the kitchen in Pandy to see her a few days later. She was surprised to see her out of bed so soon. Louisa bent down to kiss her and gave her the flowers she had picked from the garden.

"I feel fine at the moment, but I will go back to bed later to rest." Dorothy said. She pulled her dressing

129

gown around her tightly. "Look I can fasten the belt around me again now."

In the back parlour the baby was fast asleep in her cot. The cot had been a gift from Bill's parents. Louisa looked down at her smiling. "She looks very content."

"Yes. I have just fed her. She seems to be a happy baby."

"Where's mother?" Louisa asked looking around her for Mary Ellen.

"She's just popped next door for five minutes."

Louisa told her about the birth of Mary's baby.

Dorothy laughed. "Both our families are expanding. Bill's sister is expecting now."

"Do you think it's because of the end of the war? There seems to be a baby boom." Louisa suggested. She sipped her ubiquitous cup of weak tea.

"It might be. There were a lot of weddings after the war, mine included, so it makes sense that there would be more babies."

"I think Fred's older brothers and sister have finished having new babies."

"What about John? Did you say that he and Joan had two little boys?

Louisa nodded. "Yes, they are called Donald and John. Fred went to Crewe to see them soon after I brought Michael home. They don't live far from Crewe station so Fred caught the train. They are still living with her parents."

"Have you heard from Cecelia? How is she? Any news?"

"She writes to me regularly and seems to be alright. Both her two sons are fine. Neville won a scholarship and is soon going to go to Bluecoats school. Michael is doing well too.

"And how is your little Michael?" Dorothy asked. She leaned forward to gaze at her nephew who was now sitting on Louisa's knee. Louisa smiled at her sister recognising the loving motherly yet anxious expression on her face. She had seen that tender look on other new mothers when she was in hospital herself almost a year earlier.

"He's doing well now. Sitting up and taking notice of everything. He is trying his best to walk. He's not quite there yet."

Louisa turned her head towards the door behind her when she saw Dorothy's eyes suddenly light up. Bill had arrived and so Louisa got up. She bent down to kiss her sister.

"I had better go outside to see what those two girls are up to. She carried Michael with her to the garden. As Louisa suspected the two girls were helping themselves to the late raspberries in the garden. She told them off quickly and guiltily they ran out of the garden. When they weren't looking Louisa helped herself to a few raspberries too. They were her favourite fruit.

A few weeks later one Saturday afternoon Fred took a train from Gwersyllt train station to Seacombe. From there he would get a bus to see his brother Jim in New Brighton. He was hoping that later he could get a ferry to cross the river Mersey to Liverpool. This was so that he could visit Bob. He was hoping to see Tom too who had come home on leave.

During that same afternoon Louisa received a visit from her brother-in-law Bill who was accompanied by a colleague. Whilst she was happy to see Bill,

Louisa felt inexplicably uncomfortable receiving his companion in to her house.

"This is Vince." Bill said. "I'm giving him a lift home. He lives not far from you in the other phase of the airey houses on Wheatsheaf Lane."

Despite an incipient feeling of unease Louisa smiled at her brother-in-law and his work mate and offered them some tea. She watched warily as she saw the two men sit down and make themselves comfortable. Louisa didn't like the way Vince's eyes roved over her body and his eyes gleamed as he stared in to her face. Hurriedly she handed him his tea, and she was unsure if she had imagined that his hand unnecessarily caressed her own. She was pleased that Christine and Susan ran into the house just then and greeted their uncle.

"What are you doing here Uncle Bill?" Christine asked. As usual she got straight to the point. Inwardly Louisa felt proud of her daughter's ability to speak her mind. Susan was more artful, always hinting at things and less forthright than her sister. Fred often felt he had to be a mind reader to understand what Susan wanted.

Bill laughed. "I've just finished work and taking Vince home after we have had a cup of tea with your mother."

"Is that your truck outside?" Christine asked.

"Yes. It is big isn't it? Vince has had to leave his at the depot today. He came with me to deliver the last load for the new road they are building in Chester, and now I am taking him home?"

Christine went to stand by her mother. Louisa put her arm around her protectively. Susan leaned against Bill and he put his arm around the little girl. She was an affectionate child.

"Are you enjoying your new job?" Louisa asked Bill.

He had only just recently started to work in road haulage. The labour government had begun a national programme of re-constructing the roads. As well as nationalising the coal mines and railways, the government had launched a nationalisation programme of the haulage trade. This had been met with a lot of opposition from private hauliers, however from Bill's point of view it offered him a well-paid job with reasonable hours and well maintained vehicles. He had learned to drive during the war and had been in a good position to get a job working for British Road Services.

"So far, so good." Bill said. "I get to see a bit of the country and how re-construction is progressing." He drained his cup and got up. "Thanks for the tea Lou." He kissed her on her cheek and Vince followed him out of the kitchen into the back yard. Louisa had a feeling that if she hadn't moved her face away to listen to something Christine had said, that Vince would have tried to kiss her too. She shuddered and was pleased to see the back of him.

When Fred returned from Liverpool later that day, Louisa mentioned that Bill had called with his colleague Vince, though she said nothing about her feelings regarding Vince.

"Bill has dropped lucky to get that job in haulage." Fred said. "Nationalising transport and haulage is a good idea of the government, but I wish they would invest a bit more in the railways. They seem to be going to rack and ruin. They were never properly maintained during the war and now some of the smaller stations are under threat of being closed down."

He sat down in an arm chair only to be bombarded by Susan to ask him to read her a bedtime story. Obligingly he pulled her on to his knee and opened the Rupert Bear annual she gave him. The book had been a Christmas present the previous year and Susan treasured the book very much.

Before Fred began to read he mentioned to Louisa that when he had got off the train he was told by the guard that the trains were delayed running through Wrexham the previous day because there was a huge fire in Regent Street.

"Where?" Louisa asked shocked.

"The *Wrexham Leader* office. Apparently it started early yesterday morning. The blaze was completely out of control and there was a fear it might spread towards the railway station. There is smoke everywhere. I could smell something when I got off the train in Gwersyllt. The guard said they were worried the flames might get to the petrol tanks on Vincent Greenhous garage."

"I wonder how that started." Louisa mused.

"The guard seemed to think it came from the top floor of the building where that sewing factory has been set up." Fred turned a page over in the book to appease Susan's impatience. She put her hand on his face to try to get his attention.

"You don't think those new electric sewing machines they installed had anything to do with it?" Louisa suggested. She was shocked about the fire and intrigued about the sewing factory.

"It might have done if they had been left on or over worked. It must be quite a blow if that little clothing factory has lost everything. It hasn't long started up. Didn't you mention it to me not long ago?"

"Yes it is called Johnsons and they are, or at least, they were on the top floor. What a shame. It would be difficult to rescue all those machines. I hope nobody was hurt."

"I don't think so. The guard didn't say that there were any injuries. Apparently the *Wrexham Leader* Office carried on work yesterday as if nothing had happened. They have got a temporary work place in High Street."

"That was quick work."

Fred shrugged. "Well they have got a big story to write. News is news."

Susan was getting impatient and so he began to read aloud to her. Whilst he read Louisa began to think about the workers and the loss of fabric and machinery at the small clothing factory in Caxton place. Secretly she had been thinking that when Michael was old enough to start school that she might apply for a job there as a seamstress. It was a few days later when she heard that the clothing factory had re-located to somewhere else in Wrexham.

Later when all the children were in bed Louisa asked how Fred's trip to Liverpool had been. He said he was shocked that there were still slums and uncleared bomb sites in the city centre.

"It's going to take a long time before everything gets back to normal. I saw Jim and Bob and Tom and the rest of them. Little Louie and Alf are doing alright. Bob's kids weren't around when I got there. Robert and little Jim were playing football somewhere, Frances and Margaret had gone to the cinema and Celia was playing with her friend next door.

I didn't stop long at Tom's. Nancy wasn't well, so I didn't want to disturb her. Tom gave me a lift on his motorbike to see Mary. He's thinking of leaving the army soon."

"Did you manage to see Mary's baby?" Louisa looked up smiling.

Fred nodded. "Yes I saw her. I only stayed at Mary's ten minutes because Tom offered to take me to the railway station so we didn't stay long. But she is fine. The flat she is living in is cramped. She is sharing with another family but at least she has a roof over her head and seems to have everything she needs. She told me she is going to move out soon. She has been offered a job as a housekeeper and she can take the baby with her."

Fred didn't mention Mary's husband, and Louisa knew that was because there wasn't one. She and Fred had been surprised to hear that Mary was expecting a baby and had assumed that eventually they would be introduced to the baby's father.

"Well that will be useful, having a job where she can look after the baby at the same time." Louisa commented.

"Yes it is very convenient. I just hope it works out well for her." Fred agreed and said no more about the matter. Louisa knew he was a little worried about his sister, but there wasn't much either of them could do for her. She hoped that everything would turn out all right for Mary. There were so many other people in Liverpool who were living in difficult circumstances, so for now they had to be glad that Mary would be able to keep her baby and earn a living.

For the first time in ages Louisa suddenly felt a surge of relief releasing the tension in her body. The feeling felt good and in that moment she felt happy with her lot. She had a nice home, a good husband and three lovely children. Things were beginning to get better. Surely all the family deserved some happiness now.

The only thing that could improve their day to day lives now was the much yearned for end to food rationing. She hoped it would be soon. Surely they had turned a corner.

Chapter Eleven

Louisa's contentment was somewhat shattered just a week later. This disruption of peace was caused by an unwanted and altogether unpleasant visit from Vince Belling. The intervention of her new neighbour prevented what could have been an ugly scene.

Earlier that day - it was a Friday and new neighbours were moving in to the house next door. Louisa was in the garden pegging out some clothes when she saw them carrying in various objects of furniture.

A little boy and girl ran around the garden and weaved themselves around their parents. They were taking advantage of the fact that they were not in school and enjoying the freedom of the open space. Their antics were hampering their parents' endeavours and Louisa smiled as she recalled the day she and Fred had moved in almost a year earlier. Their house was on a corner plot and surrounded on three sides by a good sized chunk of garden. Fred and her father had dug most of it over and laid some of it to lawn for their children. This still left a sizeable patch where they had planted potatoes, onions and cabbages as well as rows of beans and peas in the bits that were left. On the boundary with Louisa's new neighbour they had planted raspberry and redcurrant bushes. They were still very small as they had been cuttings from William's own garden.

Louisa leaned over the bushes to greet her new neighbour and introduced herself.

The young woman put down a wooden chair she was carrying and promptly sat on it. She took a deep breath. "Hello my name is Carol Lloyd." She pointed to her husband who emerged from the front door and was hurrying down to a van on the road. "That is my husband Reggie and these are my two children Gwilym and Bethan."

Carol had a round face with a creamy complexion currently flushed with the exertion of house moving. Her auborn coloured wavy hair tumbled over her forehead and ears framing her pink face. Louisa noticed a roundness of her stomach and guessed she was in the early stages of pregnancy. Her neighbour caught her glance and smiled ruefully. "I'm due before Christmas."

"If there is anything I can do to help, please ask." Louisa said. "I've got three of my own. I know what moving house with children is like." She laughed. "We had a lot of help though."

"Thank you. We are nearly done now. My brother and his wife are coming to help soon. Ron – that's my brother - is finishing work early this afternoon so he will help Reggie with the heavy stuff. He's bringing Sybil with him and my mother. They will help me unpack."

She picked up the chair and carried it in to the house. Louisa didn't see her again for several hours and between feeding Michael and changing his nappies she got on with her own household chores.

When she heard a knock on the back door she assumed it was her new neighbour, but the ready smile on her face disappeared quickly when she saw it was Vince. She pushed a stray dark hair away from her forehead with the back of her hand and held the handle of the door with the other. She didn't invite him in but somehow his foot was on the step and she involuntarily moved back. Her action allowed the door to open wider.

"Hello Louisa I thought I would call for some tea." He looked at her menacingly, and Louisa looked over his shoulder anxiously hoping that Bill would be behind him. He saw her glance. "I'm on my own today."

"I'm sorry." Louisa said recovering herself. "I'm too busy today. Besides I have only a small amount of my tea ration left. I need that for my husband when he comes home from work."

Vince grinned. "Never mind the tea. I'm sure there is something else you can offer me." He walked towards her and Louisa instinctively stepped back. She felt panic rising inside her. Just then there was a knock on the half open back door and her new neighbour called out to her. "Hello Louisa."

Vince drew back and Louisa seized the opportunity to stride to the door. "Hello Carol come on in."

The woman was dusty and wore a scarf around her head though her wavy auburn hair was still escaping all over her face. Tendrils hung everywhere round her. Louisa was so pleased to see her. Carol looked at Vince and smiled. "Hello you must be Louisa's husband."

"No, no he isn't my husband. He is just going. Goodbye Vince." Louisa glared at Vince. He shrugged, letting a sullen smirk smear his face. He nodded at Carol and then turned to go. "I'll see you again Louisa."

As soon as he had gone Louisa breathed a sigh of relief and leaned against the sink to calm herself down.

"Is everything alright?" Carol asked. "Have I come at a bad time?"

Louisa shook her head. "No you came at a very good time. That man is a friend of my brother-in-law. I don't like him very much and I am glad he has gone. He called unexpectedly."

Louisa didn't want to explain how she felt to a complete stranger, yet Carol seemed so sympathetic. The two women bonded with each other almost straight away.

"Did you want some help?" Louisa asked.

Carol nodded. "I seem to have mislaid my kettle and all my pans. I think they are in a box still at my mother's house in Rhostyllen. Do you think I could borrow a pan or something to make some tea for Reggie and Ron?"

"Of course." Louisa strode to her cupboard and handed an aluminium saucepan with a lid to her new neighbour.

"Thank you so much. Would you like to come and have some tea with us?" Carol asked. "I've got some to spare."

Louisa glanced at the clock on the wall and hesitated. The children would be home from school in ten minutes. It was the last day of term and they were breaking up for the summer holidays.

"The children will be here soon." Louisa hesitated.

"Well it is a nice day, we could sit outside on our dining room chairs, I haven't put them in yet. From our kitchen door you will see your children coming up the path."

Louisa smiled. She liked that idea. It was nice to be able to have someone to talk to. She went to get Michael's pram and pushed him outside on to the yard so that she could see him from next door's kitchen door. He was still asleep. Carol's dining chairs were brand new and Carol and Reggie were proud of them. They were some of the articles they had managed to buy new before moving home.

"Utility furniture." She confided. "Most of the other stuff is old and donated to us by friends and family. "We've been living with my mum and dad for so long we have scarcely had time to fix up a home of our own. We are so glad to get one of these airey houses. Now my brother and sister-in-law will have a bit more space."

"That sounds very much similar to our circumstances." Louisa admitted as she explained about Dorothy and Bill having to move to Pandy.

When Christine and Susan arrived home fifteen minutes later, they saw their brother's pram in the yard and their mother drinking tea next door with complete strangers. A little apprehensively they approached the garden boundary close to where their mother was sitting. That part of the boundary was just bits of building rubble. It provided makeshift rocky steps for them to walk over to next door. Both girls picked their way carefully to speak to their mother. Christine rested a foot each on a small hump of stones. "We have finished school for summer now mum." She declared.

Just then Carol's two children came out of the house and they stared at Christine and Susan. Both girls stared back. Carol laughed.

"This is Gwilym and this is his sister Bethan. I hope you will be friends."

Louisa got up, handed her cup and saucer to Carol and stepped over the rubble to join her daughters. "Come on you two, you need to change out of your school clothes. Thanks for the tea Carol."

Christine followed Louisa into the house but Susan lingered. "Do you want to come and play with us?" she said to Bethan and Gwilym. Both children looked at their mother for consent. Carol glanced anxiously at Louisa and saw her nod her head, so the children climbed over the stones and followed Louisa and her daughters in to the house.

Once the two girls had changed into their play clothes they went out in to the garden with their new friends. Louisa brought Michael's pram back into the house and began to prepare the evening meal. She felt a lot calmer now, but worried whether she should tell Fred about the unpleasant incident with Vince. She decided not to worry him. No harm was done and she doubted that Vince would call again. Besides the children were now in their school holidays so she would have company for the next six weeks. Having the children around would make it very difficult for Vince to make any unwanted advances. In any case Louisa was sure he wouldn't visit her again. There was an added bonus that Fred had booked a week off work. It made her happy to know that Fred would be around so that they could take the children out for walks and picnics. She pushed the nasty incident with Vince to the back of her mind.

When Fred arrived home later he suggested that they used one of his leave days to drive to Rhyl for the day.

"These children have never seen the seaside or played in the sand." Fred said. "I'm sure I have enough petrol to get us there and back. The weather forecast says it will be sunny for the next couple of days. That terrible thunder storm we had recently has cleared the air."

Louisa shuddered at the memory of the storm two nights before. She hated the thunder and lightning, she could never dis-associate it with the sirens she heard during the war. First came the sirens then the sound of gunfire.

"The children will love it. Shall we go on Monday? I can boil some eggs to take with us."

The children were excited when they told them what they planned. On Sunday afternoon they walked over to Pandy and the little girls eagerly ran in to their grandparents to tell them about their forthcoming expedition the next day.

"You will be needing some lettuce and onions to take with you for the picnic." William said getting up and going outside to his garden. "Do you want some potatoes too? I don't think yours will be ready yet. You can have them cold with your eggs."

Louisa was happy to take anything her father could spare. Absently she plucked a pod of peas from the canes and began to eat them raw.

"Take some of them too, if you want." Her father said.

"Our onions and potatoes are not quite ready yet." Fred confirmed. He had followed them in to the garden. Mary Ellen stood behind him.

"The ground in your garden hasn't been planted with anything for years before they started building those houses so the soil is not so good. The building plot was just fields. Don't worry you will get something soon. Next year your crops will be better."

"I'm just glad we decided to plant potatoes and onions now that there is a scarcity." Louisa said.

Fred nodded. "We are more fortunate than a lot of people now that potatoes are on ration."

"I'm glad I managed to keep a lot of seed potatoes back before they went on ration. I have been keeping some every year." William said.

The next day the sun was shining and they set off for Rhyl. The last time Fred and Louisa had been to the seaside was on Fred's motorbike before they got married in nineteen thirty eight. He hoped he could remember the way. The journey took them an hour and a half and when he finally parked the car on the seafront, Susan had fallen asleep. The baby too was asleep.

Rubbing her eyes after being wakened, Susan couldn't believe her eyes when she saw the sea. It was bigger than she had imagined. She had seen pictures of the sea in books but had not anticipated the sheer scale of it. Christine too was overwhelmed. She put down the book she had been reading which ironically was Robinson Crusoe. She stared disbelievingly at the wide expanse of water.

"Come on let's get on to the sand." Fred said as he opened the door for the two girls to get out. He was excited as they were. Louisa laughed and followed them with Michael in the pram along the sandy path to the beach. Louisa put down an old blanket on the sand and sat down as she watched Fred take one daughter in each hand to the edge of the water. He encouraged them both to take off their socks and shoes and they nervously hung on to him as they felt the wet sand under their feet. They both screamed with pleasure when a wave came crashing down in front of them. Fred saw it in time and lifted them up before it soaked them, though the bottom of his trousers didn't escape the wet foam.

How different all this must be for Fred, Louisa thought. Playing in the water with his daughters instead of being on board a destroyer on the Atlantic Ocean. She smiled happily whilst she got Michael out of the pram and carried him to the water's edge.

"Tuck your dresses into your knickers!" she told the girls, then you can go in further without getting wet." Fred looked up at her and grinned. He had a boyish look of delight on his face and Louisa felt a fresh surge of love for him.

"A good idea." Fred said. He rolled up his trouser legs so that they rested above his knees, then grabbing the girls hands again they dashed into the water shrieking with laughter.

Much later after they had eaten their picnic salad they strolled along the promenade as they pushed Michael in his pram.

Fred hoped that they would be able to have a treat of fish and chips to round off the day and they looked for a place that seemed to have less of a queue. Fish being off ration there was often a queue. They didn't have to wait too long and they sat on a bench near the sea to eat them.

"They always seem to taste nicer outside." Fred remarked. He watched delightedly as his daughters tucked into their supper.

Louisa agreed. "Yes they do. A very nice change. It's been a lovely day." She felt relaxed and had all but forgotten the unpleasant occasion a few days ago. She had a pang of guilt not telling Fred about Vince, but she didn't want to worry him. Besides there was nothing he could have done about it. The matter was over and done with and she felt she had made it quite clear to Vince that his presence was not welcome in her home.

The children fell asleep in the car on the way home, so Fred spoke quietly to Louisa his plans for the rest of the week. He suggested they went for walks along the banks of the river Alyn and perhaps he would teach the girls how to fish.

"Maybe next year we could have a week in Rhyl in one of those holiday camps they are setting up."

"Would we be able to afford it? All our savings are going towards a new house."

Fred sighed. "Yes I think so. I know we agreed to save towards our new house, but we should allow ourselves a bit of a holiday. Don't you agree?" He took his eyes off the steering wheel to make a quick sidelong look at his wife.

Louisa shrugged. "I don't mind. It's been a good day today and to have more of them and a week's holiday to look forward to next year sounds even better. The children have loved it." She broke off to glance at the sleeping girls on the back seat of the car.

"Besides we don't know if Joan will be ready to move out next year. Things are progressing slowly with house building all across the country not just Liverpool. It's nice to have a plan. We have waited too long for a holiday. It will be nice to give the children a carefree life after all the dreary years of the past. And this little one," she hugged the baby to her, "will have a good start in life."

She gave Fred a reassuring smile and was rewarded to see a smile of satisfaction trace his suntanned features.

A few days later Vince made another unexpected and unwanted appearance. This was to be his undoing. Louisa was glad that he appeared when Fred was at home. She was astonished as well as aggrieved at Vince's persistence. When she opened the back door and saw his leering face on the doorstep she was taken aback by his boldness.

"What are you doing here?" Louisa spoke to him curtly. She glanced at the closed hall door that led from the kitchen. Fred was upstairs and she knew he would come down any second. Vince followed her glance arrogantly mistaking her gesture as an invitation to go upstairs.

"You know I won't take no for an answer Louisa. The bedroom is that way is it?" He lunged towards her and she screamed just as Fred opened the hall door. He blinked when he saw Louisa's frightened face and Vince's arm around her waist.

"Take your hands off my wife!" Fred said. He seized the man by the collar and pushed him against the cupboard.

"What are you doing in my house?" Who are you?"

"He's Vince, Bill's workmate I told you about." Louisa gasped. "I told him last week never to come here again."

Fred released the man from his grip and Vince choked. "If I ever hear of you in this house again I will call the police. Get out. My wife has told you not to come here again and now I am telling you."

"Alright, I am going. No harm done." Vince shuffled out of the door quickly. He glared at Louisa on his way out. Fred slammed the door behind him and Louisa ran into the safety of his arms. He stroked the back of her head to comfort her.

"Did I hear you right? Did you say he tried to get in here last week?"

Louisa nodded. "Last Friday when the children finished school. Fortunately Carol next door was here and I told him then he wasn't welcome. I didn't like the way he was looking at me. I didn't like him when he was here with Bill the first time, but I thought I would never see him again so I didn't say anything. I didn't want to worry you."

Fred sighed. "I don't like the look of him. I should tell Bill in case he goes chasing after Dorothy. He needs locking up."

"I shouldn't think he would bother Dorothy. She is seldom alone in the house. He lives in Gwersyllt in a house like this one on Wheatsheaf lane. He must have finished his shift and come here. Bill said that sometimes when they finish their load and take the lorry back to the quarry they are dependent on various people and other lorry drivers to give them a lift home. He must have been dropped off near the Mold Road and decided to come down here."

"If he lives in a house like this one in Wheatsheaf Lane he must have a wife and family of his own." Fred mused.

"Yes, I thought that too when Bill introduced him. I thought these houses were allocated to families with young children."

"Yes. At least that is how I understood it when I applied." Fred agreed.

"I suppose Bill didn't know that Vince is a womaniser." Louisa said.

Fred grimaced. "I've met blokes like that before. They have no shame or morals and treat women badly. Well I still think we should tell Bill and be on our guard. In the meantime, when you are alone, I think you should keep the doors locked at least for a short while. Though I have a feeling he won't be back."

Chapter Twelve

Whilst Fred was home for the week Louisa felt safe especially with the children running around the house. Meanwhile both she and Fred had got to know their new neighbours next door Carol and Reggie. The children too seemed to have made friends with the girl and boy next door. Gwilym was two years older than his sister Bethan and Christine who were almost the same age. Bethan would be starting at the same school as Christine in September and Carol was glad that the two girls had got to know each other beforehand.

"Not that Bethan is shy but I think it is nice to know a few people before you start somewhere new." Carol confided in Louisa one afternoon.

Louisa agreed. She never forgot the time she had to travel to Wallasey on her own at the age of fourteen to work as a kitchen maid. She had been nervous though determined to do her best. The housekeeper there had been very mean and spiteful. She had only been there two weeks when Arthur had called to see her. He had taken one look at her forlorn appearance and decided to take her home on his motorbike. Things turned out much better for Louisa after that. Despite being sent away from home again to work as a servant, her mother had found her a position in Broughton Hall. That place was just a few miles away from Pandy. The housekeeper there had been less demanding and Louisa had felt much happier. She also made friends with some of the other servants, two of whom she was still in contact. Olive now lived in South Wales with her husband Sidney. Another friend from Broughton Hall was Ivy. She had a sister who had gone to work in Chesterfield during the war. During the war Ivy had joined her sister Rose at the Robinsons factory where they made medical supplies. The two sisters were determined to be career girls. Rose was now a supervisor in the medical and surgical dressings department. She had been promoted after her superior Muriel had left to get married. Ivy was now a secretary in the adjoining building.

As Louisa mused over how the lives of her friends had changed, she began to think about the sacrifices that Ivy and Rose had made to be career women. They had given up being wives and mothers so that they could be independent. Louisa felt it was unfair that a woman should have to give up so much in order to follow a career. It made her even more determined to return to her sewing as soon as she could. She didn't delude herself that she could be self-sufficient from her sewing, but the small income she got gave her some satisfaction. Besides she loved designing and sewing clothes. Every now and again she treated herself to a magazine so that she could study the clothes the models were wearing. She usually bought them at the post office where she went weekly to get the family allowance.

When Fred returned to work a week later Louisa was a little apprehensive about being at home without him but was determined not to let her feelings show in front of the children. She kept the door locked when they were in the house. Meanwhile she took advantage of the good weather and every afternoon encouraged the children to play in the garden where she would read a book sitting on an old wooden chair near the hedge. Fred had planted some privet all along the exterior boundary of the garden which was growing very slowly.

Summer had turned into autumn when Louisa invited her next door neighbour's children to accompany her and Christine and Susan to go blackberry picking. Carol decided to go along too. She was quite fit despite being six months pregnant and they all walked amiably to the Bluebell wood. On the way they called for Dot and Malcolm. It had become an annual ritual to pick blackberries in the Bluebell wood. It was one of Louisa's favourite places and her children loved it too.

For the first time during all these years of gathering the fruit Dot and Harry's older son Gordon was unable to go with them. He was playing football. At nearly thirteen years of age he had started playing football in a school boy football club that had been set up in Wrexham. It was a club that encouraged school boys under the age of fifteen. Apparently he was very good at it and showed a lot of promise for the future.

Louisa had confided in Dot about most things in her life over the years and so when Carol was out of earshot she whispered to Dot about the problem she had experienced with Vince. He hadn't made an appearance since Fred threatened him and she felt confident he wouldn't call again. She decided to mention it to her sister-in-law. Dot was shocked. Have you told Dorothy and Bill? They ought to know."

Louisa shook her head. "Not yet. I haven't had the heart really. I don't want to worry them. It isn't the kind of thing I want to discuss with them. Fred said he would try to get Bill alone, but so far he hasn't been able to. They are both wrapped up with the baby." She managed a smile as she thought of her niece Ann.

Louisa heard Dot sigh with exasperation as she watched Louisa stretch towards the top of a blackberry bush. She was trying to reach a branch that was sagging with the weight of several large berries. They were tantalisingly just out of her reach. She put down her basket and tried again.

"Hold on I will hold these brambles back for you. I can see what you are trying to get at." Dot said grinning. She got hold of a thick branch and pushed it back and watched Louisa triumphantly pick the berries.

"The bigger and best ones always seem to be where you can't get at them." Louisa laughed.

"I know, but there are plenty of others." Dot retorted.

"You know Harry was telling me that Arthur was getting Bill a deal on a car. He was arranging for him to pick it up this week end, so you never know they may call to see both of us soon."

"So no side car on the motorbike for Dorothy then." Louisa smirked. "I must admit I thought it was quite fun when I used to ride in the side car with Christine on my knee."

"Well you didn't go very far though did you? The war was on and there was scarcely any petrol."

"No not really. I think we went to Farndon a couple of times."

That week end Bill and Dorothy arrived with their baby during a late Saturday afternoon. Louisa had just made them comfortable with a pot of tea when Fred arrived home from work.

It wasn't long before the conversation turned to Vince and his bad behaviour. Fred made it quite clear what he thought of the man and told Bill that friend or not he would inform the police if he was to annoy Louisa again.

Bill was appalled. "Louie I am so sorry. I had no idea he was like that."

"Next time you see him, can you tell him I mean what I say?" Fred said.

"I certainly will. I have to say I haven't seen him for a week or two. There are a few of us drivers and we don't always see each other regularly. We work different shifts and routes and contracts and so on. But I give you my word that next time I see him I will make sure he doesn't come here again."

"Do you know exactly where he lives?" Fred asked.
Bill shook his head. "All I know is, that he lives in a house like this one.

Later they went outside to say goodbye and Bill proudly showed them his Austin Ten New Ascot

Saloon. "Arthur got me a good deal I couldn't resist."

"All we need now is a house of our own instead of living with mother and father." Dorothy said. "Not that it is a problem, but it would be nice to have our own place like you and Fred."

Fred put his arm around Louisa's shoulders. "Yes it does make a difference having your own home. We are happy here aren't we?" As he said this he turned towards his wife and Fred realised that he was happy even though the house was not made of bricks.

Louisa put her hand across Fred's own hand. "Yes very happy."

The following afternoon they walked across the Pandy fields to see William and Mary Ellen. In the small kitchen Arthur and Gladys were making themselves comfortable. Outside in the garden were there two children Brian and Maureen. Happily Christine and Susan went to join their cousins.

Inside the kitchen Arthur showed Fred a copy of a book he had bought it was called *Nineteen Eighty Four* by George Orwell.

"You can borrow it after I have read it Fred." Arthur was saying. "It is very unusual. It is all about a future world in forty years' time."

"Thanks maybe I will. Let's hope we will all be alive in nineteen eighty four."

"Oh Fred don't talk like that." Louisa admonished her husband crossly.

"Talking of books and films, we haven't been to the cinema together for a while, why don't we go?" Suggested Gladys.

"Good idea." Fred and Arthur enthused.

Louisa hesitated and glanced at her mother. "Who will look after the children?"

"Bring them here. They can stay here. They are still in the school holidays so a late night won't harm them."

"What do you think Louie?" Fred said.

"Yes, if mother is sure." Mary Ellen nodded her head.

"Right. Let's see what's on." Arthur said. He picked up a newspaper that had been lying on the table.

"How about this - *The Third man*. I wouldn't mind that."

Fred looked up surprised. "Yes I wouldn't mind that either."

Both Gladys and Louisa agreed and they all looked at each other amazed.

"That was a quick decision!" Arthur said folding the newspaper. "We usually take ages to decide."

William laughed. "Don't go changing your mind then. He turned towards his daughter. "Dorothy and Bill are going to Mold for the week end next week so they won't be able to go with you. Are you going to ask Harry and Dot? They won't have much trouble getting Dot's mother to mind the boys. They are getting older now so they are less effort."

Mary Ellen laughed. "Yes they are growing up quickly."

"Yes it will be good if they can come." Louisa said. She got up to get ready to go home. "We can call on the way home to ask them can't we Fred?"

"Yes. I don't mind." He opened the door and crossed the track that ran around the back of the terraced house. When he reached the garden gate he called to the children. "Come on we're going home now."

The girls ran in to kiss Mary Ellen and William goodbye then they set off again towards the fields. Louisa checked to see if the cows were away from the path. She knew they wouldn't harm her but she didn't want to take chances with the children. Louisa handed the baby to Christine, whilst Fred lifted the pram over the stile towards Louisa. She caught it the other side and settled it down again on to the stony path. Christine helped her mother to put the baby back into the pram and together they pushed Michael along the stony path over the fields.

Fred picked up a long stick. He caught Louisa's glance. "If one of those animals come near us I will wave it off with this. They are quite timid really you know."

Louisa smiled. "I know. I'm just cautious."

When they got to Rhosrobin Louisa knocked on Harry and Dot's door and without waiting for an answer she opened it. She called 'hello" just as the two girls dived in to the hallway.

"Hey come back you little devils." Louisa called. "We aren't stopping."

The girls returned to the door followed by their Uncle Harry. He was pleased to see his sister and brother-in-law.

"Have you got time to stay for a bit? Come in for five minutes at least."

They trooped in and sat down on the three piece suite that Harry and Dot had recently bought. Fred hadn't seen it and he admired the workmanship.

"Not bad for government utility furniture." Harry said. Louisa could see he was pleased with the purchase.

"Well now the government have introduced new regulations about quality furniture it ought to be good." Fred said. "It should last many years."

"The reason we called was to see if you wanted to come with us and Arthur and Glad to see a film. We've already decided that we want to watch *The Third Man*. It's on at the Majestic and we want to go next Saturday. Can you come?" Louisa asked. She looked up at her brother who was listening to her intently.

"What do you say Dot?" Harry turned around to address his wife.

"Yes. I have read the book. It would be nice to see the film. I'm sure my mother will keep an eye on the boys."

On Friday afternoon the day before they were due to go to the cinema, Louisa took her children to the post office in Gwersyllt. She wanted to get her family allowance and to buy some stamps. When she arrived inside the small office she was surprised to find such a frenzied atmosphere. The room was more crowded than usual. It wasn't a big place. It just about served to do postal duties and sell a few odd groceries, magazines and newspapers. The children were crushed together as she waited her turn. To make more space she asked Christine to go outside with the pram and to look after Michael. She kept hold of Susan as she had a tendency to wander off.

Eventually it was Louisa's turn. As she asked for her stamps the woman at the back of her in the queue said "Well she will probably hang for it."

Louisa swivelled her head around to look at the woman behind her. She was dressed in a pink and grey fleck jacket and grey flannel skirt. Louisa took a second to admire the cut with her expert eye before asking. "Who is going to hang?"

Again the excited buzz in the post office met her ears and she was confused.

"'aven't you 'eard?" The woman behind the pink and grey flecked jacket responded excitedly. She jerked her head towards Louisa. "There's been a murder. And not far away from 'ere either. She did 'er 'usband in."

Louisa stared at the second woman. She had a dark brown scarf around her head. The edges of the scarf draped over a tan coloured blazer. Louisa paid for her stamps and moved away so that the pink and grey flecked jacket could be served. Before she spoke to the post office assistant she spoke to Louisa. "It's true, I'm afraid."

This comment started a flutter of chatter again and Louisa stared from one animated face to another. "Who?" She gasped. Somehow Louisa felt she knew what they were going to say.

Another young woman thrust a copy of the *Wrexham Leader* in front of her. "Look it is all in there."

Louisa gazed down at the two photographs on the front of the newspaper. There was a picture of a young pretty woman named Edna Webb and next to that was a picture of Vince Webb.

"Oh my god!" Louisa gasped again.

160

"Are you alright love?" It was the woman in the tan blazer. "You look as if you 'ave seen a ghost.

"I'm fine thank you. It is such a shock to see a picture of the dead man and the photo of his wife. Why did she kill him?" Louisa composed herself quickly.

"I don't know, but it is a terrible thing to kill your 'usband." Answered the woman. By this time the pink flecked jacketed woman had been served and she spoke to Louisa as she edged towards the newspaper stand. "She'll hang. I know she will." Then the woman walked away nodding her head towards the other three women in the queue. She walked confidently as if she already knew the outcome of Edna Webb's trial. The rest of the women were all muttering about the murder. Louisa paid for her copy of the newspaper and hurried outside again to find Christine and Michael.

When she got home Louisa took out the newspaper and began to read the front page article. There wasn't a lot in the report other than the wife had said that it was an accident. She had insisted that he had fallen down the stairs when she had tried to stop him beating her.

Probably true mused Louisa. She recalled the glint in Vince's eyes when he tried to seduce her. Poor woman, she was probably telling the police the truth, but will they believe her. She showed the newspaper to Fred when he arrived home.

"That's sad. People like that usually come to a sticky end."

"Yes but what about this poor woman Edna. What is going to happen to her?"

"Depends on the evidence I suppose." Fred replied.

The next evening they caught a bus to Wrexham and met the rest of their family outside the Majestic on Regent Street. As predicted by Louisa they were all talking about the death of Vince Webb. Dot hugged Louisa. "You must be feeling you had a lucky escape from that man Louie."

Louisa's brothers crowded around her protectively. Harry put an arm on her shoulder. "Are you ok Louie?"

"Yes I'm fine. It was a shock to see his photograph on the front page of the *Leader* but other than that I'm fine. I'm worrying about his wife. I think she killed him in self defence."

"It was an accident? Was it?" Gladys asked. "Did you know her?"

Louisa shook her head. "She looks a few years younger than me, and I don't think she was in school when I was there. Maybe Dorothy knew her. I wonder if they had children."

"They are bound to have children or they wouldn't have been given one of those houses on Wheatsheaf Lane." Arthur said. "And they might not be from this part of Wrexham. They might have moved from those slums the council were clearing near the old Leather works in Salop Road. I know a few people who have moved from there. I'm surprised no-one has been injured. Those old houses looked as if they were about to collapse. Have you seen them Fred?" Arthur glanced at his brother in law expecting some comment about the building industry. However catching sight of Fred's distraught face, his own expression changed.

Fred was distracted about Vince. "He must have served in the war." Fred said. A grim expression traced his troubled features. Louisa wasn't sure if her husband was recalling the day Vince threatened her, or whether he was thinking of a nasty incident during the war. "Such a shame to have survived that and then to turn into a nasty brute and…"

"And meet such a horrible end to his life." Arthur finished for him.

Harry said nothing, though he nodded his head in agreement with his brother and brother-in-law. His own countenance displayed distress. Louisa began to feel uneasy again.

"Come on you lot. Cheer up. We are here to enjoy ourselves." Gladys said. "Let's get our tickets and enjoy the film."

Chapter Thirteen

Early in September Louisa went shopping with Dot
to buy a school uniform for Gordon. This purchase
was to be Gordon's first long pair of trousers. They
went to *Lloyd Williams* the draper's shop and whilst
Dot paid for the trousers and his blazer, Gordon and
Malcolm hung back with Louisa. Gordon had been
delighted with the new trousers but was too coy to
stand next to Dot as she paid for them.

Louisa intended to buy material to make two new
skirts. Though Christine didn't wear a uniform
Louisa was going to make her a skirt that would be
suitable for the following year when she would
require one. Susan was wearing an old skirt of
Christine's. She never complained about wearing
Christine's hand me downs but Louisa wanted to
buy Susan something new. In the shop she put a
tape measure around their waists. Satisfied she had
the correct measurements she selected a bale of
material and took it to the counter to get it cut. The
material was good quality but it was expensive.
Louisa hoped that the material would be an
investment so that she wouldn't have to make new
skirts for at least two more years. The garments

would have generous seams to allow for growth. As the children grew bigger she would let out the seams. Satisfied with their purchases they went to King Street to catch the bus home.

On the corner of King Street there was a newsagent and Louisa stopped to buy a copy of the *Wrexham Leader.*

When they were seated on the bus Louisa opened the newspaper to casually glance at the articles. Amongst all the advertisements Louisa noticed that the Johnson's clothing factory that had been affected by the fire were now advertising for seamstresses part time. She showed it to Dot.

"It's a bit too early for me at the moment, but it is something to think about in a few years when Michael is in school."

"Are you not going to start your own little business again?" Dot asked.

"I would like to but I'm not sure it would pay me a regular wage. It will take years to build up a good reputation and to get people to pay for my designs. I'm not giving up on that dream totally though, I will just have to wait and see. I was thinking if I had a part-time job with a regular income, I could concentrate on my own designs in my own time."

Dot leaned over her shoulder and read the advert. "This Johnson company has re-located you know. I was told the new owner of Johnson's old place has been renovating it. The new owner is going to open up a similar factory. It is going to be run by someone called Manley. Not that it matters."

Then her eyes scanned the opposite page and caught sight of a report about the wife of Vince Webb. "Look Louie it seems that Edna Webb is out on bail

165

pending trial. I wonder who paid the bail money for her."

Louisa read the article. "Well whoever it was I am glad for her sake. I wouldn't be surprised that it really was an accident. Every time I go to the post office I seem to pick up more gossip. I've heard rumours that her face was often bruised. Perhaps she tried to run upstairs away from him and he grabbed her. She might have pushed him away to defend herself from his blows and he lost balance and fell down the stairs. Accidents do happen."

"The trouble is can she prove it? How is she going to provide evidence? I hope she doesn't hang." Dot said.

"I feel sorry for her children because even if she doesn't hang, she may have to serve a prison sentence."

"Poor woman." Dot said. "She will be able to apply for Legal Aid though I suppose."

"If she is pregnant she wouldn't hang." Louisa mused half to herself. "I think the law states that a pregnant women would not face the death penalty."

"She may still go to prison though." Dot remarked. "How awful to give birth to the baby in prison. Would she be able to keep it?"

"I don't know. Anyway that's neither here nor there because we don't even know if she is pregnant. I'm just speculating." Louisa said shaking her head in bewilderment. "It is a terrible situation to be in."

In the Post office a few days later Louisa heard more gossip about Edna Webb's coming trial. The pink checked jacket woman was nowhere to be seen. It was the post mistress herself who informed Louisa that the bail money had been raised by friends and neighbours who had organised a collection. They had also contacted various women's groups who had also contributed.

"It seems the neighbours are convinced she is innocent because they heard her scream on more than one occasion. They are convinced her husband was punching hell out of her." The postmistress said. She handed Louisa her change for her purchase of stamps. "It seems to me that her husband got his cum uppence. I hope she gets off free and can find herself a decent husband. She has three children under the age of five you know."

"Do you know when the trial will be?" Louisa asked.

"Probably a few months' time I shouldn't wonder. These cases sometimes take months even years. Let's hope it's all over before Christmas and that the jury are sympathetic."

Louisa thanked her for her change and hurried home with the children. It was late October and the weather was turning colder. In a few days it would be their wedding anniversary and she was hoping to make something nice to eat for herself and Fred to celebrate. Their anniversary the previous year had been fraught with worry over Michael and moving into their new home. She could scarcely believe how quickly the year had gone and now Michael was walking and getting into mischief. He was adored by his two older sisters and they were willing to play with him at any time he demanded their attention.

Fred also had some ideas on how to celebrate their wedding anniversary. He suggested to Louisa that they ask Dot to mind the children whilst they went to see a film and then get fish and chips for their supper.

Louisa laughed. "I don't mind, but I was thinking on the lines of a romantic dinner for two."

Fred looked surprised. Whenever he had suggested that they go out for a meal she had always said it was too expensive, now she seemed to have changed her mind. "Well that's alright with me. Do you have a place in mind?"

"No. But let's stick to your plan because there is a film I would like to see. It's a romance so it would be appropriate, and fish and chips would be a treat."

"What's the film?"

Louisa grinned. "Actually I've shortlisted three I am interested in. Two of them are musicals."

Fred pulled a face. He didn't like musicals much.

"I know you aren't keen on musicals but these are supposed to be comedies as well as romances. One is about sailors on leave. You will relate to that!" Louisa smirked. "Not that their antics are anything like yours would have been in the war. At least I hope not." She gave Fred a playful side long look. In turn he looked affronted so she hurried on. "The other one is about a summer time romance."

"And what is the third one? The one that is not a musical."

"It's more like a drama but sounds interesting." That one is called "*The Shared Rib.*"

"Hmm that's a bit of a contrast in taste. I think we would both enjoy that one more. We both like dramas. It sounds like it is going to be a battle of the sexes."

"Possibly. Anyway I am willing to see it if you are."

"Yes I think I am. Have you asked Dot to come and keep an eye on the children?"

Louisa nodded. "Yes all fixed up."

On their anniversary a few days later they walked up to Gwersyllt railway station and travelled by train to Wrexham. The Station was in Hill Street, so all they had to do was walk down the hill to Brook Street to the Odeon. Fred bought the tickets whilst Louisa waited in the foyer studying the posters of previous films. The current one caught her eye and she realised that it advertised the film they had chosen to watch. It was a court room drama based on the alleged murder of a woman's husband.

Fred joined her with the tickets and she pointed out the poster. He read it whilst he put his wallet away then gazed at his wife. "Very topical for us isn't it? Are you sure you want to watch it? I can change the tickets if you tell me now." He glanced over his shoulder at the queue at the ticket office. It was Friday night and the cinema was a popular place to go at the end of a working week. The queue wound its way all along Brook Street and almost to the corner of Bridge Street.

Louisa nodded enthusiastically. "Yes I do want to watch it." Fred followed Louisa in to the cinema and they got settled in to their seats. Then after some shuffling around with coats he handed Louisa a box of chocolates and grinned when he saw her astonished expression as her eyes lit up.

"Oh lovely. Where did you get these?"

"It was by chance, that yesterday I was in a shop where they had just been delivered. So I bought them straight away. It was almost a fight to get them. There are rumours that the government is going to rationalise chocolate again."

Louisa sighed. "So soon after taking chocolate off ration and they are putting it back on. Not that there has been much in the local shops. "I bet they cost a fortune." Louisa said unpacking the paper as quickly as she could. Fred winked. "It was nice to be able to afford a present for our anniversary." He helped himself to one of the chocolates and was satisfied to see the ecstatic enjoyment of his wife as she chewed on hers. On the way home later they discussed the film and tried to compare it with the pending case of Edna Webb.

"Do you think if we were to tell her solicitor what we know about Vince that it would help her case?" Louisa suggested. She offered Fred one of the last two remaining chocolates on the top layer of the box. She bit into hers which was fudge then put the box into her bag. They had agreed they would share the bottom layer with the children and Dot.

"I think it might." Fred said as he chewed on his truffle. "It's worth a try. If the solicitor thinks it would help we would have to make a statement and be prepared to be called up as a witness. Would you be alright with that?"

Louisa nodded her head and used her eyes to convey to her husband that she would be willing to help. She was savouring the last taste of chocolate in her mouth and didn't want to talk. Eventually she swallowed the last of the chocolate and licked her lips.

"Would you be prepared to be a witness too? Another man speaking on her behalf would probably carry some extra weight in her favour."

"Yes of course I would."

Neither Fred nor Louisa had any idea who was representing Edna Webb so on the following Saturday afternoon they decided to visit the Police Station and explain what they wanted to do. The Police station was in Regent Street not far from the Majestic cinema. A Police Sergeant told them that they would need to write down their observations in the form of witness statements. He took them in to another room to write them down. This took more time than they had anticipated and when they came out of the station they both felt exhausted but relieved.

"I could do with a drink after that." Fred said. "Let's go to the Horse and Jockey and have something."

It was just a five minute stroll down Regent Street to the Horse and Jockey. The pub was a landmark in Wrexham because of its thatched roof. The building was long and narrow occupying the corner of Regent Street and Priory Street. Louisa sat down near the door and waited for Fred to bring her a shandy. He had a pint of Wrexham lager.

"I'm glad that's over." Fred said sitting down and taking a large swallow of his pint.

"The sergeant was very non-committal wasn't he?" Louisa replied. "I suppose he can't express an opinion one way or the other."

Fred agreed. "They have to remain neutral. It's part of their job. They probably have to deal with dozens of cases every day."

"I hope they don't have dozens of murder cases in Wrexham!"

171

Before Fred could reply he felt a hand on his shoulder and a familiar voice said "What are you two doing here?"

Fred got up and faced Arthur grinning at them. He was in his working overalls and his face was slightly grimy with grease. Despite his unwashed visage his bright blue eyes twinkled with delight in finding them.

"Do you want a pint Arthur?" Fred asked leaping up to greet his brother-in-law.

Arthur shook his head. I've got one already on the bar other there with that lot." He pointed to a small group of men dressed in similar garb as his. "We've just finished work. I'll be off home soon." He dragged a stool from under a nearby table and sat down on it. "So what brings you two into town? Our Louie drinking on a Saturday afternoon!"

"Only a Shandy!" Louisa admonished her brother laughing in his face. She adored her brother, Harry too.

Fred explained their reason for coming in to town. Arthur listened gravely. "And to think that Bill introduced that Vince to Louisa is unbelievable."

"It just goes to show how people's lives can intertwine with others in the most unexpected ways." Fred said.

Arthur looked at his watch. "I will have to make a move. I'm taking Brian to that school boy football club with Gordon later. If I don't see you in the week I will see you next week at the match Fred." He bent down to kiss his sister.

"We ought to go too." Louisa said.

As Christmas approached there was no news from Edna Webb's solicitor nor about her trial.

172

Meanwhile Louisa immersed herself in the usual preparations for Christmas day.

Rations for meat were still strict but by pooling their resources as usual, Louisa, her mother and sister planned to provide their family with a roast chicken dinner. William's and Fred's garden produce would provide potatoes, parsnips, carrots and sprouts. And as bread was now off ration again Mary Ellen would able to make her bread sauce.

"It's a pity Arthur and Gladys aren't coming for dinner, he loves my bread sauce." Mary Ellen said.

"Couldn't you make some extra and give it to Gladys to warm up on Christmas day?" Louisa suggested.

Mary Ellen blinked with surprise. "What a good idea. Yes I will."

Louisa and Fred were pleased that fruit was in more supply and so when they filled the Christmas stockings for the children they were able to put in an orange for each child. Alongside the fruit they were able to put some nuts, books and homemade toys that both Fred and Louisa had made.

"I heard on the wireless that the government may relax some of the rations in the New Year." Louisa commented.

"Not before time." Fred said. "The war has been over for four years now and still we are rationed."

"At least we can have a few things more than last year. I'm going to make a trifle this year. We can have that on boxing day."

"I will look forward to that and much though I like Christmas I will look forward to hearing the end of *Rudolph the Red Nosed Reindeer!*

173

Louisa laughed. "Well it's a change from *Away in the manger* which is all we got from Susan last year!

"That reminds me. I promised them I would get tickets for the pantomime. It's on until the first week of January at the Majestic."

Which one are they doing? It was *Robinson Crusoe* last year I think."

"No that was the year before. This year it is *Puss in boots*."

Fred frowned trying to recall the performance from the previous year. "I think it was *Aladdin*. It's hard to remember because we didn't go. I didn't know about it." He looked up from filling stockings to glance at his wife. "We had other things to worry about last year."

Louisa smiled her agreement whilst listening to her husband.

"Walter Roberts the shop keeper in town used to organise them. Someone at work said that he started to do it to raise money for charity. I think some of the proceeds went to the hospital. I'm not sure who is organising this one."

"Well whatever it is I'm sure the girls will love it."

Chapter Fourteen

1950

Gordon didn't want to go to the pantomime he preferred to play football.

"He seems to live and breathe at the *Under Fifteens Club*!" Dot remarked.

On the first Saturday afternoon in January, Fred and Louisa took their two daughters as well as Malcolm and Maureen to the Majestic cinema for the pantomime. Brian had a cold and wasn't well enough to go with them. Dot and Harry were looking after Michael.

After the performance, the little group arrived back in Rhosrobin to collect Michael. They rushed into the house to get out of the cold biting wind.

Dot had made vegetable soup and sandwiches as well as sultana scones for everyone. The children and Fred sat down gratefully to eat them. Louisa checked on the baby first before helping herself to a paste sandwich. "Has he been alright?" She asked Dot.

"As good as gold. He's been asleep all the time you have been out."

"Where's Harry?" Louisa asked looking around for her brother.

"He's gone to fetch Gordon. I didn't want him to hang around waiting for a bus in this cold weather."

The food was rapidly disappearing and Louisa looked up guiltily as she finished her soup.

"Don't worry. I've got more in the kitchen. I kept some back for Harry and Gordon. Arthur can have some too when he picks up Maureen. I've got plenty of vegetables, I only wish I could say the same about meat."

A few minutes later Harry and Gordon arrived. Arthur was behind them having just parked the car behind his brother. A rush of cold air blasted down the hallway and everyone shivered as the three of them entered the room. The trio greeted the rest of the family quickly as they made their way to the fire where they held their hands to the flames.

"It's getting colder. I think we will get some snow." Arthur said. He lifted his daughter and Susan up from an arm chair so that he could sit down. Each child perched on one of his knees. Both girls put their warm hands on each side of his cold face. They both giggled when Arthur made loud sighs of contentment.

Meanwhile Harry asked Malcolm and Christine if they had enjoyed the pantomime. Those two were sitting at the table polishing off the rest of the scones. Dot made fresh tea.

"Any news on that court case Louie?" Harry asked.

Louisa shook her head. "Not yet. We have had a letter from the solicitor asking us if we would act as witnesses and that is all. I suppose the courts

176

haven't started hearing cases again yet, so soon after Christmas."

"Where will it be held? The Assizes court I suppose." Harry answered his own question.

Both Fred and Louisa agreed.

"I think that you are both good to do such a thing to help the woman." Dot said. "Especially you Fred. It could make all the difference you know. It is still a man's world despite the work women did in the war. Some men still think that all women are good for is cooking and sewing."

"And cleaning!" Louisa added. "We are not so weak and feeble as some men think. And we can think for ourselves too. The war changed that for a lot of women and it is about time that their husbands woke up to that fact!"

All three men looked first from Dot and then to Louisa. Each wore a half amused expression on their face.

"Well the war didn't change you much Louie." Fred started to say before her brothers pitched in.

"No indeed it didn't. You always were feisty, if anything the war has made you worse." Harry commented. "The arguments you had with mother about that bike of yours. The times I had to mend it for you."

"Yes. I agree." Arthur said. "She was. Look at the fight she put up when Mother tried to send her away to Wallasey to work."

Louisa sighed. "Not that it did me much good. I still had to go."

"You negotiated a deal with mother though before you went. That's what made it easier for me to bring you home when I did. You were barely there a fortnight!"

Arthur grinned remembering the day he arrived in Wallasey to see his sister on her hands and knees scrubbing a floor. As soon as she laid eyes on him she had abandoned her cleaning and thrown herself at him. It hadn't taken much persuasion to convince her to drop everything and return home with him.

Suddenly they heard the baby crying and Louisa went to check on him. She emerged from the front room with Michael in her arms. "I will just change him and then I think we should go." She glanced at Susan who was now half asleep on one of Arthur's shoulders. His daughter was almost in the same position leaning on his other side. He held both children safely with an arm each.

Fred got up to get their coats. Gently he lifted Susan from Arthur's shoulder. He stretched his arm with some relief from the removal of the weight. He shifted Maureen to a more comfortable position and declared that he too should go. The three men made arrangements to meet up at the next home game in Wrexham.

On the way home in the car, Fred commented about how Louisa had become more confident during and since the war.

"It was a case of having too." Louisa replied. "It's just that some women have quietly gone back to being housewives whilst others feel they have been pushed aside without any recognition. I think I am somewhere in the middle."

"I think there was a lot of bewilderment amongst those men who returned home hoping to pick up the pieces where they left off. Some had lost their homes and families and it took a lot of time to come to terms with their emotions. Then on top of that they find there are no jobs and women doing the jobs that they used to do. A shock for them and a shock for the women too." Fred said.

"I know. It has been difficult for everybody. We all had to re-adjust. I know I say it a lot, but we are the lucky ones." Louisa sighed.

In the darkness of the car Fred said quietly so that Christine could not hear. In any case she was half asleep and not listening.

"What hurts the most for me is not being here when you gave birth to Susan. Then when I saw how much pain you were in with Michael, it brought it back to me how I felt so helpless."

Louisa put her hand on his arm and squeezed it. "I know you cared and that's all that matters."

At the end of February Louisa and Fred received a letter from the solicitor defending Edna Webb that there would be a hearing in the middle of March.

Meanwhile another court case that was dominating the news at that time was regarding a German scientist of the name Fuchs. They discovered that he had been an intern in Canada during the war and then spent some time in the United States of America working on plutonium.

"I think he is the man who contributed towards creating that atomic bomb that was dropped in Japan." Fred said when they heard that he had been arrested in Britain.

"Is that why he was arrested?" Louisa frowned. "It was a terrible bomb. That plutonium caused a lot of devastation."

"The reason he was arrested is because it is alleged he leaked secrets about explosives to what the Germans considered to be their enemy. As a German he is deemed to be a traitor I suppose."

The case was heard on the first of March and Fuchs was sentenced to fourteen years in gaol.

It wasn't long after Fuchs's trial that Louisa and Fred found themselves in the Assizes court to be character witnesses at the trial of Edna Webb. They were told to wait outside the courtroom until they were called. The solicitor had warned them previously that they may not be called.

Sitting on a long bench outside the court room Fred and Louisa waited for the small crowd of journalists and other on lookers to disperse and for the trial to start. The bench they sat on was at the top of the stairs. Seated next to them on the long wooden bench was a Mrs. Mason and two other witnesses who introduced themselves as Mrs. Roberts and Mrs. Ellis.

Eventually the defence solicitor appeared. He was a tall man with dark hair and a moustache. Louisa gauged his age as mid-forties.

"How long do you think they will be?" Fred asked the defence solicitor.

He shrugged his shoulders. "It could be half an hour it could be hours. But in my opinion I think probably an hour. There isn't a lot of evidence to consider. The jury have witness statements to read and of course they have to consider what will be said in the court room. I doubt there will be an adjournment."

"I hope not. I have had to take a day off work without pay for this." Fred said.

Mrs. Mason was called as the first witness. She looked very nervous when she got up to go and Louisa swallowed hard. She too was getting nervous.

Louisa learned much later that Mrs. Mason had been able to confirm Mrs. Webb's statement. The prosecution had asked Mrs. Mason if she had ever seen Mr. Webb hit his wife. Mrs. Mason said she had not but she had heard her screaming several times and had heard her asking her husband to stop. She assumed that he was beating her.

The prosecution then asked Mrs. Mason if she felt that screaming was evidence of Mr. Webb beating his wife. To this Mrs. Mason said no but she had seen bruises on Edna's arms and face.

The prosecution asked if the bruises were evidence of a violent man. Mrs. Mason felt that they were, but seemed less confident when the prosecution suggested that Mrs. Webb may have got the bruises from falling or perhaps struggling with her husband who was trying to save himself from her pushing him down the stairs.

For a little while Mrs. Mason had got confused and said in a quiet voice that she didn't know. Then she remembered that she had seen bruises on Mrs. Webb's face before the death of her husband.

She said afterwards to Louisa, that she managed to recover her confidence when the defendant's solicitor asked questions about Mrs. Webb. She was asked if Mrs. Webb ever confided in Mrs. Mason about her husband. To this Mrs. Mason replied no, but she felt that she was being loyal to her husband. The solicitor then asked if she had frequently seen bruises on Mrs. Webb's face and arms or was it just on one occasion. Mrs. Mason said she had seen bruises on her face and arms more than once. She noticed that Mrs. Webb tended to wear long sleeved clothes. She said that after each occasion when she had heard screaming she didn't see her outside in the garden very often so was not sure about her face. Even in the summer when it was hot she seemed to stay indoors or wear long sleeved blouses. Mrs. Mason noticed that Mrs. Webb put her washing on the line very early in the morning or late at night.

Two more neighbours were called as witnesses and Louisa began to worry that the case was not going well for Edna Webb. Despite feeling sick at the thought of giving evidence Louisa hoped that she and Fred would be called. She was not disappointed. The defendant's solicitor called her name and Fred squeezed her hand to encourage her.

Facing the jury and members of the public Louisa felt even more nervous. She swallowed hard as she held on to the wooden banister in front of her.

The prosecution asked Louisa how she knew Edna Webb. Louisa replied that she did not know her and that she had been introduced to her husband a year ago by her brother-in-law. She explained how her brother-in-law William who she called Bill had called to see her one day on his way home from work. He had brought his workmate with him Vince Webb. She explained that she had felt uncomfortable in his presence and took an instant dislike to him.

The prosecution asked if she felt that taking a dislike to the victim would help the court to resolve the case. Louisa hurried on to explain her feelings. She then described the two occasions when Vince Webb had forced himself on to her in her own home. She said that fortunately for her, the second time Vince called at her house, her husband was at home and rescued her.

There was an audible sigh in the court house at these words. Louisa heard it and felt emboldened to say. "I feel quite sure that if my husband had not been there I would have been violated by this man who would not listen to me. I asked him to go and he would not go and furthermore he started to manhandle me."

Again Louisa felt the mood shift and was relieved when the defendant's solicitor stood up to ask her more questions. He asked her how she had managed to avoid Vince Webb's advantages the first time he tried to push himself into her home. Louisa replied that her neighbour next door had knocked on her kitchen door at a moment when Louisa had managed to break free from her would be attacker.

When Fred was called to the stand the prosecution asked him if he trusted his wife. Fred was furious at such a question and said that of course he did. He was then asked to describe the scene he had found in the kitchen when Vince was with Louisa. After this the defence asked Fred if he had met Vince Webb before. Fred replied that he hadn't met him, but his wife had told him he had been in the house before because he was a colleague of his wife's brother-in-law.

"So your wife told you that both men had called to see her on a previous occasion."

Fred replied that she had.

"Did she tell you about the second occasion when Vince Webb tried to gain entry into your house?"

"At the time she didn't. But after his second attempt she told me about the incident."

"Why do you think she didn't tell you?"

"She didn't want to worry me. Besides my wife felt she had dealt with the situation and that he would not try to harass her again. As far as she was concerned the matter was closed.

There were no more questions and no more witnesses. The prosecution and then the defence were permitted to make their views known to the Jury. After this the Judge asked members of the public and the witnesses to leave the court room and that they would be called back when the jury had formed a verdict.

Once again Fred and Louisa sat on the seat at the top of the stairs to wait for the verdict. Mrs. Mason; Mrs. Roberts and Mrs. Bellis joined them. Eventually the defence solicitor Mr. Meredith appeared.

"How long do you think they will be?" Fred asked the defence solicitor.

He shrugged his shoulders. "Hard to say. It could be an hour it could be longer. As I said earlier, there isn't a lot of evidence to consider. However, I believe you have time to get a cup of tea if you want to wait for the verdict. There is a teashop just around the corner from here."

"Well we have come this far we may as well stay to the end." Fred said. "I have taken a day off work for this."

They stood up to go outside and were surprised that the three other witnesses followed them down the steps.

"I hope you don't mind if we accompany you?" Mrs. Mason asked nervously. Both Louisa and Fred said they didn't mind at all. In fact they were quite pleased to have someone with whom they could discuss the case.

Between them they managed to piece together what information they had. Mrs. Mason nor the other neighbours had known much about Mrs. Webb prior to the accident. They had got to know more about her circumstances when she was home on bail.

They discovered that Edna Webb had first met her husband in 1943. She was sixteen and he was twenty. He had been home on leave in the small village of Bersham whilst serving in the army. Mrs. Webb also from Bersham, had said that Vince had been very attentive and loving and that he had promised to marry her after the war. They met again a year later where he discovered she had a baby boy.

At the time he accepted that the child was his and they married as soon as he was discharged from the army in August 1945. After a short while living in cramped conditions with Vince's mother and grandparents she became pregnant again. Soon after the birth of their second child – a girl - they had been lucky to get a house in Gwersyllt.

Mrs. Webb claimed that when they moved house she had noticed a change in his character. He became moody and was often violent. He began to hit her in bouts of unexplained anger then suddenly quieten down again. When he was quiet he would be kind to her.

She gave birth to another daughter in 1947. Each time after she had given birth he was very attentive but then would fly in to fits of temper. Whilst in a

185

rage he always accused her of lying when he was away in the army and that their son was not really his son. As the years went by his aggressive behaviour increased and he started to punch her more often. At that stage he didn't hit her in the face. A fit of temper usually started before he began to hit her. Normally she would take the beating but couldn't stand it when he began to hit her in the face. Attacking her face was a more recent occurrence. It was then she screamed for him to stop. At this point he would walk out of the house and not come back until much later.

On the night of his death he had returned home from work in a violent mood and she had run upstairs to avoid him. He had chased her and in fright she had pushed him away from her but not before he had landed a blow to her face. He had let go of the banister so that he could hit her again but had lost balance. He fell hitting his head on the wall before sliding backwards and hitting his head again on the stairs. She knew he was dead as soon as she saw him and had called for a neighbour to help. The neighbour Mrs. Mason had called the police.

As they sat around the table stirring their tea no-one spoke for a minute or two. Louisa was horrified at what she had learned.

"It wasn't very pleasant in there was it?" Mrs. Roberts started the conversation. "They made me feel as if I was a liar."

"The prosecution were trying to make out we were unreliable witnesses." Fred remarked. "I suppose they were only doing their job. They have to consider all the angles. Still I agree it wasn't nice."

After listening to each other's experiences in the witness stand they again commented how they felt.

Mrs. Bellis was indignant when she heard about Fred's encounter with the prosecution. "I don't like what they were suggesting about your wife. It's like as if they were saying that she were encouraging that Vince to your house."

Louisa nodded. "Yes that wasn't nice at all."

"Do you think the jury will clear her?" Mrs. Mason asked. She sipped her tea and looked nervously around the table at her companions.

Louisa sighed. "It's hard to tell. I suppose she has a fifty fifty chance. The jury surely can't dismiss Fred's statement. That Vince was a violent man."

"The trouble is, his violence could give his wife a reason to kill him. So the jury have to be convinced that she didn't deliberately push him down the stairs, and that he fell." Fred said.

They all sighed.

For a few minutes they were silent. Then out of the blue Mrs. Bellis said wistfully "I wish we had more sugar."

This broke the tension and they all laughed. Everyone they knew craved for more sugar.

"There's no evidence that she pushed him." Louisa said suddenly. She had been deep in thought, thinking about the case. "Surely you can't convict someone of murder if there was no-one to witness it or no evidence to prove it."

Fred looked at his watch. "I think we should go back and find out for ourselves."

Outside the court room a crowd was gathering. The steps outside was heaving with journalists waiting for the verdict. Louisa and Fred and their companions made their way back up the steps and into the foyer. There were even more people milling around inside and then Fred caught sight of the defence solicitor running up the stairs towards the court room.

"Come on. It looks like the jury have made their mind up."

They hastily moved up the stairs and found seats in the court room. The legal representatives and other witnesses were making their way back in followed by the jury then the judge.

Fred and Louisa held hands tightly as they waited for the verdict. When the jury announced that they found the defendant "not guilty," they hugged each other with relief.

There was a huge cheer in the court room and whilst they hugged each other Louisa and Fred turned to see the smiling faces of the three women with whom they had just shared a pot of tea.

The next day Louisa walked to the post office to get her family allowance and to buy a newspaper. As usual the post office was buzzing with excitement about the news.

"Of course, I knew all along that she would get off." The post mistress said.

Louisa smiled. That's not what you were saying a few months ago she thought. She paid for her newspapers and left the post office with Michael in his pram as quietly as she could. She rushed home quickly, eager to read about the trial in the newspapers. She had bought two papers so that she could compare the articles. The *Wrexham Leader* and the *Liverpool Post*.

As soon as she got home she poured over both papers and compared the stories. She was amazed at how the reports differed even though they both covered the same story. In any case the front headlines on both were satisfying. One read "Housewife cleared of murder," and the other "Battered wife innocent of murder."

She showed them to Fred when he arrived home. After reading them he commented that "It's a shame that Vince Webb died in such a way after serving his country."

He made the same comment a few days later when sitting in the front parlour in Pandy chatting to his brothers-in-law. All the family had gathered that afternoon. Fortunately it was a nice spring day and most of the children were playing outside in the yard. Gordon sat on the edge of a chair next to his father.

"It is a shame that he died the way he did." Gladys reiterated quickly in response to Fred's comment. "But whether he served in the war or not he shouldn't go round beating up his wife and attacking other women either. If his wife didn't kill him, she may have later on, if things got worse."

Arthur ignored his wife's comments. He didn't approve of attacking women but he had become interested in where Vince had served.

"Which regiment was he in?" Arthur asked. His eyes asked Louisa then he rested his gaze on Fred.

"At court they said he was in the Welsh guards and had served in North Africa and Italy." Fred replied.

"I was in the Welsh Guards." Bill said. "The third battalion. I recall having this discussion with him when we worked together. He said he had been in

Algeria and Tunisia. I was there too in nineteen forty three. We didn't know each other then of course. We were amongst thousands so the chance of meeting each other was very remote." He sighed for a little while as he recalled those war years. "I was only twenty years of age then."

"Yes you are quite a bit younger than the rest of us." Harry said. "I was twenty three when war broke out. Both Arthur and I joined the Welsh guards. Arthur was twenty one and both of us married with children. We were in different battalions, though we both went to North West Europe first of all."

William looked watchfully at Harry as he listened to him speak. It was very rare for him and Arthur to mention the war. As William switched his glance to Arthur he could see that Arthur regretted opening the conversation.

Despite surviving many battles and earning promotion to a sargeant Arthur preferred not to talk about the war if he could help it. Never one to dwell on the past he liked to move forward and to see what he could make of life. It was the mention of the Welsh Guards that had triggered some interest in him as well as in those men gathered around him at that moment. Each of them had witnessed death and destruction in places they would never want to see again.

Harry was aware that Gordon was sitting at the side of him listening to the discussion and decided he didn't want to say any more about the war. However he told his son eager for information that Arthur had been one of the thousands evacuated from Dunkirk.

Arthur acknowledged this with a nod and tried to make light of it with a wink at his nephew whilst he listened to his brother. He knew that inevitably Gordon would want to ask about when Harry was taken a prisoner of war by the Japanese. Harry still hadn't got over that and so they rarely discussed it. He certainly didn't want to talk about it in front of his son.

Fred didn't want to talk about the war either. He had lost his youngest brother Eddie in the war. He had been killed at sea in a submarine. Mentally Fred calculated that he would probably have been about the same age as Bill.

Louisa sensed that they were wandering on to a sensitive subject and she steered the conversation away from the war.

"At least this business with Edna and Vince Webb is over and done with." Louisa said. "This is a triumph for women against violence."

"Yes it is." Dorothy declared as she walked in to the room with Ann who had just woken up from her nap.

The tense atmosphere lightened considerably after this last remark. Mary Ellen pleased they had avoided a heavy subject got out of her chair. "More tea anyone?"

Chapter Fifteen

A few months after the court appearance there was
some general excitement in the post office regarding
food rationing. It had been announced the day
before on the wireless that chocolate biscuits, jelly
and dried fruit was off the ration.
"Tinned fruit too and syrup and treacle." The
postmistress advised her customers. She had said
this proudly several times that day and wasn't fed up
of saying it.
Fred was pleased that petrol was also off the ration.
"We'll be able to go to the seaside more often now."
He told the children. He promised them both that he
would take them to Rhyl again. Ever since the day
the year before when they had a day out they had
been asking when they could go again. Secretly both
Fred and Louisa had been scanning advertisements
in the newspapers and had sent away for holiday
brochures. They were hoping to save enough money
to stay in a caravan for a week.

The scurry for chocolate biscuits and tinned fruit soon outstripped the stock of all the local shops and so it was another fortnight before Louisa was able to proudly display her loot to her family. She waited until Fred came home from work at six o clock and had eaten his main meal before she produced the goods.

"This is your pudding she said to the children." She enjoyed the gasp on their faces when their eyes alighted on the biscuits. Fred also looked delighted.

"We can have two each and then we can have two each tomorrow." Louisa said.

They didn't need much encouragement, and Louisa too savoured the taste of something that had been denied them for so long.

"Christmas will be easier this year." Dorothy commented when she visited her sister with her baby a few days later.

"Mother is ecstatic that we can now get dried fruit, syrup and treacle to make cakes and mincemeat without worrying about ration books."

"Yes and I can make some trifles with the tinned fruit. I am going to make one next week for Christine's birthday."

"It's my wedding anniversary too." Dorothy smiled. "Bill is taking me out for a meal. Mother is looking after Ann. It's hard to believe that Christine will be eleven!"

For the first time in her young life Christine had been promised a tea party and was able to invite three school friends. Louisa made paste sandwiches and a trifle for the occasion. Christine would be moving to the seniors section of the school in September and to mark the occasion Fred and

Louisa had bought her a set of encyclopedias. They had been expensive but they knew she would appreciate them as she was an avid reader and interested in many things.

One of Christine's guests was Bethan Lloyd from next door. Whilst Christine's friendship blossomed with this little girl, so had the friendship between Louisa and Bethan's mother Carol. She too attended the little tea party and later helped Louisa to wash up. Her baby, born just before the previous Christmas was now asleep in the sitting room. She had called her Shirley. As Carol finished wiping the pots she confided in Louisa that she was thinking of looking for a part-time job. Her mother had offered to look after Shirley for a few days a week.

"Where would you work?" Louisa asked.

"They are looking for part time sewing machinists in Manley's in the town centre. They are thinking of expanding again. You know when Johnson's had that fire above the *Leader* Office in Caxton place?"

Louisa frowned. "Yes."

"Well they had temporary headquarters in High Street. Then they moved to Salop Road and now they have moved again."

Louisa was confused. "Yes I know Dot told me. So what has that got to do with Manley's?"

Carol took a deep breath. "Sorry I am not explaining this very well. Manley's have taken over the old factory in Salop road. They have renovated the building and are expanding. It looks like they can afford to take on more staff."

"I was thinking I would like to work with fabric again." Louisa said. She was beginning to feel excited at the idea of working with her sewing machine once more. She hadn't done much lately. Her sewing machine had sat in the corner of the sitting room unused for several months.

"Why don't you apply? It would do no harm." Carol said. "We could travel together on the bus."

"Who would look after Michael?" Louisa frowned. Even if she asked her mother and she agreed, she would still need to take him to Pandy. She wondered if it was worth the effort. She casually mentioned it to Dorothy when she visited her a few days later.

"|Louie I think you should apply. You know you have always wanted to get a job in the fashion industry."

"I would like to, but I have to think of Michael."

"No problem. I will look after him. I'm not ready to look for work yet, so I can come here on the days you need to work and I can bring Ann with me." She glanced at her daughter as she slept in her pram.

Louisa stared at her sister in amazement. "But are you sure?"

"Of course I am sure. It will give me something else to do. There is only so much dusting and cleaning to do at home, especially with mother helping. As you know I'm not much good at knitting and sewing. I spend most of my free time reading and walking in between looking after the baby. I can walk over here easily enough and read a book when Michael and Ann are asleep. Honestly I can spare two days a week." She watched the little boy playing with his building blocks that Fred had bought for him.

Louisa got excited about the plan. "Well alright. I will apply. I might not get the job anyway."

She talked things through with Fred. His main concern was that she may tire herself out. She assured him she would be fine and so sent a letter of application to Manley's. A few days later she was surprised and delighted to receive a letter inviting her for an interview.

"They want me to take some samples of my work." She told her mother and Dorothy when she got to Pandy feverishly excited. She had wrapped Michael into his pram that morning and pushed him as quickly as she could towards Pandy. When she reached the fields that she would normally use to take a short cut between Rhosrobin and Pandy she became exasperated that she couldn't negotiate the kissing gate with the pram. There was no one around to help lift him over the stile. It was a damp July morning and most people had stayed indoors. Resignedly, Louisa chose the lane that circled the fields and continued her journey. Her enthusiasm returned as soon as she reached the end of terrace house where her parents and Dorothy and Bill lived. Bursting through the door she had scarcely entered the kitchen when she waved her letter in the air for her mother and Dorothy to see.

Dorothy was pleased for her sister. Mary Ellen was more reserved in her reaction. She didn't want to dampen her daughter's spirits but she was worried she may get exhausted with working and looking after three children. It was true that Christine was eleven now and didn't need much looking after. Susan was prone to running to Pandy on her own even though she had been told not to do it, and Michael was still wearing nappies.

Louisa caught her mother's expression and guessed what was going on in her mind.

"It's only for two days a week mother. The money will boost up the family allowance and help towards paying for a holiday in Rhyl. Fred is determined to take the children away for a week during the summer holidays."

"Well as long as you are sure." Mary Ellen got up suddenly to rescue the pan of milk that was boiling on the fire in front of them.

She poured the milk on to three cups of instant coffee. It was her treat to have coffee in the morning, even though it was now off ration it was very expensive. It was rare for her to share her coffee as she guarded it closely, but on this occasion she had decided to treat her two daughters. She was fortunate that William did not drink coffee, and most of the men in the family preferred tea.

She handed the hot drinks to her daughters and sprinkled a few grains of sugar in to hers. Dorothy and Louisa had weaned themselves off sugar in their drinks years ago and now disliked the taste of sugar in their coffee.

Michael was beginning to get restless in his pram and Louisa lifted him out and sat him on her knee. He smiled at his grandmother and slipping off his mother's knee tottered across to Mary Ellen. She gathered him up on to her own knee and he settled down there for a little while. He very soon got bored and walked the few steps to the sideboard. Bending down he pulled out a box he knew was there. It was a game of dominoes. He loved playing with the small rectangular shapes as indeed his two older sisters and cousins did too.

"Taking two samples of your work won't be a problem for you." Dorothy laughed. "You should take that beautiful dress you made with the material auntie Nancy gave you. I still have mine. It is probably the best thing in my wardrobe."

"And mine!" Mary Ellen agreed.

When Louisa returned home a couple of hours later she saw Carol in the garden and called to her to tell her the news about her interview.

"I got a letter this morning too. I called to tell you but you were obviously out."

"Yes. I went to Pandy. When is your interview?"

Next week – Thursday morning."

"Mine is the same day. Half past ten." Louisa said.

"I'm at eleven o clock. Have you got any samples to take with you? I've got a few."

Louisa laughed. "Yes I have plenty."

On the day of the interview Louisa suddenly felt nervous. The last time she attended an interview for a job was many years ago when she had started work at the dairy in Pandy.

When she got off the bus in King Street, she made her way to Salop road where the factory had opened the new work shop. She carefully carried with her a package of the three dresses that belonged to herself, her mother and her sister. She had wrapped them up in brown paper. When she unwrapped the paper in the interview room she hid her smile of pride when she heard a gasp emit from the mouths of the two people who were on the interview panel. One was a young woman about twenty five the other person was a man about twice her age. He introduced himself as Mr. Manley and the woman as Miss

Gloria Manley. Louisa wondered if the woman was his daughter.

"They are beautiful." Gloria Manley breathed as she fingered the silk.

"And you assure me that you made these yourself?" Mr. Manley asked.

Louisa nodded. She explained where she got the fabric from.

"I see. Well you were very lucky to come by such fabric. You have done an excellent job. If this is the quality of your work I wouldn't hesitate in offering you a job. I understand you want part-time hours."

"Yes please." Louisa couldn't believe her luck.

They agreed on two days a week. She was to start at nine o clock and finish at four o clock. Louisa was happy that she had arranged two days that were not consecutive and that one of the days was when Dot didn't work. They had agreed that if Dorothy wasn't well Dot would help out with looking after the children. Carol, who had negotiated different days would help too.

Fred was pleased when Louisa told him the news, though she could see there was anxiety in his eyes when he tentatively asked "When do you start?"

"Not until September, so the children will be back in school." She grinned when she saw the relief in his face.

"So that won't affect our plans for a summer holiday in Rhyl."

Fred hugged her. "You must have read my mind." He handed her the newspaper. "I just hope the weather improves. According to the forecast in the newspaper we are going to have heavy rain and thunderstorms tomorrow. With a bit of luck this

unsettled weather will turn to sunshine in two weeks
and we will have a sunny week in Rhyl."

Chapter Sixteen

Unfortunately, the weather remained unsettled for the rest of July and early in to August. However the wind and rain had cleared away in to the second week of August, and as Fred and Louisa packed their luggage into the car they were hopeful they would have at least dry weather.

Fred put the pushchair in to the boot of the car and they set off towards the North Wales coast.

The caravan was quite small, but it wasn't far from the beach and the children were delighted with their new accommodation. Having to walk across a field to a toilet and wash room shared with other campers was not a problem for them. They had been used to having to go down the garden to a toilet in Pandy. In fact they loved the idea of walking across a sandy field to get to the washrooms.

It was more inconvenient for Louisa having to make sure that the three children didn't splash water everywhere as they washed!

Though the sun didn't shine during that week, they managed to take the children on the beach every day even when it was dull. The clouds remained grey but at least the weather was dry. Both Louisa and Fred gave up trying to keep sand from getting into the caravan. Michael seemed to get covered in it every day, and try as they might to keep it out of his hair he seemed to like putting buckets of sand over his head. This was amusing at first but proved to be a tiring escapade of his as the days wore on. It was useless taking the bucket from him as he would cry forever until he got it back, so they relented and took it in turns to clean the little boy up as best as they could.

On the day they had to vacate the caravan, Fred under instructions from Louisa took the three children for a walk along the promenade. She wanted to clean the caravan of every last grain of sand then she was going to pack all their clothes ready to be loaded in to the car. Two hours later she was exhausted but satisfied with her effort. She sat on the caravan steps to rest and saw her family striding towards her. They were licking ice creams. Fred was balancing two cornets in his hand whilst pushing Michael's pushchair. He tried his best to lick dripping ice cream off his hand but wasn't making much of a success of it. Louisa got up to meet them and took one of the proffered ice creams. She licked it greedily, savouring the cool creamy taste to quench her thirst.

Near the entrance to the caravan park was a long stone wall that edged the caravan park and then continued for a mile or so along the promenade serving as a boundary between the promenade and the beach. Fred parked the pushchair close to the entrance and the family sat on the wall to enjoy their cold refreshments.

By the time all the ice creams had been consumed, the three children had managed to smear their faces with it. Fred laughed as he wiped his hands on his handkerchief.

"This would make a good photograph. I will just get the camera."

He ran to the caravan and stopped quickly at the door when Louisa called. "Don't forget to take your shoes off. There's bound to be sand on them."

Fred obeyed then came out of the caravan grinning with his camera. Hurriedly he put on his shoes and then got everyone to pose for a photo. Satisfied that he had taken enough photographs Fred put the camera on the driver's seat of the car and then motioned to the children to get into the vehicle.

"Are we going home now?" Susan asked petulantly.

"Yes, don't you want to go? Fred asked.

Susan shook her head and so did Christine.

"We can come again next year if you like."

Two heads nodded vigorously.

The holiday had done them all good despite the lack of sunshine. Louisa could see that Fred was more relaxed than he had been for a long time and she was glad. This made her happy too and she smiled to herself as they drove home. The hair pin bends on the road made the two girls laugh as Fred manoeuvred the car along. The weaving motion sent Michael to sleep, so they carried him carefully into the house when they got home, hoping he would sleep a little longer whilst they unpacked. Within a few hours they had all drifted back into their normal routine. The dark clouds which had followed them home burst and the rain that had threatened them all the way home came pouring down.

Fred grinned. "Home just in time." He got out a pack of playing cars and before long he and the two girls were playing 'rummy' a card game they were all very fond of.

The unsettled weather continued throughout August with some very bad thunder storms and gales. Louisa was glad she was at home and not having to deal with unseasonal conditions whilst in a caravan.

The week end before the girls were due to start back to school Fred suggested they went to Liverpool to see his sisters and their children.

"I didn't get to see Cissy last time so I would like to see her first and her two boys, then we can go and see Mary and her little one." Fred said. "It will be nice for the girls to meet their other cousins."

As luck would have it the sun shone brightly that Sunday morning as they headed for Birkenhead and the Mersey tunnel. Fred explained to the girls how the tunnel was completed in nineteen thirty six and that it took ten years to build. They were both frightened when he told them that they were driving under the river but were amazed that there were lights in the tunnel. Louisa recalled the first time she went under the tunnel with Fred when she was on the back of his motor bike. It was when he had taken her to meet his mother and all of his brothers and sisters. Most of them were living together then in a house in Islington. A huge part of that area was bombed during the war and there were still areas that had not yet been re-built.

Cissy lived in a top floor flat in an old house in Old Swan. The house had been slightly damaged in the war but it had been assessed safe to live in. The flat consisted of three attic rooms and a shared bathroom and kitchen on the second floor. Climbing up the rickety stairs with Michael in her arms, Louisa wondered who exactly had assessed the house as safe. One look at Fred's face confirmed her worry. He greeted his sister warmly and she fell about hugging him in surprise and delight. There were tears in her eyes when she caught sight of the two little girls and Michael who had now woken up. He was anxious to be put down on his own two feet.

Presently they all sat together on an old sagging leather sofa that had seen better days. Cissy sat on one of three wooden dining chairs.

"The two boys are out playing in the street somewhere. They will be pleased to see you I'm sure." She got up again. "I'll go down stairs and put the kettle on then I will see if I can find them. They won't be far."

When she went downstairs, Fred followed her under the pretence of helping her to bring up the drinks. Louisa guessed he wanted to have a quiet word with his sister and to make sure she was alright. She knew he worried about both of his sisters.

Presently they both re-appeared with a tray of tea followed by Cecelia's two boys Neville and Michael. Louisa produced a packet of chocolate biscuits she had brought with her and they shared these between them. Little Michael explained that his cousin was also called Michael.

"So what's the position on housing now?" Fred asked. "Have you got your name down for a council house?"

Cissy nodded. "Yes, but I'm thinking of moving out of Liverpool and going to Manchester. I've got a friend living in a three bedroomed house. Her parents have died and she has inherited the place. She's never married and got no kids, so she said I could live there with her. I'll have to pay rent of course, but there will be more space for the kids. I will get a job too."

"Do you think you will be able to get a job?" Fred asked anxiously.

Cissy nodded. Irene seems to think so. She said she would put a good word in for me at the bakery now bread is off ration again."

"That was a stupid thing the bread rationing." Fred said. "When it was first introduced a lot of bread was unsold and went to waste!"

Cissy nodded her head. "Yes I know a wicked shame. Anyway as soon as Irene lets me know, I am going."

"How are you going to get there with all your stuff?" Fred glanced around the room. She didn't have much furniture, though there were a lot of books on a shelf.

"Bob said he would take me. This furniture isn't mine. The flat came with the furniture. So I won't have much to take. Irene has everything I need."

Fred nodded with relief, glad to know that his older brother would help her. "Well good luck."

Cissy smiled. "Thanks." She turned her attention to the photographs that Louisa was showing her of their recent holiday in Rhyl. Cissy asked if she could keep one or two and Louisa said she could have the ones of the children eating ice cream and another one with their father which Louisa had taken on the beach.

Eventually they said their goodbyes and headed off to the other end of town to see Mary and her baby Stephanie.

Fred's youngest sister had written to Fred a few weeks earlier to tell him that she had moved out of the cramped living conditions that she had been sharing. She was now living in a large house where she was housekeeper. She had a couple of spacious rooms of her own with access to a bathroom and large kitchen where she was expected to make meals and do the laundry. As she had explained to Fred previously she was allowed to have her baby with her, so for the present time she was satisfied.

It was late afternoon when Louisa and Fred with their family arrived at the house where they received another rapturous welcome. Mary hugged their children whilst Louisa peered at Stephanie asleep in her cot.

"She's very good." Mary said. "She sleeps a lot, so I can get on and do things." She put the kettle on. "I expect you would like some more tea. I know you will Fred!"

Her brother grinned. "I never say no to tea."

Not only did Mary give them all tea, she found some lemonade for the children and then made them all an assortment of sandwiches. "You must be hungry, it's nearly tea time."

Both Fred and Louisa looked astonished at the array of food.

"Don't worry, there's plenty of food here. I don't do too badly." Mary urged them to eat and so they helped themselves.

An hour later completely restored they got ready to leave.

"Are you going to see the others?" Mary asked.

Fred shook his head. "We haven't time. These little ones need to go home now, they start back to school again tomorrow. We will see them next time."

There were tears in Mary's eyes as she waved them goodbye. Louisa hoped that things would turn out well for her. After the visit she felt that Fred was relieved that his two sisters seemed to be happy. He knew it must be hard for them bringing up children on their own. Later when the children were in bed she asked Fred if Cissy had told him if she had heard any news from Jack. He shook his head. "I asked her, and she said she had heard nothing. She said she had seen his mother and she didn't know where he is either. It's a mystery. There must be a very good reason for him to stay away from his family. I hope for his sake he is alright."

"Do you think he may have been posted overseas during the war and then decided to stay there to make a new life for himself? He may have been badly injured or ill and couldn't face coming back."

Fred shrugged. "I suppose it's possible. The war affected people in different ways. Some men were shell shocked and a bag of nerves when they were de-mobbed. Many felt worthless. Look at your Harry he still can't forgive himself for being a prisoner of war. Even now he feels responsible for the surrender, yet it wasn't his fault. He was just obeying orders."

Louisa sighed. She knew that Harry had never reconciled himself to being a prisoner of war. After his capture in Singapore in nineteen forty two he had been treated badly in Changi. He was also ill-treated when forced to work on the Burmese railway. The indignity of capture and the cruel prison conditions had left more than the scars on Harry's back. He was still battling unhealed scars on his mind.

Since his return home in nineteen forty five he had put on weight again and looked much better than the skeleton they had met in Liverpool docks. On the surface he began to look like his old self, but on the inside, Louisa was not so sure. Sometimes during unguarded moments, Louisa noticed anguished expressions on Harry's face. Just occasionally she recognised similar expressions on the faces of both Arthur and Fred. She guessed they were reliving uncalled for bad memories. She knew it would take more time for all those mental scars to fade.

Chapter Seventeen

The children went back to school the next day. After she had waved to them both at the gate, Louisa walked back with Carol, both of them pushing their prams.

"Are you looking forward to starting work tomorrow?" Louisa asked Carol.

Her neighbour nodded. "Yes. I'm a bit nervous though. What about you? You start on Wednesday don't you?"

Louisa admitted she was a little nervous too. "Once we get the first day over with I expect we will feel better. Will you have time to come and see me for a few minutes tomorrow night when you get home?"

Her new friend promised that she would.

So when Louisa started work on Wednesday morning she had the advantage of knowing what to expect. Dorothy had arrived as promised at eight o clock with Ann fast asleep in the pram. Louisa had made sure that the two girls were washed and dressed ready for school. They had been reluctant to get out of bed an hour earlier than usual. Susan despite having a lot of energy once she was up, at the age of seven was always reluctant to get out of bed in the mornings. She never wanted to go to bed at night time either. Even though she could read, she would only settle if Louisa or Fred read to her a bed time story. She was very fond of fairy tales, especially when Fred substituted his daughters' names for the fairies. He also used familiar place names to make it more realistic. So much so that the two girls often wandered around the garden looking for fairy glens.

"Are you nervous?" Dorothy asked, as she picked up Michael to cuddle him. The boy loved seeing his aunt who always took time to play with him.

Louisa gulped down her tea and shrugged herself in to her jacket. "I'm looking forward to it, but anxious at the same time. But at least I know what to expect. Carol came round last night and gave me an outline of what would happen. She said it was fine, but it took some time getting used to the noise of the sewing machines."

"How many machines are there?"

"Carol didn't say. Anyway I must go before I miss my bus." She kissed her sister goodbye. "Have a good day. Hopefully I will be home before half past four."

At the factory Louisa was met by Gloria Manley who introduced her to Audrey Manley a younger version of herself.

Gloria laughed. "Yes we are sisters in case you were wondering, and Mr. Manley the boss man is our father. Many people think we are alike."

"I have a sister too, and people think we look alike too," Louisa started to say. But Gloria cut her off as she started to explain things. Louisa realised that they weren't interested in her own sister. She stood silently listening to Gloria.

"Audrey looks after the machinists and will be your supervisor. I work in the office alongside father and do the accounts. I hope you will be happy here Louisa."

Audrey beckoned Louisa to follow her to a small room where there were dozens of lockers. She was told to put her coat and bag in a locker and was then given the key and an overall. When she was ready she was led into the machine room. There was no mistaking where it might be because the noise got louder and louder as they approached.

Eventually Louisa was led to a machine which was located at the back of a column of nine machines. The column was the third of six columns. Audrey handed her an instruction sheet on how to use the machine and told her to practise for ten minutes on a piece of rayon before being given some work to do. Tentatively Louisa threaded the machine and then practised a few lines with the machine. It was faster than hers and she had to get used to lowering and pressing her foot on the machine pedal. When Audrey returned she felt confident she could use the machine. She was given a basket full of sleeves and was told above the noise that she had to sew the seams. She was handed another basket to put in the finished seams.

All day long Louisa sewed the seams which she realised were part of a man's shirt. Each time she emptied her basket and had placed the articles in to another one, her work load was replenished and she would start again. At the end of her shift she took off her overall and hung it in the locker ready for her next shift at the end of the week.

On the bus home she was glad to get away from the noise and also glad that she had a day of rest in between the next shift. She got off the bus at twenty five past four and walked down the road to her house conscious of a slight buzzing in her ears. Dorothy had the kettle boiling as she walked through the door and she slumped into a chair. She grinned at her sister as Michael crawled on to her knee.

"Have a good day?" she poured the water on the teapot and brought a tray with the tea things on to the table.

Louisa nodded. "Yes I suppose it was alright. The noise is the worst thing, and of course it is repetitive work." She explained how she had spent the day sewing sleeve after sleeve.

"Perhaps you will do cuffs next time?" Dorothy suggested.

"I don't know. They will tell me when I get there I suppose. I feel as if I have earned my fourteen shillings per day."

Dorothy poured her tea. "Think of the money. And remember you don't have to do it. Some people are desperate for work. You have a skill that some people don't have."

Louisa sipped her tea then put her cup down. She was still wearing her coat. She lifted Michael off her knee and stood up to take off her coat. "Yes I am grateful for the extra money. It's to pay for little luxuries like going out for the day with the children." She took another sip of her tea. "I'm grateful that you have helped me to do this so I am willing to share my wages with you. I couldn't do it without your help."

"Don't be silly. You know I am always glad to help and play with the children."

"It's still a commitment Dor. It's not as if you come now and again. I must give you something. I know you are saving for things for your own home."

Dorothy shrugged. I don't know when that will be, houses are still hard to come by. We will be low on the housing list."

They agreed that Louisa would give Dorothy four shillings for looking after the children. Dorothy refused to take any more. Both women were satisfied with the arrangement. When Louisa told Fred what they had agreed he was content with the outcome too.

"We mustn't get tempted to spend it." Fred said. "The money should be for what you intended. Family outings and the benefit of the children. But before we do anything like that you should treat yourself to something nice Louie. I've got a feeling I know what you want too."

Louisa gazed at her husband as she saw a smile edge across his face.

"What?" She asked puzzled.

"I will give you a clue. It has something to do with an item just come off ration."

"Soap!" They both said and laughed.

It was true, Louisa had frequently been bemoaning the fact that not only did she have to scrimp with the butter, she had to scrimp with soap too. She was determined that when she was paid she would buy herself the biggest bar of soap she could find.

As autumn passed into winter and Christmas began to get nearer, Louisa had the satisfaction of seeing her wages adding up to a nice little sum.

On her way home from work she passed a poster advertising *The Lion, the Witch and the Wardrobe* that was due to be shown in the Majestic. She felt her two girls would love to see that and she mentioned this to Fred.

"What about Michael? He's too little to watch that."

"We could ask Dot to look after him and then we can take Malcolm too. Gordon may not want to see it. He might think it is too babyish for him."

As it turned out, Gordon said he would like to see the film, and Dot agreed to look after Michael. When Maureen and Brian found out about it they wanted to go too. So Arthur agreed to meet them at the cinema with his children. Gladys was happy to stay at home with little Arthur.

"I hope the children won't be disappointed." Fred grinned wryly.

"So do I." Arthur said. "I'm looking forward to a snooze whilst they are watching it."

"Working too hard?" Fred asked sympathetically. He knew Arthur was working all hours to save money for a bigger house.

"Yes, but I decided to finish earlier today otherwise you and Louie would have had all the children to look after." He laughed. "I couldn't do that to you mate."

As it turned out Arthur didn't fall asleep. He seemed to have enjoyed the film as much as the children. He said as much to Harry when they all got to his house in Rhosrobin.

Harry laughed. "I'm glad you enjoyed it, but I'm just as happy relaxing here than being in the cinema with you .Thanks for taking the boys." He turned towards his sister. "Have you got any more outings planned Louie?"

"Not yet. But I will keep you posted." She kissed both her brothers goodbye and then Dot. "Thanks for looking after Michael."

A month or so later soon after Fred's thirty fifth birthday in November, Louisa came up with another idea for a family outing. This time it didn't involve her own brothers, but it would, she knew involve Fred's brothers.

"We could take the children to Liverpool to see the Christmas lights." Louisa suggested. She recalled with pleasure the first time Fred had taken her to John Lewis's at Christmas time. She had been spellbound by the lights. Momentarily a hint of sadness touched her face as she remembered that her visit was before the destruction of the war. Amongst other victims she knew that the Lewis's store had been hit during an air raid.

"Good idea." Fred's face lit up at the thought of going back to his beloved Liverpool. "Perhaps we could call to see Jim and maybe Bob too?"

Louisa laughed indulgently. She knew Fred would say that.

The Saturday before Christmas Fred had the whole day off work that year. Christmas day was to be on Monday and after a lot of thought his boss had told his employees to finish work for Christmas on Friday evening.

After a leisurely breakfast on Saturday morning the family set off for Liverpool. They arrived at Jim and Annie's house shortly before mid-day. Fred had written a note to his brother telling him that they would call. Louisa had enclosed the note with the Christmas card that she had sent.

"I hope he got the card." Louisa said when Fred parked the car outside his brother's house in New Brighton.

"You sent it to the New Brighton address and not Wallasey didn't you? I forgot to check the envelope when you gave it to me to put the note in it."

"Yes I'm sure I did."

They all got out of the car and Fred knocked on the door. His brother was obviously expecting them and they were ushered into the house and given a warm welcome.

Fred was very fond of his oldest brother. He had acted more like a father figure when he was a child. Their father had been killed in nineteen seventeen in Passchendale when Fred was just two years of age and Jim was thirteen. Fred was fond of Jim's wife Annie too. She had sheltered him several times during the war when his ship had docked in Birkenhead or Wallasey and he had just twenty four hours leave. Sometimes he had only had twelve hours leave. He had made his way to see Annie where she had provided some temporary solace from his war weary travels. Fred had always appreciated even a few snatched hours of being in a proper home rather than on a battle ship. That way he had managed to see his niece Louisa and his nephew Alfred. Both children were similar ages to Christine and Susan. The four of them were getting to know each other as they had not met before.

"I'm hoping that this will be the beginning of more visits Fred." Jim said as he watched Annie pour tea for everyone. She managed to find some lemonade for the children. Louisa handed Annie a loaf of bread, some eggs and a chicken that her father had given her to take. Mary Ellen had plucked it ready for the oven. They both went in to the kitchen to make some egg sandwiches. Annie covered the chicken with a tea towel and put it near the window to keep cool. "Thank you very much for this, every little helps."

"Well we couldn't expect you to feed us all." Louisa said.

Annie showed Louisa some mince pies that she had made. "I'm glad mincemeat is off the ration. These will be nice warmed up after the sandwiches."

"Are you going to see Bob?" Jim asked Fred much later. Fred glanced at his watch, it was three o clock.

"What do you think Louie?"

"It would be a shame not to, since we are so close. " Louisa replied. "What time will the lights be switched on?"

"As soon as it goes dark, about five o clock." Jim replied.

"It would be nice to see him just for half an hour." Fred said. "I didn't tell him we were coming so it will be a surprise, that's if he and Maggie are in."

Half an hour later they were sitting in Bob and Maggie's kitchen drinking more tea. Fred explained that they couldn't stay long and Bob understood that they wanted to take the children into the city.

"Did you know Cissy's left town?" Bob asked.

Fred shook his head. "No, I know she was thinking of going to Manchester. When did she go?"

"Last week. She said she would let me know her new address. I haven't heard from her yet."

218

"I expect she is still settling in." Louisa suggested. She gazed around the room to watch her children acquaint themselves with Bob's children. He and his wife had two boys and three girls. The two oldest Jimmy and Margaret were almost the same age as Christine. The young Robert and his sisters Frances and Celia were closer to Susan's age. Celia was the youngest of them all. They seemed to be getting on well.

After a short visit and hurried goodbyes, they finally left and Fred parked the car as close as he could to Liverpool city centre. The shops were still open, where last minute shoppers were hurrying along looking for suitable gifts. The children were in awe of the lights. Louisa took advantage of their excitement and whilst Fred kept them busy, she dashed into a large book store and bought albums for the three of them to put in their Christmas stockings. *Treasure Island* and *Alice in Wonderland* for Christine, *Peter Pan* and *Rupert* for Susan. She was unsure about *Rupert.* Susan was seven now and Louisa thought she might not want it any more, yet she still read the previous year's annual. She had kept all their books for Michael for when he was older. That day she bought him the newest *Noddy* annual and a colouring book. She rejoined her family at the huge Christmas tree that was in the centre of the city.

"Got everything?" Fred asked trying not to arouse interest from his two daughters.

Louisa nodded smiling broadly. She held on to her shopping bag tightly as she walked beside Fred pushing the pushchair. The children were distracted by the lights and they didn't notice Louisa's stuffed shopping bag. They didn't notice it either when she put it in the boot of the car before they drove home.

As usual Louisa, Dorothy and Mary Ellen pooled rations for Christmas dinner. Somehow they all squeezed around the table in the back parlour. The roast chicken was shared out and with the ample supply of roast potatoes and vegetables they were all satisfied with the food. Mary Ellen was especially pleased to be able to serve a plum pudding as well as mince pies that year. "Let's hope even more food comes off the ration next year." She said.

Chapter Eighteen

1951

When Louisa returned to work in the New Year she was informed along with the rest of the workforce that they would be working on the new summer collection for Ladies. The company had a contract for two of the main chain stores in Britain and was excited about the order. Louisa was pleased not to be making shirt parts. She had sewn sleeves, cuffs and collars but had never been asked to finish the complete garment. She knew this was because she was part time. However on this occasion she had been singled out to sew up one side of seams on the dresses. When she saw her workload she was able to fathom out how the finished article would eventually look like. The dresses were made from a new type of rayon and Louisa wondered if she was able to buy the material somewhere. She was hoping to make some summer dresses for herself, Christine and Susan. When she mentioned this to Carol she suggested that they might be able to buy it from Manley and perhaps get a discount. Carol was also thinking of making some new clothes for herself and daughters.

"I know some of the full time girls get a discount because I have heard them talking in the canteen, I'm not sure if we part-timers would get a discount."

"Well perhaps we could ask Moira. She is quite friendly. I will ask her when I get a break." Louisa offered.

Moira told Louisa that the staff were entitled to discounts on the finished garments before it went to the shops. "Sometimes there are rejects, too badly done for remaking and then we can have them for next to nothing. They don't give them away but they are very cheap. With a bit of patience and know how you can usually transform a reject into something useful."

"What about fabric?" Louisa asked. "Would they sell some of that to me?"

"I don't know. I've never asked. But if you are happy to make do with remnants I know they sometimes have end of rolls in the cutting room which they sell off cheaply. You have to be quick though because some of the other girls go looking for it."

"How come I didn't know about that?" Louisa asked.

Moira laughed. "It's a bit of a secret. The less people know, the more there is for the others."

Louisa pulled a face. "So where do I go and who do I ask?"

"I'll give you a tip. You finish earlier than us on a Friday. If you are willing to miss your bus and get the next one, you should go down to the cutting room and ask for Archie." Moira blushed. "We have a special arrangement. Just tell him I sent you and he will show you some of the best bits. I've got enough to be going on with at home. I daren't take any more home me mam will kill me even though I have made stuff for her too! It's taking over the house."

Louisa looked taken aback at this admission and Moira had the grace to look ashamed that she had taken so much. She was pleased she had asked Moira and told Carol what she had found out. Carol didn't normally work on a Friday but decided to accompany Louisa on the following Friday.

Fortunately Moira had told Archie that he may get a visit from Louisa. He wasn't expecting Carol too, but he was happy to show the two women what was in the remainder tub. "Have a look in there. You can have as much as you like as long as you pay what's on the ticket price. When you are ready take it over there to Charlie. He checks it out on the till and will give you a receipt. You are in luck today, we came to the end of several rolls yesterday."

Carol and Louisa couldn't believe their eyes when they saw the amount of cut offs. Some of the lengths were long enough to make dresses for Christine and Susan. The price on each remnant was so cheap that Louisa bought enough to make them two dresses each. The lengths for herself were not quite enough however she found that two lengths of the same fabric and colour would serve just as well. After some rummaging she found enough material to make two dresses for herself. Carol also chose enough for herself and Bethan. They both clutched their parcels delighted with their finds as they rushed to King Street to get their bus home.

"This will keep us busy at home." Carol said.

Louisa agreed. Despite the late January wind biting through her neck as she sat on the seat next to her friend, she could visualise how lovely her two girls would look in their new clothes.

Dorothy looked in awe at the material when Louisa got home. Louisa promised her sister, that she would get some for her too very soon. There was still plenty of time to sew before the summer.

During February Fred and Louisa listening to the wireless one evening, were informed that Herbert Morrison the Labour Member of Parliament had plans for a huge festival that was going to be in London on the South Bank. It was going to be an event to make British people feel good again. There would be ships traveling to various ports for people to be able to go aboard and get a glimpse of the pageantry that praised Britain.

Very soon after this announcement Christine came home from school with a note from the teacher to say that a coach party from Wrexham would be taking school children to London to see the Skylon.

What's this all about?" Fred asked when he saw the note.

"It seems that Herbert Morrison or Lord Festival he seems to be called nowadays has arranged for something – I'm not sure what - to be suspended in midair and it is called a Skylon. In any case she would get the chance to see London, so I think she should go." Louisa declared.

Fred gazed at his wife. "It's a long way and she's only eleven."

"Nearly twelve!" Christine said folding her arms resolutely. "Bethan is going."

"Has she asked her mum already?" Louisa frowned as she spoke to her daughter. "I've only just read the note myself. I don't think Carol has come back from work yet. I'm sure Bethan's mother hasn't had time to make a decision."

"Well Bethan wants to go and I want to go too." Christine said stubbornly. Then added "please." When she saw her mother's stern expression.

"I suppose it is a good opportunity." Fred said slowly. He inclined his head towards his wife. Then smiled at his daughter. He wouldn't refuse his daughters anything if he felt he could help it.

"Alright." Louisa said. "I'm sure we can afford the fare. It's a long way to London though. Are you sure you want to travel that far?"

Christine nodded eagerly.

"I will have to get a move on and finish those dresses for you." Louisa hesitated. "I suppose you will be going in school uniform?"

"I don't know." Christine said. "Thanks mum, dad. I will ask tomorrow."

When Susan found out that Christine was going to London she wanted to go too. It took a lot of explaining that she was too young and that when she was older they would take her to London. A few weeks later at a home football game Arthur mentioned to Fred and Harry that his son and daughter were going on the school trip to London.

"My two are going too! Harry said.

"And mine!" Fred added.

Arthur grinned. "Well if that's the case we ought to do something whilst the kids are out of the way. They won't be back until late. If mother will look after little Arthur and Michael we can all go out together."

"Don't forget Dorothy and Bill." Harry said. "She'll have to look after Ann too. Three little ones and Susan might be too much for her, even our mother!" He grinned wryly. He knew his mother was a very capable woman but she was approaching sixty and it didn't seem fair to ask her to look after three children under the age of three.

Arthur pulled a face. "Perhaps I could ask Glad's mam, but I'm not too hopeful."

When Fred mentioned the plan to Louisa, she suggested that she could ask Carol to look after Michael and Susan. That way her mother would only have to manage Ann and possibly little Arthur too.

Arthur and Gladys put off asking her mother, because they dreaded her answer would be no. She didn't approve of them going out and leaving the children. Meanwhile Louisa and Dorothy asked their mother to look after Arthur as well as Ann. Mary Ellen was pleased to look after both infants so it was settled.

Arthur beamed when Louisa told him and she could see relief spread on his face.

"For goodness sake Arthur are you that scared of your mother in law?" Louisa teased her brother.

"You know what? I think I am." He replied grinning. "I'd rather face an enemy tank."

Louisa burst out laughing.

They were sitting in Louisa and Fred's house in Gwersyllt one Saturday afternoon. Arthur had taken a bride to Gwersyllt church to her wedding and had called on his way back to Wrexham before returning with the Limousine. The Wedding reception was in the church hall so his services wouldn't be needed until much later in the day. Clark's garage where Arthur worked as a mechanic also hired out limousines for weddings and Arthur performed the task of driver. It was extra income for him.

"Have you done the football pools this week?" Fred asked him. He pulled out his own copy from his wallet and put it on the table in front of him.

Arthur checked his watch. "Yes I have." There's still half an hour to go before the results are in. I had better get a move on so I can check them when I get home. Mind you, if I don't get there in time Gladys will check them for me."

Later that evening Fred turned on the wireless to check the football results and was delighted to find he had won twelve shillings. "That will go towards Christine's day out in London."

The day of the departure to London arrived on the third of May and Louisa and Fred got up early to walk to the school with Christine. Once they saw that she was sitting on the coach with Bethan, Malcolm and Gordon they smiled and waved as the coach left to pick up the other school children in Rhosrobin School. Brian and Maureen went to a school in Acton and would be travelling on a different coach.

Fred and Louisa picked up Harry and Dot on their way to the cinema. Arthur and Gladys were collecting Dorothy and Bill. They had arranged to meet at the Majestic.

As usual they discussed the films they would like to see. Fred and Louisa got distracted as they gazed at the poster advertising a Hitchcock film about

227

strangers. "I would like to see that when it comes out." Fred said.

Harry came to look over their shoulders. "So would I." He said. "It looks good. Anyway it looks like the best choice for tonight is the "*man in the white suit.* We have agreed so you two are outvoted even before you start." Harry winked at Louisa.

Fred grinned. "That's fine with us."

Once they were all settled in the cinema, Harry turned to Fred and asked his opinion on the government's plan of the Festival of Britain.

"Well they've thrown a lot of money at it." Fred said. "But not everyone can get to London, and what will happen to the new buildings that have been purpose built? That's what I would like to know. I would have preferred them to spend more money on re-building the bombed cities. A bit of metal hanging in the air doesn't change your life style does it?"

Harry agreed with him. "I think you are right Fred. The project is supposed to make us feel good. But I don't think it will. It won't have a long lasting effect on the workers. The children will love the day out to London and will probably remember it for many years to come. I dare say. But for us…" Harry sighed.

Louisa who was listening intently to her brother, was sitting sandwiched between him and Fred. She noticed how Harry shook his head as if to dismiss darker thoughts coming to the surface. He began to speak again. More roughly this time.

"But they shouldn't be allowed to forget those people who are still living in misery because of the war. I get the feeling the government are just papering over the cracks." He looked squarely at Fred. "We survived! We are the lucky ones! That's what we are continually being told."

He looked so solemn that Fred was taken aback.

"Yes we are the lucky ones." Louisa said. "No-one can forget the past. Those of us alive know how much suffering there was, but Harry we have to try to draw a line under it all. We have to move forward for the sake of the next generation." She put her hand on his shoulder to try to comfort him.

"I know Louie, I am trying to think forward, but somehow this display of gaiety on such a grand scale reminds me of all those people lost."

"I think I know what you mean." Fred said. "It is an emotional time. People pulled together when the war started, and they rejoiced when the war was over. Now there will be crowds again and the thought of it, well, it does play about with your emotions. So you are bound to feel a bit sad. I do." Fred sighed deeply then spoke again.

"I think the government want to move on away from the war. Plus the fact they want to remind the people that they won the General Election last year! They want to advertise to the people that the Labour Party have given the nation permission to be happy." Harry relaxed a bit then. Louisa guessed he just wanted to get things off his chest.

The lights were dimmed and the film was about to begin, but for a while Fred couldn't forget Harry's grim face. Eventually he settled down to watch the film and slipped his arm around Louisa's shoulders. Louisa leaned forward a little and looked down the row to see what the rest of their little party were doing. She smiled to see that each couple were now leaning into each other settling down to watch the film.

After they left the cinema Harry and Dot returned to Gwersyllt with Louisa and Fred. They waited together for the children to return from London.

Louisa quickly went next door to collect Michael and Susan who were both fast asleep. She reluctantly woke Susan who sleepily followed her mother home. She soon fell asleep again in her own bed. Michael who had not stirred settled easily in to his own bed too.

Gordon and Malcolm had been instructed to walk with Christine and Bethan back to Louisa and Fred's house when the coach arrived. From there they would walk home with their parents. Fred offered to drive them back but Harry said the exercise would be good for the children after sitting so long on the coach. Harry seemed more cheerful now after his conversation with Fred. He beamed at his two children who appeared to have enjoyed the excursion.

"I hope Harry will be alright." Louisa commented after they had gone.

"Don't worry. He will be fine. It's this pageantry that provokes all kinds of emotions. Not long ago the country was mourning its dead and now we have bunting and flag waving. It messes with your emotions."

"I suppose so." Louisa pursed her lips.

"It's only natural he feels like that. We all have highs and lows. Arthur and Bill do too." Fred said. "Time is a good healer. So they say." He grinned. "Still the film was good wasn't it? At least we all managed to laugh."

Louisa agreed. "Yes it was. And the children seemed to have enjoyed themselves judging by their smiling faces even though they were a bit tired. Christine seems to have spent all her pocket money on souvenirs." She picked up a badge that had fallen on to the floor and laid it on the table so that her daughter would see it in the morning. "I hope she remembered to buy Susan something."

Christine was tired the next day when she got up but still excited about the school trip. She gave her sister some souvenir pencils and a badge. The badge was not dissimilar to the one that had fallen off her school uniform the night before.

"What was the Skylon like that everyone seems to be talking about?" Louisa asked her daughter.

Christine shrugged. She evidently wasn't that impressed. Louisa laughed, guessing that her daughter was probably more interested in the musical festivities and the Festival Hall Exhibition stands.

"It was just a bit of metal hanging from a ship." Christine replied. "The ship was good though and the river Thames is huge."

The government minister Herbert Morrison had arranged for the festival of Britain to be celebrated in as many ports around Britain as they could muster. A few weeks later Fred received a letter from his brother Jim to tell him that the HMS Campania an aircraft carrier was sailing up the Mersey in to port at Birkenhead as part of the Festival of Britain exhibition. His son Alf was going to go with his neighbour. Jim thought that Fred might be interested, seeing as he was always hanging around the dockyards when he was a child and that he was in the Royal Navy when he served in the war.

Fred was indeed interested and suggested to Louisa that they take the children.

"I think you should take the girls. I will stay home with Michael. He's too little to take him around a ship."

"Are you sure?" Fred said. "I could carry him."

Louisa shook her head. "No, you will enjoy it more with the girls."

So a few days later Fred drove to Birkenhead with his two excited daughters to look out for HMS Campania. Christine tried to be blasé about the ship saying that she had seen it before, but she was still awestruck when they finally sighted the vessel. Eight year old Susan was mesmerised at the sheer size of the ship and worried about how it would keep afloat.

Fred kept a look out to see if he could see his nephew Alf, but there were so many people around it was like finding a needle in a haystack. He said as much in a letter to Jim a few days later.

Soon after this trip both Christine and Susan caught measles and had to stay off school for a fortnight. Louisa didn't like the idea of leaving them when she went to work, and Dorothy was worried she might pass them on to Ann. Mr. Manley was sympathetic but whilst he agreed to let Louisa have time off, his company was not willing to pay her sick leave.

"You should join a union." Fred said.

"I would if there was one, but there doesn't seem to be one where I work. I will have to make enquiries. No-one has ever approached me to join one."

Louisa shrugged. "I'll just have to put up with it. I can't take a risk with the children."

No sooner did the girls recover than Michael caught the measles too. Then he got mumps. Bethan eventually caught the disease and Carol's baby Shirley also got measles and mumps. So both women were off work for a considerable time.

"I don't think they will have us back." Carol said at the end of July. "In any case it is the school summer holidays soon, I would have to negotiate more time off to take the children away. We are going to Rhyl to the same camp you went to last year. Are you going away again?"

Louisa sighed. "I hope so. Fred hasn't booked anything yet because we wanted to make sure the children are well enough. I'm going to be in the same position as you. So if I've lost my job there's nothing more I can do about it. I may as well try to get away if I can."

"I think we should go and talk to Mr. Manley." Carol said.

The day before the school closed for summer Louisa and Carol went to the factory to see Mr. Manley. Both women were interviewed separately and the outcome was that if they were both looking for work in September then they would be considered to work on a new assignment. The company had agreed a new contract and would need extra staff. Mr. Manley knew he would probably have a few vacancies soon because one of their machinists was due to get married and moving away to Oswestry. It was too far away to travel to work so she would be leaving. Another two seamstresses were leaving to have babies.

233

"These are full time posts though. I would consider you both for those if you were interested. Two other part time vacancies are coming up in October and November."

On the way home on the bus, Carol suggested to Louisa that they could look somewhere else for work. Louisa was not so keen. She enjoyed her work even though it was noisy. An idea began to form in her mind. "What if we shared a full time job between us? I know its more hours because we would have to work two and a half days, but we could do it."

Carol looked doubtful. "I don't think that would work Louie. The extra hours are too many, and sometimes the full time staff are expected to work overtime and Saturdays."

Louisa shrugged. "Just an idea."

When Louisa talked it over with Fred and then Dorothy, they agreed it was too much of a commitment. Disappointed, Louisa reluctantly agreed.

Meanwhile, Fred had been asked by his employer to take a late holiday from work that year and though he agreed, he discovered that the bank holiday week end in August was a difficult time to book a caravan. Eventually after sending countless letters of enquiry they eventually managed to find a vacancy. Fred was ecstatic. He was looking forward to a break and he knew that Louisa needed one even though she said that she didn't. He knew she was disappointed that she couldn't go back to work again.

"We can manage without you working Louie. So why don't you enjoy the summer holidays and then consider going back in October or November when those other women leave?"

Louisa shrugged. There wasn't much she could do about the situation. She had set her mind on working again in September. She knew it wasn't much longer to wait, but she was getting impatient.

As July rolled into August, and the children appeared to be fit and well again, Louisa too began to relax. She had been worried about their health and she realised that she had worked hard looking after them and needed a rest too. So she shelved the idea of going back to work until later in the year. Meanwhile Fred suggested they had an outing to Snowdonia National Park.

"It's still a few weeks before the bank holiday week so instead of waiting for our week in a caravan, I reckon we can afford a night in a bed and breakfast place somewhere near Snowdon."

Louisa's eyes lit up at the thought of a night away where she would have a break from cooking and cleaning.

It was a gloriously warm week end when they drove to Port Madoc and checked into a B and B near Borth y Gest. The children loved playing on the beach and managed to clean themselves up again so that when they went to a café nearby for a fish and chips supper, they had got rid of most of the sand off their shoes and clothes!

Driving up the Snowdonia mountain passes, the beautiful scenery entranced the children and Fred. On the other hand Louisa who had no head for heights, became nervous and was glad when they started the descent.

The week end helped Louisa to unwind a bit. She realised she had worked herself up into a nervous state looking after the children when they were sick and then worrying about losing her job.

Fred too felt more relaxed and was already looking forward to their next adventure. Both of them commented upon the freedom they felt now that petrol was off the ration. It had made such a difference to their lives.

"Mind you as far as getting to Rhyl is concerned, we could get the train you know." Fred commented when they were home again.

"I know, but we would have all the bags to carry and then worry about where the children were. At least when we are all in the car together, and the luggage is in the boot we don't have to worry for a while."

Fred smiled. "Yes that is a big advantage. Not long now before we go on our travels again. I hope the sun shines."

The sunshine Fred wished for appeared once or twice, though more often than not it disappeared behind clouds. However the temperature was warm which allowed them to spend time on the beach. Michael being a little older they were able to encourage him to paddle into the sea with his sisters.

When the holiday was almost over, Louisa groaned when she was faced once again with the task of removing sand out of the caravan. Good humouredly she grabbed a brush to do it. Meanwhile she sent Christine and Susan to the camp tap to wash all the sea shells they had collected as well as the buckets and spades. "Leave as much sand behind as you can." She told them laughingly as she watched them dragging everything with them to the camp tap.

Michael ran after them. Eventually they were ready to leave. Louisa felt refreshed and ready to face the rest of the year. The week away had helped her to think about her future career prospects, such as they were. Fred too seemed to be in good spirits.

Dorothy resumed her visits to see Louisa twice a week as she had before, though not so early in the morning. She had got in to a routine when her sister was working. She missed the walk to Gwersyllt and looking after the children. Ann had not contracted measles nor mumps but as Dorothy said she would probably get them when she started school.

"But that will be a few years yet." Dorothy said. "Who knows where we will be living then. I hope we won't still be in Pandy."

Louisa smiled sympathetically. "I know what you mean. Mother and Father have been good to us but it is nice to have a place of your own. I'm so glad that Fred suggested we put our name down for this house. It is modern and it was a god send after Michael was born. He was so ill."

"Bill wants to save as much as we can so that we can move towards Chester so that he is closer to work. We are both quite content at the moment really, and we have more space in Pandy than what we had in Mold. Ann has a room all to herself. The one that used to be mine and yours!"

"But you would like a place of your own." Louisa said sympathetically. "You will soon I'm sure. Things are improving slowly."

A few days after the new term at school had started, Susan went missing again. Christine was next door playing with Bethan. Louisa had been dusting and cleaning upstairs, whilst Susan was reading a book on the sofa. On Louisa's return to the living room she discovered Susan wasn't where she had left her half an hour ago. Louisa assumed she had gone to join her sister. When Carol told her that Susan wasn't with her, Louisa began to worry.

"She's probably gone to Pandy the little minx. "Do you mind looking after Michael whilst I go and look for her?"

Carol came back to her house to get Michael and Louisa hurried into her coat to walk to Pandy. She half walked and half ran stopping only for a few minutes to see if Susan was with Malcolm at his Granny's house. Dot's mother lived just a few houses away from Dot and Harry. It was Friday and Dot would be in work. Malcolm and Gordon usually stayed with their Granny after school. Mrs. Weaver said she hadn't seen Susan. She called Malcolm to the door and he shook his head. No he hadn't seen his cousin. Louisa thanked her and hurried on feeling sure that Susan had gone to Pandy.

However when she reached her parent's house Mary Ellen and Dorothy said they hadn't seen her either. Louisa slumped into a chair. "Where can she have gone?"

Louisa was getting worried now.

Suddenly Dorothy got up and grabbed her coat. "I think I know, and if I'm right, I'm sorry. The other day I told her about the Roman Gypsy caravans parked on Bluebell lane near the Chester Road. She was fascinated about the caravans, I think she may have gone to see them. Come on, I'll come with you."

238

For a moment she hesitated then glanced at her mother. Mary Ellen nodded as if reading her mind. "Go on, I will look after Ann. Louisa was already at the door and Dorothy followed her out her coat belt trailing on the floor as she caught up with her sister. "Louie, I'm sorry."

Louisa grimaced. "Don't be sorry. It's not your fault. She's been told not to go wandering off on her own. I just hope she is alright."

They both hurried around the corner and on to Bluebell lane. The lane was a good half mile long and led on to the Chester Road. On the edge of Bluebell lane before it met the road was a huge field where every year Roman Gypsies camped for the bank holiday festival. Often they extended their visit for two extra weeks.

They soon found the gaily decorated horse drawn caravans. Within minutes Louisa spotted Susan sitting on the steps of a brightly coloured caravan that was decked in ribbons the colours of the rainbow. When Susan saw them approach she grinned and called to them "Mummy, Auntie Dorothy, come and see the caravans."

Dorothy and Louisa looked at each other and laughed. They were both relieved.

"What am I going to do with her? How can I be cross with her when she looks so happy?" Louisa sighed.

A middle aged woman with a bright scarf around her head lifted Susan from the steps of the caravan. Taking her by the hand she led her to where Louisa and Dorothy were standing. Susan loosed hold of the woman's hand and ran to her mother.

"Is this yer daughter?" The woman asked.

Louisa smiled. "Yes, she keeps running away. Thank you for looking after her."

The woman grinned and returned to her caravan.

Dorothy took hold of one of Susan's hands and Louisa the other and together they walked away from the field and back along Bluebell lane. Once again Louisa reminded Susan that she was not to go wandering off on her own. The little girl promised she wouldn't but Louisa knew that the girl was so headstrong and independent, that no doubt she would do it again. She just hoped that no harm came to her. She vowed to keep a keener watch on her until she felt she was old enough to go out on her own. Christine was now twelve, but even she was told not to go to Pandy on her own. Not that she ever seemed inclined to wander away from home as much as Susan did. Christine was happy to play with her new friend Bethan or read her books.

Chapter Nineteen

Early in September after the girls started back to school Louisa and Carol decided to pay Mr. Manley another visit to let him know that they were still interested in part time work. He seemed pleased to see them but told them the situation was still the same as he had told them previously.

"I'm glad you have come though. At least I know you are sincere about working here. I'm expecting a new contract soon for next spring so when you start in November you will be working on that. As I told you before I have two women going off to have babies."

What will we be sewing?" Louisa asked. She was interested to know what would be in the shops the following year.

Mr. Manley smiled secretly. "That I am afraid I cannot tell you. It is confidential. You will just have to wait and see."

Both women were cheerful on the bus going home. "At least we know we will have some work soon." Louisa said.

"Yes Carol replied. "It was a good idea of yours to go and see him. Let him know that we are still interested."

The football season had started again and Fred went to the match with Harry and his two boys. Susan said she wouldn't mind going to the football match but Fred said she was too little. Fortunately he managed to fob her off with a promise to take her for a walk to the woods the following day.

Dot walked up to keep Louisa company whilst their husbands were at the game. Soon after she had arrived Dorothy knocked on the backdoor and without waiting for an answer, she pushed Ann in to the kitchen and called "Louie" at the same time.

"Bill's gone to the match with Arthur. I suppose they will be meeting Fred and Harry when they get there, so I decided to come here. Gladys is with mother. I suggested she came with me too but she wanted to stay in Pandy with mother. She is going to see her own mother afterwards."

"How is Gladys?" Louisa asked. "I haven't seen her for a while."

"She's fine but she's complaining she hardly ever sees Arthur. He seems to be working all the time."

"Yes he does seem to be working a lot. He wants to buy a bigger house and the only way to do that is to earn more money. The children are growing up and will need more space soon."

Dot nodded. "Yes, Brian is twelve now and Maureen is eight. Arthur is two months younger than Michael. They must be cramped now in that small house."

Louisa sighed. "I know. I keep thinking of Joan with her four children in my two bedroomed house. She came to see me the other day. She's decided to move back to Liverpool."

Both Dot and Dorothy looked up in surprise at this statement from Louisa.

"So has she found a house?" Dorothy asked excitedly.

Louisa shook her head. "Not exactly. It seems Joan's had an offer from her deceased husband's aunt Molly. Apparently Molly's husband has died and as she is not in good health herself has decided to move in with her brother and sister-in-law. Molly's house is three bedroomed and she has said Joan and their family can live there for now. The house is in disrepair but more or less habitable. It means they might have a better chance of a council house in Liverpool. As they have four children they may get something quicker than staying here in Wrexham. They realise now that they could be waiting years. She is determined to go back to Liverpool."

"So what are you going to do with the house? Are you going to move back?" Dot asked.

Louisa shook her head again. "It's too small for us now. We are going to sell it and bank the money. We have plenty of space here and there is still a shortage of houses. Fred would so like to have a brick house. Being a builder he would feel that way." Louisa shrugged. "For now though we are content."

"Bloody war." Dorothy burst out. "If it hadn't been for the war we would all be better off by now."

"Bloody Hitler." Dot said suddenly.

"I agree." Louisa said. She got up "Let's have another cup of tea."

Dot turned to Dorothy. "Would you and Bill be interested in buying Louie's house?"

Dorothy sighed then glanced at her sister. "A year ago I might have been interested, but now Bill has another job it would be better to move closer to Chester. I must admit we haven't made much of an effort to look for anything. At the moment, we are in a better situation than most." She grinned.

When Fred, Harry his two boys, Arthur and Brian arrived a couple of hours later, the women were surprised that they were not still discussing the match as they usually did. The subject that was causing some heated remarks was the oncoming General election.

Fred was defending the Labour government by reminding his brothers-in-law that the welfare state including the National Health Service was down to the Labour Government.

Arthur insisted that the government had not fulfilled all its promises and had squandered the money they got from America, and Harry was insisting that the money spent on the Festival of Britain was also a waste of time and money. On this last point the three young boys who had enjoyed their recent school trip were now defending the Festival of Britain. When Christine and Susan heard them arrive they too chipped in about the good things about the Festival of Britain and so Harry good naturedly gave in. The children had worn him down with their vehement protestations.

Arthur on the other hand insisted that the government could have done more for the people and that there was a good chance that Clement Atlee would be replaced by Churchill.

Fred shook his head. "Do you really think Churchill has a chance of being Prime Minister again when he failed to get the people's vote in nineteen forty five?"

"He might." Arthur replied. "I hope not, but the Labour Government didn't get a huge majority last year as you well know. If they don't win more seats this time, and Fred I don't think they will, then Churchill will be back in the driving seat."

Fred sighed. "I hope you are wrong."

"Well we will just have to wait and see." He laughed and got up from his chair. "Come on Brian lad, we'd better get back to Pandy to pick up your mum and baby brother."

"Where's Maureen?" Louisa asked.

"Playing with her friend Della." Arthur replied. "She lives in the same street as us and is in Maureen's class at school. Thick of thieves they are." He grinned.

Harry, Dot and their two boys also decided to go. Half way down the path Arthur hurried back. "Dorothy do you want a lift back to Pandy? It's getting dark out here now?"

"No, no. I'm alright. I prefer to walk. I'm going soon. Don't worry."

"I'll take her." Fred said.

A few weeks later Arthur's pessimistic prophesy turned out to be correct. The Labour government was knocked out and Winston Churchill became the Prime Minster once again.

"They didn't get a huge majority though." Fred said to Arthur when they met up in Pandy the Sunday morning after the election.

"Maybe not. But they got more seats than Clement Attlee got last year."

"I just hope they don't wreck the National Health Service and the Welfare State." Fred replied.

"Do you think they will?" Louisa asked. She knew that without the National Health Service they would have been in debt for a long time after the birth of Michael.

"Well Atlee's government has already put charges on glasses and dentures. Will the Tories take it a step further? I hope not." Fred said. He gazed at his wife a troubled look of concern on his face.

"No they wouldn't dare!" Arthur said. "They would have revolt on their hands if they did that. It's one of the finest things the Labour Party created and the people have got used to having it."

Arthur looked ready to explode.

"The Tories promised to build more houses. That's why they got in." Harry commented. "If they fulfill that manifesto promise, then Churchill is on to a second term."

"If he lives that long?" Gladys snorted. "He's getting on for eighty now!" She puffed on her cigarette and blew rings of smoke into the air. Christine and Susan stood watching her fascinated as the smoke rose. Maureen leaned against her father unimpressed. She had seen her mother blow cigarette smoke circles lots of times.

"Churchill also promised to get rid of rationing as well." Louisa commented. As far as she could see the country was still in debt and dependent on America for many of the goods that Britain imported. Continued rationing to her mind was probably going to be for the next year or two at least.

"We're paying for that wretched war in Korea. That's why there has been little house building." Fred said. "Churchill has used the situation in Korea to boost his own ego with the fact he was in power during the war."

Harry sighed. "The Labour Government was in a mess. It's a shame Stafford Cripps has had to resign and Ernest Bevin has died. They relied too heavily on the feel good factor from the Festival of Britain."

"Oh not that again." Louisa commented. She glared at her brother.

"Where's Dot today?" Gladys asked, before Harry could retaliate "and the boys?"

"Dot is looking after her mother. She's got a bit of flu. The boys are playing football somewhere."

"How is Gordon getting on with that club he has joined?" William asked his son. He had been quiet for a while smoking his pipe and listening to the conversation about the General election results. He had voted for the Liberals all his life and had no intention of changing. The Liberal Party had not done very well at the recent election and he chose not to mention it. Fred was a committed Labour supporter and Trade Unionist. His two sons he knew had voted Labour but were not so enamoured with that political party's politics as their brother-in-law. All three of them would attack William over the Liberal party, so he stayed silent whilst enjoying their company and their conversation. Now he felt it was time to steer the conversation to more domestic events.

"He's doing well and enjoying it." Harry replied proudly. "Malcolm is coming along well too. He goes with Gordon to the *Under Fifteen Club* now."

Fred nodded his head in agreement. "Yes I've seen them both play. They are both talented.

Arthur grunted that he too had seen his two nephews play well.

"Gordon has been talent spotted by Bolton Wanderer's Manager." Harry added. His face beamed with pride.

Arthur blinked at that news and so did Fred. Both men congratulated Harry.

"Is Gordon going to play for Bolton then?" William asked excitedly.

Harry nodded. "Yes when he is old enough. He's starting work soon. He's going to be an apprentice painter and decorator like me." Harry Laughed. "At least for the time being."

"What about Brian? Isn't he playing with them?" Mary Ellen asked.

Before Arthur could reply, Gladys answered for him. "Brian likes going to the matches and playing at school, but he's not so committed to the game like Gordon and Malcolm. He would rather stay in bed late on Saturday and Sunday mornings than get up to go to the club. He goes with his friends for bike rides instead. That's where he is now." She finished her cigarette and got up.

"I think we ought to be going. Mam will have our dinner ready soon. You know she likes to get it done early."

Arthur got up and followed his wife and daughter to the door. "See you next week."

Harry got up too. "I suppose I had better go too." He grinned. "We will continue our discussion next week."

248

As soon as Harry had gone Louisa and Mary Ellen began to peel the vegetables for their dinner. Dorothy and Bill had gone to Mold to have a meal with his family, so for a change Louisa and Fred were having a meal with Mary Ellen and William in Pandy. Over their meal Louisa told her parents about her and Fred's decision to sell their house.

"Does that mean Joan has left?" Mary Ellen asked surprised.

Fred nodded. "Yes, she and her family went a few days ago. I had planned on building an extension before selling it, but I have changed my mind now. It would take up too much garden space and probably spoil the view for the neighbours, so we're going to sell it as it is. There is still a housing shortage, so I'm sure it won't take too long to sell."

"We'll save the money towards buying a bigger house of our own sometime in the near future." Louisa added. She helped herself to more vegetables and passed the dish around the table.

"Aren't you happy where you are?" William asked. "You have a modern house with plenty of space and a big garden to grow vegetables."

"We are very happy." Fred said.

"It's not made of brick though!" Louisa supplemented. She knew that was the only thing that troubled Fred. He was a builder, from a family of builders. Yet both of them conceded that the house met all their requirements and more. Several times Fred had tried to convince himself that it didn't matter if the house was made of steel. He knew he was fortunate to have such a good place to live. The garden, being a corner plot was huge and he knew William was envious of the plot. In fact he had put in a lot of his own hard work to help Fred dig it over.

"We can wait." Fred said. "In any case it will be nice to have some money in the bank."

Very soon after this conversation, Christine came home from school one day and asked if she could have piano lessons. Apparently her music teacher in school had asked the children if any of them would be interested in learning the piano. She knew someone who was starting to offer lessons.

"We haven't got a piano. How would you practise?" Louisa asked.

"Miss Jones said that I could practise on the piano in school during dinner times or after school in the afternoons."

Louisa talked this through with Fred. They agreed that Louisa would contact the piano teacher to find out how much she charged and what books she would need to buy.

"This might be just a passing fad." Fred said. He grinned. "Anyway it will be cheaper and easier than buying a pony. She seems to have gone off that idea."

"That's because she finished reading *Black Beauty* ages ago! Louisa laughed. "The trouble is, Susan is reading it now, so we could get requests for a pony again!"

Christine started her piano lessons at the middle of October. That month Louisa and Carol visited Mr. Manley and were told they could start work at the beginning of November. Both women were pleased. However, before Louisa could start work Michael became seriously ill and was admitted to hospital.

At first Louisa thought his fever and runny nose was due to another cold that he had picked up. However he started to cough and looked as if he was struggling to breathe. She became very worried and took him to see her doctor who immediately arranged for an ambulance to take Michael to hospital. Louisa stayed with him for most of the day and only left him to go home to tell Fred when he returned home from work.

Later they went to the hospital to see their son. The Staff nurse advised them that Michael had whooping cough. They had isolated him as whooping cough was contagious. They said his breathing was stable and that they were feeding him with liquids.

"This is like when he was a baby all over again. We had to feed him liquids through the insides of a fountain pen." Louisa told the Staff Nurse.

Fred squeezed Louisa's hand reassuringly. "He was a tough little fighter then. I'm sure he can fight this too." Fred said this to comfort both his wife and himself. He tried not to let his anxiety show in order not to distress Louisa any further. But he was very worried.

After a few hours, Louisa decided to stay at the hospital. Fred left to look after the two girls and to get some rest before he went to work the next day. He watched them carefully to make sure they were not displaying the same breathing symptoms Michael was experiencing. The doctor said the condition was contagious and he wasn't taking any chances.

Louisa stayed at Michael's side for the next week only leaving him to return home for clean clothes. Carol, Dorothy and Dot took it in turns to look after

Christine and Susan, and to give Louisa a rest at the hospital. But she didn't want to leave him longer than it was necessary to wash, feed and clothe herself.

Finally a few days before Christmas the doctor told her he had passed the crisis point. He was responding to the antibiotics and should be able to go home in a few days.

"I would like him to stay here over Christmas though. I prefer he didn't get excited during all the usual activities." The doctor advised.

Louisa smiled with relief. "That's a small price to pay doctor. Thank you."

All thoughts of returning to the sewing factory had gone from Louisa's mind. She was pleased that Carol had managed to get some work though. Louisa concentrated on looking after Michael and planning what she could for Christmas.

Though everyone was relieved that Michael was recovering, it had put a strain on the family. Louisa cooked a Christmas meal for Fred and their two daughters at home that year. She was exhausted but grateful that Michael was recovering. It was also a relief to spend time at home preparing the Christmas meal. It was the first time they had their Christmas meal in their own home.

"Actually we said last year that perhaps there were too many of us now to keep going to Pandy." Fred commented.

Louisa nodded her head. In many ways she could see the advantage of having their meal at home. She enjoyed having the visits during various intervals that day from her brothers and their families. They had staggered the visits so that everyone got to see each other and spend quality time together.

Carol popped in and other neighbours too. All of them had shown their support when they had heard Michael was unwell. Dorothy had managed to do some Christmas shopping for Louisa so that Christine and Susan had something to open on Christmas day. Fred too had also managed to procure some things, especially the Christmas Annuals that he knew his two daughters would like. He had also indulged in a wooden train set for Michael. The little boy had been given lots of soft toys to play with whilst in hospital and so he was able to amuse himself.

When Michael was discharged from hospital a few days before New Year's Eve everyone was reassured. Let's hope the next year will be a good one." Louisa said happily as she lovingly watched her son now returned home again.

Chapter Twenty

1952

Having been away from the sewing factory for so long, Louisa doubted very much that Mr. Manley would give her another job. However encouraged by Carol and Fred she decided to go and at least ask.

She knew that Fred wasn't really keen for her to go back to work. He felt she could do with a rest but he knew she loved working at the factory even though it was noisy. She had often admitted that she was glad she had a day off in between the two days she worked.

Some of the factory workers wore ear plugs to keep out the noise, but Louisa usually stuffed cotton wool in to her ears.

Michael was fully recovered now. So at the end of February Louisa caught the early morning bus with Carol to Wrexham and when they got to the factory she asked to see Mr. Manley. Despite his delight upon seeing Louisa again and telling her how happy that her son had recovered, he said he was unable to offer her any work.

"I had to employ someone else when you were not available and I have given her a permanent contract. Your replacement has no responsibilities so I know I can rely on her. I'm sorry."

"So you are saying that because I am married and have children to consider I am not reliable." Louisa said bitterly.

Mr. Manley said nothing. He looked away from Louisa's unhappy face and repeated "I'm sorry."

Louisa felt indignant and totally disappointed. Instead of going straight home, Louisa caught the Chester bus to Pandy. For two days she had felt anxious and had worked herself up in to a tangle of nervous energy before going to see Mr. Manley. Her disappointment overwhelmed her and she felt queasy in her stomach. She had an urge to talk things through with her mother.

However the door to the house in Pandy was locked. Mary Ellen wasn't at home that morning. It was Monday and Louisa remembered that her mother usually went to the beast market on a Monday in Wrexham. So Louisa started the trek back to Gwersyllt. When she got to the railway bridge she had an impulse to take a short walk to the Bluebell wood. It was a dry day despite the time of year. She felt she would feel better if she could walk in the woods for a little while. It was somewhere she used to go as a child whenever she felt upset.

It took her only a few minutes to get to the stile and then walk down to the kissing gate. The path was still well used by the coal miners as they walked back and to from the colliery at Gresford. Her favourite place usually swathed in honeysuckle in the summer was now bare. The sparse hedgerow with the filbert and hawthorn trees stripped of their fruit did little to cheer her up. After a few minutes of idly looking around her she retraced her steps, then leaned on the kissing gate for a while to settle her mood. A robin came and perched close by and began to tweet as if it was talking to her. She found herself smiling and talking to the bird. It seemed to be listening to her until it eventually flew off. Louisa felt she should go too. Her mood lightened and she felt better as she walked back across the fields in the direction of home.

As she passed Harry and Dot's house in Rhosrobin she glanced towards the window. She knew nobody would be in. Dot had started working full time hours now at Woolinghams, Harry would be in work, Malcolm at school and Gordon had now started to work as an apprentice painter and decorator. She hardly saw Gordon these days. When he wasn't working he was playing football. His brother Malcolm also seemed to spend as many hours as he could at the *Under Fifteens football club*. Both boys were encouraged by their father.

"How did you get on?" Dorothy asked when Louisa reached home. "Judging by your face not very well."

Louisa shook her head. "Never mind. I wasn't too hopeful when I went. I realise I have had a lot of time off work and the company need to have someone reliable. I'm not too disappointed."

"At least you tried." Dorothy sympathised. "It does seem unfair that married women get passed over for work. Though to tell you the truth, you look a bit relieved actually. Let's have a cup of tea." Dorothy got up to go to the kitchen. "I've brought some extra with me. I swapped some potatoes with Mrs. Dawson next door for her tea. She doesn't drink as much tea as we do. Now the government have increased the rations we can afford to drink a bit more than usual now and again." She grinned and Louisa returned her grin.

Although she didn't confide in her sister that day, Louisa's subdued disappointment over Mr. Manley's refusal to give her work was owed to something else preying on her mind.

On the bus journey from Wrexham to Pandy she realised she was expecting another baby. Louisa consoled herself that in many ways it was just as well that she had been refused work. It would have meant taking time off work because of her morning sickness. She felt it would have been another negative mark on her work history. She realised that she was exhausted. The strain of looking after Michael had taken a lot of her energy. Her disappointing interview with Mr. Manley had left her feeling drained. She knew she had to look after herself for the sake of the new baby.

Louisa drank her tea appreciatively. "The Ministry for food said on the wireless that tea rationing would be lifted completely by the end of this year."

Dorothy held the teapot high and managed to squeeze out another cup of tea for each of them. "I look forward to it."

Fred was delighted when Louisa told him her news about the baby though he was anxious about her health.

"You must take it easy and if you think there is something wrong we must get it sorted straight away. Remember how you were with Michael."

Louisa nodded. She couldn't agree more. They decided not to say anything to the family for a little while until Louisa had confirmed her suspicions with the doctor. However there was no doubt in Louisa's mind that she was expecting her fourth child.

The day after her appointment at the doctor, the country was informed that King George VI had died and that his daughter Elizabeth would be queen. Everyone was talking about the King's death and so Louisa waited to tell them her news. It was a few weeks later that Louisa told her family about the expected new baby. She knew that apart from the excitement about the news, that her close family would be concerned about her health and would be advising her to take care of herself.

She assured them that at the moment apart from morning and evening sickness she felt fine.

During the spring as the evenings became lighter, Fred spent some time renovating their old home ready to put it up for sale. It didn't take too long as structurally the house was sound. Harry helped him to clean it up and freshen the walls with paint. When they finished on the last day of April they both walked through the house for the last time.

"It doesn't seem so long ago that I was painting this house ready for you and Louie to move in." Harry remarked as he wiped his hands on an old cloth before removing his overalls.

Fred nodded his head ruefully. "Yes I know. We were both so excited to move in here after our wedding. We had such plans before the war started."

"You can say that again. Bloody Hitler. But let's not talk about the war. We can't undo the past." Harry sighed. "Come on. I'll buy you a pint at the Wheatsheaf later. You deserve it."

Just before Christine's birthday on the fifth of June, Fred and Louisa received an offer for the purchase of their house. The offer was exactly the asking price that they had hoped for and so Fred made arrangements with a solicitor to organise the sale.

"Does this mean that you can afford to buy me a piano?" Christine asked innocently when she overheard her parents talking about the money that would be put in to the bank. "It's my birthday soon." She added.

"The money is for our future home." Fred told his daughter. He regarded her thoughtfully. He was amused by Christine's impertinence.

"Yes." Louisa added. She was startled at Christine's assumption that any spare cash would be spent on her.

"We have a home." Christine replied primly.

Fred was just about to tell Christine off and not to intrude on his and Louisa's discussions regarding finance when Bethan knocked on the door and Christine went outside to play with her friend.

Later when both Christine and Susan were out of earshot, Louisa and Fred discussed the possibility of spending some of the money from the sale of their house on a piano.

"It would be a good investment for both Christine and for Susan if she shows an interest in playing." Louisa suggested.

Fred agreed. "Let's wait until the money is in the bank before we decide what to do with it. We still have to pay off the mortgage. We will also have solicitor fees to pay."

Soon after Christine's birthday Louisa contracted a heavy cold that turned into flu. Another virus on top of the flu rendered Louisa very weak. She stayed in bed for several days whilst Dorothy valiantly came to look after her sister and the children. Fearful of the virus spreading to Michael, Dorothy took him to Pandy with her. Mary Ellen looked after him and Ann whilst Dorothy traveled every day to look after Louisa.

All the family took it in turn to make sure Louisa was comfortable. Mary Ellen took it in turns with Dorothy to visit her and brought Louisa some home-made chicken soup.

Meanwhile Fred was worried that Louisa might have the same problems she had with her pregnancy with Michael.

Towards the end of June, Louisa felt a lot better though still weak. Her mother commented that she had more colour in her cheeks.

"You are beginning to look more like what a woman five months gone should look like." Mary Ellen commented. She examined her daughter's face keenly and was presently satisfied with Louisa's countenance.

"Thank you mother. I feel a lot better. Just tired."

However a week later, Louisa's health suffered a major setback when she and her family received the devastating news about a fatal accident that claimed the life of Harry.

The day started like any other day until William and Mary Ellen knocked on Louisa's kitchen door then opened it to let themselves in. Louisa was sitting at the table in the dining room and got up in surprise when she saw them. Her ready smile slipped from her face immediately when she saw the serious expressions on their own faces. She began to panic. The panic increased when behind her parents she saw the sad profile of Arthur.

"What's wrong?" She asked barely whispering the words.

"I think you had better sit down again love." William said as he came to her side. His face was grave and his blue eyes that normally twinkled were bright with anguish.

"It's Harry. He's had a bad accident. He's dead."

At these words Mary Ellen moaned and Arthur guided her to a chair as her daughter screamed "No." Louisa half stood up in her distress and then sat down again as William, grief stricken himself managed to help her back into her chair. His face was ravaged with torment. He pulled up another chair to sit beside her. Arthur stood behind his mother's chair. Mary Ellen gripped his hand.

Through her distress Louisa could see the agony and pain that her brother was making great efforts to control. The four of them huddled together around the dining table each at different stages of their grief.

"It's as if he was on borrowed time." Mary Ellen sobbed. "All those years he suffered as a prisoner of war by the Japanese and just as he was getting better this happens."

"How did it happen?" Louisa asked weakly. She was still unable to take in the terrible news.

Arthur faced his sister. "He was working at Bersham colliery. He had to cross one of the railway lines to get to the depot for some new paint brushes. As you know he was contracted to paint at that colliery as well as Gresford and Hafod."

Arthur breathed deeply in an effort to overcome his grief. He glanced at his father his face wrought with his own sorrow.   Steadying himself, Arthur continued.

"He didn't see the truck shunting coal coming towards him, it knocked him down. He was killed instantly." Arthur explained. He met Louisa's red rimmed eyes mirrored with his own. "I don't think he felt anything."

William sadly nodded his agreement.

"Where's Dorothy?" Louisa asked.

"She's with Dot. They are going to the school to fetch Malcolm. I told her to tell Christine and Susan to come straight here." Mary Ellen said. She wiped her eyes again with a handkerchief.

"They aren't going to tell Malcolm until he gets home. I thought it would be better to tell Christine and Susan yourself."

"Dot's brother Rob has gone to fetch Gordon from work." Arthur added. "Gladys has gone to the school in Acton to fetch Brian and Maureen. Her mother has got little Arthur."

Arthur got up. "I will go and see if I can find Fred, then I'll come back to take mother and father home. We'll pick up Dorothy on the way. I expect she will come back here in the morning to keep you company."

The next few days were a very sad time for all the family. Each time they saw each other they saw their own grief reflected in their eyes.

On the day of the funeral as they followed the cortege to Gwersyllt church, Louisa noticed that the lane all the way up to the church and into the church yard was lined with white flowers. So many friends and neighbours had laid their wreaths as a mark of respect for Harry. He had been a popular man and well known in the surrounding villages.

After the funeral her mother told Louisa that she must concentrate on looking after herself for the sake of the unborn child. But Louisa was heartbroken. Her emotions were making her ill and she felt she couldn't eat. Recently recovered from a virus she was still weak. The death of her beloved brother had rendered her helpless. Twice she fainted due to lack of food and so Dorothy began to stay with her every day to make sure she was alright. Both sisters tried to comfort each other over the loss of Harry.

Dot was inconsolable over the death of her husband and had to take two weeks off from work. She said she doubted that she would get her job back but in any case she was too grief stricken to work. Besides Gordon and Malcolm needed her.

To help take her mind off things Dot also spent some time with Louisa and Dorothy. Being together gave them a small measure of comfort. Dot knew she had to be strong for the sake of her two sons. She encouraged Gordon to return to work. Malcolm returned to school and was supported by his cousins Christine and Susan. They had only two more weeks before the end of term for the summer.

Mary Ellen heartbroken over the los of her son was comforted by Gladys and her neighbours. William could only find comfort by going to work. Similarly Arthur too worked relentlessly driving himself hard every day.

As best they could, Fred and Arthur tried to help Gordon and Malcolm with their loss and throughout the summer took them to the cinema whenever they could. They also encouraged them to play football. Arthur keenly felt the loss of his brother. Fred deeply felt the loss of a good friend. As time passed things began to return to normal, though everyone was aware of the huge gap in their lives that had been left with Harry's demise.

Meanwhile Louisa's health began to slightly improve. On the 1st October Dorothy read out an article from the newspaper to Louisa. "This will make you smile Lou. The government are going to lift rationing completely from tea as from the third of October."

Louisa did smile. "That will please Fred. I suppose the price will go up as well."

"Probably." Dorothy replied. She gazed at Ann and Michael sitting on the floor playing with their toys. "I wonder when butter and margarine will come off ration."

"And sugar!" Louisa added. "It's a good job I don't crave for sugar with this pregnancy." She fished out a piece of soap from her pocket and brought it to her nose.

"It's funny how you always crave for the smell of soap when you are pregnant." Dorothy laughed.

"Yes Fred says the same thing." She patted her stomach. Not long now. Another week."

Dorothy glanced at her sister's swollen stomach. She didn't seem very big to her and she worried that she might have the same complications that she had with Michael.

When Louisa's date for giving birth passed, Dorothy wondered if the date had been wrong. The doctor told Louisa that her grief over the loss of her brother may have contributed to messing up her hormones therefore causing the delay.

It was two weeks past her due date when Louisa eventually went into labour. The day before she caught a heavy cold and wasn't feeling very well. The birth itself proved to be a difficult one and Louisa was in a lot of pain. She found she had little strength and the doctor became very worried about both her physical and mental health. All day Louisa struggled then finally she gave birth to another little girl.

"What shall we call her?" Louisa whispered to Fred's anxious face.

"Do you like the name Pamela?"

Louisa nodded then fell asleep.

As the days followed it became obvious that Louisa was too weak to look after the new baby and so Dot took the baby to Rhosrobin to look after. It gave her something to focus on.

Dorothy continued to visit Louisa every day accompanied by Ann. The little girl played happily with her cousin Michael whilst Dorothy tried to encourage Louisa to eat and get fit again. Twice a week Mary Ellen accompanied Dorothy. They were both very worried about Louisa.

"I don't want to lose another child." Mary Ellen confided in William one day. He had called at Gwersyllt to see how Louisa was recovering. He shook his head sadly. "She's strong. She will pull through this. She's had a rough two years, what with Michael being ill, then Harry's accident." He sighed heavily remembering his son. He turned away from Mary Ellen as he gathered himself together.

"At least some good has come out of Louisa's illness. Harry's two boys are delighted with having the baby to look after. The little thing is also keeping Dot occupied."

It was not until Christmas that Louisa's strength returned. As she recovered the whole family heaved a sigh of relief. Despite their delight that Louisa was recovering well, the family were half-hearted about making plans for Christmas.

Once again Louisa and Fred decided to have Christmas at home. It was a sombre time for everyone. Dorothy and Bill stayed in Pandy with Mary Ellen and William so they were not alone. Dot and her two boys celebrated Christmas with her mother who lived close by.

Whilst everyone was sad that it was to be the first Christmas without Harry, they were all pleased to hear that Dorothy and Bill were expecting their second child. Dorothy had kept her news until Christmas Eve before telling everyone. She thought the news might lift their spirits.

Meanwhile Louisa and Fred discussed once again the possibility of buying a piano.

"Let's wait until after Christmas." Fred suggested. "We can tell both the girls that this is an investment for the family and not a Christmas gift. Otherwise they will think they can have expensive gifts every year." He laughed.

Louisa laughed too.

Chapter Twenty One

1953

Soon after Christmas there was a lot of speculation on the wireless and in the newspapers about rationing being lifted off sweets. Then on the fifth of February it was announced that this had finally happened.

Louisa and her three older children queued up outside the local shop on Dodd's Lane hoping to buy some sweets. The new baby was with them in the pram. Louisa's mouth salivated at the thought of buying some liquorice or nougat. Carol and Bethan were standing beside Louisa in the queue. Carol was six months pregnant and had decided a month earlier to finish working at the sewing factory.

"I hope they don't run out." Carol said. "There have been queues all day."

"So do I." Louisa replied. She nodded and smiled at Mrs. Lewis who walked past with her two children. Each of the trio had a bag of boiled sweets. More and more of their neighbours walked passed with bags of sweets and Louisa worried that her children would be disappointed. She was looking forward to sweets too.

As their place in the queue drew closer to the shop entrance, Louisa stood on tip toe so that she could peer through the doorway.

"I can see rows and rows of empty jars. I hope Mrs. Davies has got another supply." Louisa groaned.

Carol who was a little taller put her arms out on Louisa's shoulder to steady herself as she stood on tip toe. She was just in time to see Mr. Davies replenish the shelves with jars of liquorice and jars of what she thought might be pineapple chunks. She stood up straight again and laughed.

"Don't worry. I think there will be plenty of everything for us."

Eventually it was Louisa's turn and she had the pleasure of buying her children sticks of barley sugar, sherbet and liquorice fountains and some raspberry drops for herself. She also bought some toffee.

When Fred came home and saw all the sweets on the table he was flabbergasted. Louisa handed him a sherbet fountain. She knew he liked them. Before he ate it he disappeared into the hallway to fetch his coat. From his pocket he handed Louisa a parcel.

"I don't suppose you want these then?" He said as he tried to keep his face straight.

Louisa unwrapped the parcel and found a box of chocolates. Fred was gratified to see the smile spread across his wife's face.

"It's like Christmas." She cried.

A few months later the piano arrived. Fred and Louisa had decided not to tell the children about the piano. The removal men brought it to the house during the middle of the afternoon before the children arrived home from school. Louisa met the children from school, then with Michael walking beside the pram with the new baby, they strolled to Pandy. The plan was to wait for Fred to collect them all from her parents' house so that he and Louisa could surprise the children with the new musical instrument.

When the children were out of earshot, Louisa whispered to Mary Ellen and Dorothy what they had planned. Her mother smiled. She was knitting a matinee coat for the new baby and seemed happier than Louisa had seen her since Harry's death. Dorothy was blooming with her pregnancy and she too smiled when she heard the secret about the piano.

"How are you feeling?" Louisa asked. She hadn't seen her for a few weeks now. Dorothy was experiencing morning sickness again. She had just two months to go before the birth, and had been fine, but suddenly the morning sickness had come back with a vengeance.

"I'm alright in the afternoons. I'm sorry I haven't been to see you much lately."

"Don't worry. You must look after yourself now. I've brought you some barley sugar. I'm not sure if it helps but it tastes nice." She grinned as she broke off a few pieces of the stem to share with her mother and sister.

Mary Ellen grinned. "We don't know ourselves, now that sweets and tea are off ration." She got up to pour more tea from the teapot.

"There's talk that butter and cheese will come off the ration soon." Dorothy commented. She sucked hard on her barley sugar.

"I'm looking forward to that." Louisa returned.

Fred arrived at five thirty and after packing the pram and the four children in to the car they set off for Gwersyllt. When he parked the car he spoke to Christine, Susan and Michael sternly.

"Now I want you three to stay in the porch for a few minutes before I tell you to come in to the house."

Instantly he was attacked with bewildered comments of "why?"

"What's up dad?"

Fred tried to keep a stern face and helped Louisa with the pram and the baby into the kitchen. He then locked the kitchen door leaving the three perplexed children in the porch. They pressed their faces against the glazed window of the back door trying to look inside. Louisa took the baby out of the pram then followed Fred into the sitting room. Giggling they unwrapped the cardboard and paper that was around the piano and cut away the straps that was holding the pedals in place. As soon as they had discarded the wrappings they stood back to admire it. Fred ran his hand across the smooth lid of the keys. Gently he pressed down on one of the keys.

"I suppose we ought to get it tuned." He said.

"Yes the delivery men told me that we should. They brought a letter with them from the shop with instructions and the address of a piano tuner."

"Shall we let the tribe in?"

Louisa beamed at him. "I think they have suffered enough."

Fred went to the kitchen door and unlocked it. Louisa sat down on the sofa with the baby on her knee. She could hear Fred telling the children to come in to the kitchen to wash their hands before going in to the sitting room. She sensed Christine's puzzlement over their father's strange behaviour because she kept asking Fred what was going on. Susan mimicked her, though Michael was just happy to follow his two sisters about. Finally they all entered the sitting room and Fred and Louisa were rewarded with the look of astonishment and joy on the faces of their children.

At once Christine went to the lid and began to press the keys.

"Go on let's hear what you can do." Fred suggested. Christine didn't need a second bidding. Grabbing a chair she began to play *God Save the Queen*. Fred looked bewildered at first then realised that the children at school were being prepared for the Queen's coronation due to take place early June.

"Very good. Do you know anything else? Fred asked encouragingly. Christine then played a little melody from Bach which impressed her parents. Susan then wanted to have a go, however since she had no idea how to play there was just a jangled sound coming from the keys. She was soon accompanied by her brother who contributed to the din. After a few minutes Fred put the lid down and told his children that they needed to learn properly how to play.

"We will need to get it tuned first." Louisa said.

Later when the children were in bed, Fred said he felt it was worth spending so much money on the piano to see the joy on the little ones faces.

Within a few days Louisa managed to get a piano tuner. She also arranged for Susan to have lessons with the same teacher that taught Christine.

Listening to the children's progress on the piano helped Louisa cope with her grief for Harry, especially during the last few weeks of June and early July. The anniversary of his death on the sixth was approaching and she felt sad as she remembered her brother. She knew that her parents, Dot, Dorothy and Arthur were thinking about that fateful day. They all dreaded the first anniversary. Yet not one of them wanted to talk about it. The subject was too painful to bear.

So in many respects it was a relief when Dorothy started to go into labour on the twelfth of July giving everyone something else to think about. Bill had taken Dorothy to Trevalyn hospital in Rossett just before midnight and the next day on the thirteenth she gave birth to a little boy.

Louisa and Mary Ellen went to see Dorothy and the new baby. Bill obligingly went outside to talk to William and Fred who were looking after all the children. Bill had Ann in his arms and he was grinning widely. Fred shook his hand.

"Congratulations mate. One of each now."

"Yes. Thanks very much." He put Ann down for a moment then restrained her gently at his side. Both he and Fred turned around to witness Arthur driving up in his car with Gladys and their three children.

Bill laughed. "You will all have to take it in turns to see her. The nurses are very strict about only two visitors."

"That's alright." Gladys said. "I don't mind waiting until Arthur has been in." She lit up a cigarette.

Bill looked at his watch then at Arthur. "Perhaps you can go in now with Fred. I'll watch the little ones."

At Dorothy's bedside, Louisa and Mary Ellen were getting ready to leave. They kissed Dorothy's cheek and headed out of the ward as they saw Fred and Arthur approach. Outside Mary Ellen took charge. She said that William should go next and that he should take Gladys with him.

"So what have you called your son?" Gladys asked Bill.

"Christopher."

Gladys put her cigarette out. "Are there any other Christophers in your family?"

Bill shook his head. "No. We like the name though."

"Has anyone told Dot?" Louisa asked her father. William nodded. "Yes I went to tell her." He answered quietly. "She said she would come and see Dorothy when she is home with the baby."

A day later Louisa waited for Fred to come home from work so that she could leave the children with him. She then walked half a mile down the road to see her sister-in-law. Dot was alone when she arrived at her house. Both Gordon and Malcolm were at the Football Club. They seemed to spend more and more time there since Harry died. Louisa assumed they went to help overcome their grief of losing their father.

Dot smiled when she saw Louisa and gave her a hug. "This is a nice surprise."

"I thought I would get some fresh air. It's a beautiful evening."

"How's Dorothy? Is she alright?" Dot asked anxiously.

273

"She's fine and the baby. They are going to call him Christopher." Louisa replied.

"I will go and see her next week when she is home again in Pandy."

Louisa nodded. "Yes, Father told me. How are you Dot and the boys?"

Dot gazed at her sister-in-law through moist eyes before answering. "Oh you know, some days are better than others. You know what it is like. A year has gone by yet it seems like days." Her eyes brimmed with tears and Louisa felt her own eyes welling up. Dot felt in her apron pocket for her handkerchief to wipe her eyes.

"I'm worried about Gordon though. He seems to be angry all the time. In many ways he is like Harry when he first came home from the prisoner of war camp. Do you remember how angry he was about the surrender to the Japanese?"

Louisa sighed. "Yes. It took him a long time to get over it."

"Well it seems like Gordon has inherited Harry's anger. I suppose it's his way of dealing with his grief. Malcolm of course is grieving too, but he doesn't have angry outbursts like Gordon does. I suppose Gordon remembers those years when Harry was missing during the war, whilst Malcolm scarcely remembered his father. It was the same when Fred came home and Christine didn't recognise him."

Louisa recalled vividly the memory of when Fred arrived home from the war and how Christine had shied away from him. Susan on the other hand had welcomed him even though she didn't know him.

As she walked back home, Louisa was unsure whether her visit had cheered Dot up or made her worse. She herself had mixed emotions. She missed Harry very much but she knew she had to think about the future. Dorothy's new baby would help them all to focus on something new and to get on with their lives.

Very soon after Dorothy's return to Pandy with her baby, Arthur unsettled the family again with some surprising news of his own. The news wasn't completely welcome by Mary Ellen and William though they tried to hide their dismay. He had for some time been saying that though he enjoyed his job, that it wasn't leading to anything and that he should be looking for something else.

"I don't want to be the same old mechanic at Clarks Garages forever," he explained one Sunday morning over coffee. "A new haulage company in Ellesmere Port has started up and they have offered me a good job as manager of their workshop. I am going to take it."

"Does that mean you will be moving house?" Fred asked the question that was on Louisa's lips.

Arthur nodded. His eyes were on his mother's face who looked upset at the news.

Fred shook Arthur's hand. "Congratulations old mate. When do you start?

Arthur smiled whilst all the time watching the expressions on the faces of his parents. He knew this was going to hurt them, but as he explained, Ellesmere Port wasn't too far away. He could visit them often.

"I'm going to start work next month. Then try to find somewhere to rent. As soon as I have done that,

I will put my house up for sale. When the house is sold Glad and I will move. It could take a few months, but I hope before Christmas." He went to put his arm around Mary Ellen's shoulder. "Don't be sad mother, it's not as if I am going away to war. We will see each other regularly."

Mary Ellen patted Arthur's hand. "I'm glad for you really, but I never thought you would be moving away."

William shook his son's hand. "Well done. Good luck to you." He took out his pipe and began to make a fuss about cutting tobacco to put in it. Louisa and Dorothy could see that he was anxious about his remaining son leaving the area and was struggling to come to terms with it.

Dorothy tried to make light of the news. "Well it will be a new place for us to visit." She went to hug her brother and Louisa did the same. "Yes, you try to keep us away." She said lightly.

Arthur shot his sisters grateful looks and then headed for the door. After dropping his bombshell he wanted to get home to Gladys.

On their way home with the children Louisa and Fred speculated how long it would take for Arthur to sell his house.

To their surprise and to Arthur and Gladys's delight their house was sold within two months. On a bright but cold day in November they packed up their furniture and moved to a rented house on the outskirts of Ellesmere Port.

Just before Christmas, Bill and Dorothy announced that they too would be going to live in Ellesmere Port.

Dorothy came to tell Louisa herself. It was Friday morning the last day of term for the children at school before breaking up for the Christmas holidays.

"Arthur told Bill that there were vacancies for drivers where he works at *Floyds and Marsh* and that the money was better than what he was earning. So Bill applied and he got a job." Dorothy exclaimed. Her face was beaming with delight. "Arthur has found us a place to stay too. So we can move straight after Christmas!"

Louisa stared at her sister in disbelief. She didn't know whether to laugh or cry. Not only did she see less of Arthur, now she was going to see less of her sister. Meanwhile Dorothy was dancing around the room holding hands with Michael and Ann. There was so much joy in her face that Louisa realised that it must be a relief for her that she can have a home of her own at last. She got up from her chair and hugged her sister.

"I'm going to miss you though."

Dorothy sighed. "I know. I will miss you too and of course Mother and Father. They took the news well. I suppose they knew that one day we would move out."

"Have you told Dot? She is going to miss you too."

Dorothy shook her head. "I thought you would come with me to tell her. I thought it might help to soften the blow."

They waited for Fred to come home to look after the children, then Louisa accompanied Dorothy to Dot's house. This time both Gordon and Malcolm were home. Having both boys there, somehow helped Dorothy tell Dot her news a bit easier.

Dot was delighted for Dorothy and Bill and got up to hug her sister in law.

"We all knew that one day you would find your own place." Dot said.

Louisa laughed. "Yes, but we didn't think you would be going to Ellesmere Port."

"You will be able to spy on Uncle Arthur." Gordon said with a grin. Malcolm sniggered at this remark. Louisa was pleased that both boys seemed happier. She had been worried about them, especially Gordon. Recently he had received a letter from the government to say that he would be conscripted to do National Service. He would be leaving soon for eighteen months in the army. Louisa thought it might depress him but he seemed to have taken it in his stride. Dot was upset about losing him, but reminded herself he was not going to war. They clung to the good news that on his return he had been promised a place on Bolton Wanderers football team.

Soon after Christmas, Louisa and Mary Ellen helped Dorothy to pack up the few pieces of furniture and books that they owned. It didn't take long to get ready to leave Pandy. Fred and Bill had loaded up their cars with as much as they could carry to take them to their new home. Arthur returned from Ellesmere Port on that cold January Saturday morning to help too. His visit pleased both Mary Ellen and William. Dot and her two sons came along too to see them off. When they were ready to leave, Louisa stood at the end of the road with her parents and Dot to wave goodbye. They shivered in their winter coats. The sun was shining but it was still very cold.

The five children automatically lined themselves up to wave goodbye. Arthur who was in front of the cavalcade couldn't resist winding down the window of his car before he drove off.

"This is like a military send off." He called. He hooted his horn and then drove off followed by Bill then Fred. The spectacle made them all smile as they went back in doors.

"A cup of tea." I think Mary Ellen said seizing the kettle.

Sipping hers slowly Louisa felt that her world was changing rapidly around her. She wondered what the following year would bring.

Chapter Twenty Two

1954

Louisa soon had an inkling what was in store for her
that year. Early in February she realised that she
was expecting another baby.

Fred was of course delighted, but when they
imparted the news to their older daughters there was
mixed reactions. Christine, almost aged fifteen was
incredulous and did nothing to conceal her disgust.
Susan was unsure what to think. At first she
followed the lead of her sister but within hours
changed her mind and decided to be excited about a
new baby coming to the house. Christine however
was unwavering in her evident revulsion. Michael at
the age of five seemed pleased he was going to have
another sister or brother to play with.

Dot laughed when Louisa told her about Christine's
horror at the thought of another baby in the house.

"She'll soon change her mind when the baby is
here."

"I hope so. At the moment she keeps giving me
some strange looks."

"How is she getting on with her piano lessons? She's
done very well so far hasn't she? Is she still keen?"

"She is practising for her fourth grade exam with the Associated Board for the Royal School of Music in June. We keep hearing the same pieces of Haydn and Bach. Susan is less diligent. She likes playing but doesn't practise. When she does lift the piano lid she wants to try to play songs she has heard on the wireless."

Dot laughed. "The boys keep humming songs they have heard on the wireless too. They have told me they want a record player so they can play records."

"Fred is going to buy a new gramophone soon so we can listen to the wireless or play records. We can all listen to our favourite songs then. It's what we used to do when we were young after all. We didn't have record players or gramophones then as you well know."

Louisa smiled as she recalled those evenings in her youth listening to the wireless and humming songs as she watched her brothers tinker with their motorbikes. She glanced at her sister-in-law, she knew she was thinking the same, especially about Harry.

Dot got up abruptly from the chair to get ready to go. She glanced outside as is to check the weather. "Well I would rather do that than spend time looking for flying saucers which my neighbours seem to be obsessed about."

"Do you believe there are aliens watching us?" Louisa asked. She got up too and went to stand next to her sister-in-law. They both looked out through the window and gazed at the sky. Dot looked so intense that Louisa half expected to see a flying saucer outside.

Dot fastened her coat. "No of course not. The country has gone mad. The newspapers are full of it these days. We'll be flying to the moon next."

As the summer passed Louisa's health and general well-being improved. So much so that when Fred's brother James and his wife Annie visited one Sunday afternoon they commented how well Louisa looked.

"I keep busy and I am lucky to have plenty of fresh vegetables from the garden."

"Do you dig the garden Fred or your father-in-law?" Jim winked as he asked the question. He strolled into the garden with a cup of tea in his hand to have a look. Fred followed him with Louisa and Annie in his wake.

"William did help me get it started. It is a big plot, and we've managed to get some good crops."

"I suppose the garden had a lot of building material buried in it when you first moved in?" Jim asked with a wry smile. He knew a thing or two about builders.

Fred shrugged. "Yes there was a bit. But we managed to get rid of most of it. The worse thing was the clay. William brought me some horse manure from Stansty farm so that helped."

"You've done well." Jim remarked. He drained his tea.

"Will you carry on when the rationing ends?" Annie asked.

Fred grinned. "I expect so. At least for a couple of years. When the rationing ends next month there might still be food shortages." He shelled a pod of peas and handed them to Annie to try.

"They taste good. Any more?" She smiled.

282

Fred gathered a generous bunch and handed them to her. Louisa went back into the kitchen to get a paper bag to put them in for Annie to take home.

"It seems the government are lifting the rations on everything at the beginning of July." Jim commented. "So we will be back where we were in nineteen thirty nine. Though not much better off."

Fred leaned against a garden post and sighed.

"It's hard to remain positive when you see the devastation of the towns and cities."

He stopped to light a cigarette and offered one to his brother. Jim took one and neither man spoke again as they smoked.

They didn't need to speak, they each understood how the other felt about their home town.

The companionable silence was broken by the approach of the four older children. Christine and Susan had taken their cousins Louisa and Alf for a walk along the banks of the river Alyn. The river ran through farmland and a wood. The path alongside the river bank eventually led walkers away towards paths to either Gresford colliery or to Pandy. They had found the path through the Bluebell wood to Pandy and had decided to call to see Mary Ellen and William. This made a convenient stop for the children to get a glass of water. The four children were tired and a little dishevelled when they arrived home. It had been a long walk. They flopped clumsily on to any chair that was available. Their faces were flushed from the exertion of the walk, whilst their gangly legs and arms hung in a tangled mass over the sides of the chairs. However they were not too tired to make short work of the sandwiches and cake that Louisa had provided for them.

Jim and Annie's visit seemed to herald the beginning of a trail of visitors from Fred's many brothers and sisters that summer. Each one brought something for the new baby that was due in September. As rationing was lifted more goods became available and so new babies were being presented with an assortment of items. Certain foods they brought amongst the baby items had not been seen for many years. Amongst all these were other new imported goods not ever seen before.

When Louisa finally went in to labour during the early hours of eighth of September the expected baby was already well endowed with clothes and soft toys. Visitors to the ward brought even more new gifts.

After excited discussion with Christine and Susan they had decided to name their new sister Lesley. Fred had nodded his approval and was pleased that at last Christine had reconciled herself to the birth of the new baby.

Months later she explained that when she had been told that Louisa was expecting another baby she had been worried. Louisa had been so ill when she was expecting Michael and then with Pamela that she had fretted thinking that the next one might kill her mother.

Cradling her baby girl swathed in her new clothes and shawl at Trevalyn hospital in Rossett, Louisa gazed down at her new daughter.

"New clothes and new beginnings for us all." She bent down and kissed the baby.

THE END

Author's Note

This novel is based on true events. It was inspired by the stories I was told by my parents, and my grandparents. The desire to know more about my family history also contributed towards writing this novel.

During my childhood, attempts to build a picture of life during World War Two for my father, my many uncles and aunts was always difficult. They couldn't or wouldn't talk about it. It was too distressing.

I have discovered that this was the case for many families as well as my own. Writing this novel has made me even more aware of how the effects of World War Two reverberated for many years later.

In an effort to tell their story I have relied on fragments of information from my cousins, my sisters and commonly known historical facts.

All the places referred to actually existed except for Manley's factory. In the nineteen fifties similar places sprouted up across the UK. I modelled

Manley's factory based on my research. Any similarity in names is coincidental. The neighbours too are fictitious.

After some considerable research on domestic violence I was able to create a fictitious murder scenario and the trial. Any similarity to a murder trial in Wrexham or anywhere else, is also pure coincidence. The story was inspired by the sad experiences of an old acquaintance of my mother's.

Thanks to my sisters Christine and Lesley for their contributions to this novel. Thanks also to my cousins Alfred, Margaret, Celia, Neville, Malcolm and Christopher. Also thank you to Neil Mosley.

Gresford Colliery Explosion occurred in the early hours of 22nd September 1934. The shock and sorrow reverberated across the North Wales Coal Field.

Descendants of many of the families who lost loved ones in the disaster continue to respect the memory of these men. In my novel I have mentioned just two of those families – Jones and Clutton.

Acknowledgement and thanks to

Wrexham Evening Leader

17759659R00169

Printed in Great Britain
by Amazon